COERCIÓN

Coercion

Goddess of Fate

Book 3

Tamara Hart Heiner

paperback edition
copyright 2019 Tamara Hart Heiner
cover art by Tamara Hart Heiner

Also by Tamara Hart Heiner:
Perilous (WiDo Publishing 2010)
Altercation (WiDo Publishing 2012)
Deliverer (Tamark Books 2014)
Priceless (WiDo Publishing 2016)
Vendetta (Tamark Books 2018)

Goddess of Fate:
Inevitable (Tamark Books 2013)
Entranced (Tamark Books 2017)

Kellam High:
Lay Me Down (Tamark Books 2016)
Reaching Kylee (Tamark Books 2016)

The Extraordinarily Ordinary Life of Cassandra Jones:
Walker Wildcats Year 1: Age 10 (Tamark Books 2015)
Walker Wildcats Year 2: Age 11 (Tamark Books 2016)
Southwest Cougars Year 1: Age 12 (Tamark Books 2017)
Southwest Cougars Year 2: Age 13 (Tamark Books 2018)

Tornado Warning (Dancing Lemur Press 2014)

After the Fall (Tamark Books 2018)

My dear reader:

I made it up.

I know it's hard to believe, but this series is a work of fiction. None of it is true. None of these things ever happened, including much of the Latvian mythology. Latvian mythology is one without a lot of sources. The Latvian people didn't have written stories to begin with, and so each story was passed on from family to family, generation to generation, and each family had a slightly different version.

And then Christianity entered the picture, and the gods and goddesses changed to Saints, and the rites and rituals changed to holidays, and, well, you get the picture.

This was good and bad. It didn't give me a lot to draw on, but it left a lot of room for creativity. So I've twisted the Latvian mythology to fit my plot. I did my best to immerse myself in what documents I could find, but that wasn't many. A lot more is written about Lithuanian mythology, but they are a little different, so I learned what I could and tried to make sense of it. I had a lot of fun with this fantasy world, and I hope you enjoy it as well.

CHAPTER ONE

The three of us stood there in a circle, facing each other. I looked at my younger sister Beth and recognized the determination on her face. Beside me was Meredith, my closest friend. No, she was so much more than that. There was no defining our relationship, at least not in mortal terms.

I looked down at my hand, at the cell phone cupped in my palm. It was time.

"Ready, Jayne?" Beth asked.

I lifted my head to my sister, her eyes unwavering as she stared at me. I nodded. "Ready."

It had been two days since the three of us ran away from home. Two days since the mythological Latvian pantheon took over our corner of New Jersey, resulting in countless suicides and abandoned families. Two days since Aaron was swallowed up by hell.

COERCION

And now it was time to call home.

I powered up my ghetto flip phone and pressed the button to call my mom. Next to me, I saw Meredith doing the same to her smart phone, only she was calling her dad.

My mom answered an instant later, her voice breathy with panic and hope and relief. "Jayne? Jayne, is that you?"

"It's me, Mom." My throat unexpectedly closed up, and I thought I would cry. Never had I wanted my mother more than right now, when my whole world was literally falling apart.

Her sobs echoed through the phone. "Where are you? Are you okay? Where is your sister? What happened?"

I took a deep breath and answered her questions, spitting out the lie the three of us had already fabricated. "I don't know what happened. When I woke up this morning, I wasn't at home. I don't remember leaving, but I'm with Beth and Meredith and we're all okay."

She latched onto those words. "So you're okay. You're okay."

"Yes," I said, glad to keep her focused on that sentiment. "We're on our way home. We should be there in a few hours."

"Jayne," my mom said, her voice barely above a whisper. "The world has gone crazy. You're not the only person to vanish. I hope all of those missing people are heading home now too."

I gave a little shudder and closed my eyes. They weren't. Those people weren't heading home because I had failed. I couldn't even save my boyfriend, let alone the faceless masses whose fates had been changed by a rogue goddess.

"I hope you're right," I said instead. "We'll see you soon, okay?"

"Hurry. I put out a missing persons report for you, and I'm not going to tell the police you're home until I see you myself."

I couldn't help the tiny smile that pushed against my lips. My poor mom had been through enough of my shenanigans to know not to expect me until I was present.

How completely different from a year ago, when I was the very predictable, reliable older daughter.

2

"Okay, Mom. Call me anytime."

As soon as I hung up and lowered the phone from my ear, it was flooded with a dozen other missed calls and texts and voicemails. I started at the top, playing them as Meredith finished up her conversation with her dad.

"Well?" Beth asked from beside me.

I held up a finger as I listened to Dana's message. Dana had been my best friend for years, but since she left me for college over the summer, we had sort of drifted apart. I hadn't been able to keep her on top of all the crazy stuff in my life.

"Jayne, I've called you five times and you're not answering. I'm freaking out, your mom is freaking out, half of New Jersey is freaking out. The epidemic of missing people has spread into Delaware and Maryland, and I just know this has something to do with you. Call me back. Call me back as soon as you get this."

While prone to theatrics, I knew from the tone of her voice that she was sick with worry. She knew more about my secret talents than anyone else, except present company and perhaps my boyfriend. She also knew that I had been on the trail of the rebel goddess, trying to bring the destruction of souls to a halt.

I pressed the return call button and spoke to Beth while I waited for Dana to pick up. "Mom's fine. She was crying, but she didn't question our story." Yet. "Meredith, are we ready?"

"Yes." Meredith slipped her phone into her pocket and moved to her car, parked in the long grass on the side of a lonely country road. Behind it sat the cottage where we had spent the past two days recovering and planning. Recovering from the battle we lost and planning to win this war.

I climbed into the passenger side, and Dana answered as I pulled on my seatbelt. The car jerked when Meredith plowed off the grass and onto the road.

"Please tell me you're alive and have a very good reason for not answering your phone," Dana said.

"I'm alive and have a very good reason for not answering my phone," I said.

3

"Jayne, thank goodness," she breathed, and I could picture her closing her eyes and letting out an exhale. "Now spill it," she said, her voice lightening. "What's going on?"

Where to start? I hadn't even told her everything before this went down. "It was Karta. Or rather, this girl Samantha who used to be Karta. She thought she could buy her own immortality by stealing souls. She summoned hundreds of people to her to build a little army. I tried to stop her, I tried to free them, but I failed."

"Wait, slow down, I'm lost," Dana said. "Karta? Refresh me. Who is that?"

"Karta is one of the goddesses of fate," I said. "She's my sister-goddess, the one in charge of adults. She works with me under Laima's direction." I was, after all, the other goddess of fate.

"So isn't she one of the good guys?"

"Was." I glanced at my sister in the back seat, her gaze out the window as we drove down the two-lane highway. "When Samantha went on her power trip, Laima took away her powers and gave them to Beth. Beth is Karta now." I felt a surge of pride in my sister, in her ability to step up and take charge in this situation.

"Whoa. This is freaky crazy."

I took a deep breath, preparing myself to confess the biggest loss. "She took Aaron."

Dana's gasp echoed my own horror. "What does that even mean? She took him? Like, his soul belongs to her?"

"Exactly." The tears pricked my eyes. Aaron, my boyfriend of almost six months—until he broke up with me, of course. "He's one of her minions now."

"But you can get him back, right? I mean, she's not even a goddess any more."

"You can bet on it." I closed my hands around the edge of the door, my knuckles whitening with the tension. "We've already started on a plan." Samantha—her mortal name—might not be a goddess anymore, but she'd paired herself with a powerful god, and he supported her plan. We would

4

have to stop them both to save Aaron and the other souls.

"Can I help?"

I had Dana's undivided attention, something I hadn't had since she started school a few weeks ago. She was always so distracted with boys, or classes, or boys, or, well, that was about it. "I wish there was something that could be done, but this is on us."

"Will you let me know?"

Her voice sounded so pinched and worried that I nodded. "Of course. If I think of anything at all, I'll let you know."

We said our goodbyes, and I continued down the list of voicemails. The next one was from an unavailable number, and I wasn't surprised to hear Lieutenant Bailey's voice carrying across the line. The car slowed as Meredith put on her turn signal, and I looked up in time to see we'd merged onto the interstate. My stomach fluttered. We'd be home sooner than I wanted.

"Jayne, this is Lieutenant Bailey from the Lacey Township Police Department. Your mother put out a missing persons report on you and your sister, and due to our previous interactions, I thought I would personally call to see if you're all right. Please return my call as soon as you get this, thank you."

Oh, how sweet. He was worried about me. I went to the next voicemail.

"Hello, Jayne?"

The English accent filled me with dread, and I knew who the speaker was before she said.

"This is Elizabeth Chambers, Aaron's mother. I haven't heard from him in two days, and I wondered if you might know his whereabouts. It's not like him to be so irresponsible. If he is with you, please tell him to call his mother. Thank you."

Her words dripped with sarcastic innuendo, implying that if Aaron was acting irresponsible, it was totally my influence.

How I wished she were wrong.

I took a deep breath and held it. Then I looked at Meredith.

"That was Aaron's mom. Wanted to know where he is. What do I do? Do I tell her?"

Meredith shot me a quick glance before turning her attention back to the steering wheel. "And say what? That he tried to save you by giving up his soul to a demonic Latvian god? I don't think that's gonna go over well."

I snorted, realizing how insane that would sound. "I should tell her he's missing, right?"

"What good will that do? She knows that much, doesn't she? She wants answers, Jayne, and unless you're able to give them to her, I would just play dumb."

Meredith was right. I didn't have any new information, no light to shed on the mystery.

I hit the number to call Mrs. Chambers back. She answered almost as quickly as my own mother had.

"Hello, this is Elizabeth." The crisp British accent had an air of restless expectancy to it.

"Mrs. Chambers, this is Jayne," I said. "Sorry, I've been away from my phone."

"Where is Aaron?" she demanded, cutting me off.

For a moment I lost my train of thought, visualizing Aaron as I'd last seen him: pressed khaki pants, sweater vest, and empty, black eyes. Face devoid of emotion. I gathered my wits about me and said, "I don't know. I haven't seen him." I racked my brain, trying to think of how I would be acting if I really didn't know anything. "Are you sure he didn't tell you where he was going? How long has he been gone?"

"You're not fooling anyone, Jayne," she said, her voice cold. "He told me he was going to your house. That he was going to break up with you, Jayne Lockwood. Now I demand to know what you have done with my son."

Chills went down my spine. She didn't just think I was a bad influence; she thought I might have hurt him.

Which was crazy ironic, because the first time I saw a vision of Aaron's future, it involved him being murdered by his future ex-wife.

"I haven't seen Aaron," I said.

"So if I talk to your parents, they won't have seen him either?"

My mom might have seen Aaron when he came over to break up with me. "He came over, just like you said, but then he left. He broke up with me because of you. Happy?" I managed to throw some genuine indignation and hurt into my voice. "You told him I wasn't good enough for him, that he needed to go back to England and get away from me. So that's exactly what he did. It's not my fault he doesn't tell you everything. Why don't you check the flight records and see which one he took back?"

My voice had taken on quite an angry energy, and I realized I was expressing my true feelings toward her, even if the circumstances were false.

Silence reigned on the line, and my conscience pricked me. I shouldn't have spoken to her that way. Before I could apologize, she spoke again.

"All right, Jayne. If that's how you want to play this. But I will definitely let the police know you were the last person who saw my son before he disappeared."

I would have hung up on her, but she beat me to it. "Argh!" I tossed my phone onto the console, but not so far away I couldn't reach it. I had a bad habit of throwing it across the room when I was angry and then having to track it down later.

"What?" Meredith asked, her voice tense. "What's wrong?"

"That was Aaron's mom. She said she's going to tell the police I was the last person to see him before he disappeared. Definitely threatening me."

"Sounds like you'd have a happy family with your in-laws," Beth said from the back, her voice way too chipper.

"They're not my in-laws," I growled. Although, truthfully, I hoped they would be some day.

"She's just making idle threats," Meredith said. "Doesn't she know anything? Maybe it's different in England, but here in America, adults who disappear aren't considered missing persons until there's suspicion of foul play, which there won't be since it looks like half of New Jersey disappeared over the weekend, but even if that weren't the case, they would just consider him a runaway or someone hiding from his parents—"

"Thanks, Meredith," I said, cutting her off. Her logic reassured me, but I wasn't nervous about Mrs. Chamber's accusations. It was the thought that someday I would have to share Aaron with that offensive woman that really

7

got under my skin.

Provided, of course, that I really had successfully changed his fate and he wasn't going to end up married to his ex-girlfriend Libby.

But what did any of that matter? Samantha had single-handedly changed the fate of hundreds of people, for the worse, and without Laima's approval. Once again everything I knew about my powers descended into a confusing kaleidoscope around me, and I pressed the palms of my hands to my head before I couldn't tell which way was up or down.

"I'm going to need gas in about twenty minutes," Meredith said.

I lowered my hands away from my face and looked at her. "I'll pay this time." She'd covered the bill this entire trip and hadn't even asked for help. "Hey, what about your dad? What did he say?"

"He handled it about the same as your mom, it sounds like. Just relieved to know I'm alive. My brother is well, he didn't take off or anything, but lots of people did."

My skin tingled with alarm as I thought of all the people who had received Samantha's brainwashing poem. The majority had abandoned their homes and families to join her army. A small handful, however, had reacted badly, and a shocking number of suicides had plagued our township for the past few weeks.

"And how are we on the suicides?" I asked.

Meredith spared me a glance. "Well, I don't really know. I haven't looked it up."

I didn't blame her. Samantha had used one of Meredith's poems to brainwash people. But Meredith had written another to remedy the problem. "Remember the police have the cure. I'm sure it's been printed in the newspaper, maybe even shown on the news. Samantha won't be able to abduct more people with your poem."

Meredith pressed her lips together and nodded. "If only her power ended when she ceased to be Karta."

If only. I exhaled.

"Yeah, about that," Beth said. "I'm the new Karta. Everyone should have to listen to me."

I gave a dry laugh. "It doesn't exactly work that way."

Meredith pulled off the interstate to a gas station. "If you need to stretch or use the bathroom, do it now. We won't be stopping again until we're home."

I didn't need to use the bathroom, but I did want to stretch. And my stomach was growling at me, even though we'd had a very filling breakfast of scones and orange juice at the sprite's—no, what was the proper word for him? *Kaukas*. The *kaukas* had been very hospitable, providing food and beds for two days.

I followed Beth into the gas station, and we stood next to each other as we perused the chips.

"I'm almost as tall as you," she said with a grin.

"Shut up," I drawled back, bumping her shoulder with mine. It was true. Only in eighth grade, and Beth had nearly caught me. We could probably pass for twins, standing next to each other like we were, with the same wavy brown hair and fair skin. The biggest difference between us was her brown eyes and my blue-green ones. She picked a bag and turned slightly, her eyes scanning the rows around us.

And then she stiffened for half a second before her legs bent beneath her and she crumpled to the ground.

"Beth!" I dropped beside her, panic firing through my veins. Had something gone wrong? Was this a lingering effect of the battle we'd fought two days ago, of Beth receiving the goddess powers?

She looked up at me, tears glistening in her eyes. "Help me, Jayne."

"Help you what?" I had my phone out, ready to call 911.

She closed it with her hand and pushed it away, then got to her feet. "To the car."

"Okay." I obliged her, abandoning her would-be purchases and helping her outside.

By the time we got to the car, she was walking on her own, though she still clutched my wrist. Meredith was just putting away the nozzle from the gasoline hose.

"What happened? Is she okay?" Meredith hovered like a frightened bird.

"I don't know," I replied, my tone short and tense with worry.

"I'm fine." Beth pulled free of me and ran a hand through her hair before taking a deep breath. "I think I just had my first vision."

I reared back, replaying in my mind the events in the convenience store. The way she'd looked around, the expression on her face right before she collapsed to the ground. "Did you?" I gasped. "What happened? Tell me about it!"

"It was awful." Her lip trembled, but she kept going. "It was that man behind one of the coolers. Did you see him?"

I shook my head. I hadn't noticed anyone except us.

"I didn't know that was going to happen. I just glanced at him, and when he looked at me—" Her voice choked up. "I saw him die. No, I didn't see it, I felt it! I was him, and I was on a motorcycle when I hit a patch of ice and lost control. I was terrified. I couldn't stop, and I knew—" Beth's breathing was coming in hard, fast. "I knew I was going to die. And then I did." Her hands shook as she grasped mine, the tears welling up in her eyes. "Is that what it's like, Jayne? Is that what's going to happen to me?"

I squeezed her hands, my heart constricting for her. I knew she wasn't asking if she was going to die in a motorcycle accident. She was asking if every vision was going to feel like she'd died. And I had no easy answer for her.

"Yes, Beth. They're all like that."

She closed her eyes, the tears rolling down her cheeks. "I don't know if I can do this," she whimpered.

I wrapped an arm around her shoulders and pulled her against my chest. I wished I could tell her it would get easier, but it wouldn't. Every time I had a vision, every time I saw how someone was going to die, it tore me up inside. I died over and over and over again.

I pulled back, remembering the silver lining, the one ray of hope that saved me from going insane. "If you feel like he wasn't supposed to die that way, you can petition Laima. You can change the outcome."

She looked at me with shining eyes, hopeful. "What should I feel if I'm supposed to change it?"

I looked away, my own frustration over my inability to answer this question bubbling over. I still didn't know. I didn't feel something when I saw the visions, other than terror. Instead I used logic and tried to weigh the odds and decide whose life was more valuable than someone else's. I didn't know if I was being fair, even though that was my job as a goddess of fate.

"I don't have the answer to that. Maybe you'll get better at this than I am. You have to judge. You have to decide. But remember, every time someone's life is prolonged, the years are taken off someone else's life. The balance must be maintained."

She didn't say anything, but her eyes sort of glazed over. She muttered something to herself. I knew she was having second thoughts about taking on this role. "You've been doing this for years. If you don't know, how am I supposed to?"

"I've been having visions for years, yes, but I didn't figure out I was a goddess until a few months ago. I'm still learning."

Meredith stood beside us, leaning against the car, obviously reluctant to intrude. She cleared her throat when we paused. "I'm all gassed up. Shall we get out of here?"

I gave her a smile and climbed into the car. Beth got in behind me, still looking shaken. I turned around to face her, thinking of another question.

"What did you smell before you had the vision?"

"Cinnamon rolls. Just like Mom's. That's why I looked around."

I faced forward again. Cinnamon rolls. A better smell than lemons, but now she would never be able to eat another cinnamon roll without thinking of dying people.

I never should've let her get involved in this.

CHAPTER TWO

66 **L**et's go over the plan again," I said as we got closer to home. It was my turn to drive, and I was taking my time, not anxious to get back and face a future certain to be fraught with danger. I tried to get Meredith to talk with me an hour earlier, but both she and Beth had fallen asleep. They didn't seem to feel the same anxiety I did.

But then, I had more to lose. My boyfriend's soul was on the line.

When Meredith had blinked her eyes and pushed upward in her seat, I gave her all of two minutes to come awake before speaking. Now she looked at me, apprehension and worry on her face.

"Okay," she said.

"We need to get Trey out of the mental institution," I said.

Meredith nodded. "And then we have to get his powers back to him."

I enclosed my wrist with one hand, rubbing it gently. Trey had been sent to protect me, but Samantha and her minions stole his power. When I visited him, he indicated I was the key to getting it back, but I had no idea how I was supposed to do that. I hoped he knew.

"And then we have to track Samantha down and free those souls," I continued.

That was it. That was our game plan. If the details seemed a little vague, Meredith didn't comment. We really had no idea what we were doing. All we knew was that it had to be done.

"Right. One thing at a time. How will we get Trey out?" she asked.

I chewed on my lower lip. I'd already been considering this. "I might be able to get the police department to pull a few strings for me."

She arched an eyebrow. "You think Lieutenant Bailey is going to do anything for you after this weekend?"

My friend in the police department knew more about my abilities than the average person. "Let's hope so."

When we finally arrived in Forked River, New Jersey, Meredith dropped me and Beth off and left in a hurry. I wasn't sure if she was that anxious to get home or if she was avoiding a lecture from my mom.

The front door was unlocked, and I opened it, letting us in.

"Hello?" I called, waiting for my mom to appear.

"Jayne! Beth!"

My dad surprised me by stepping out of the living room and wrapping his arms around us, squeezing tight. I hadn't expected him to be home, since he was working out of town and wasn't due back for a few more days. But I welcomed the comfort of his embrace.

"Dad!" I said. "What are you doing home?"

He squeezed us tighter. "Are you serious, Jayne? My daughters disappear during a mass exodus of the tri-state area, and you think I'm just going to stay at work? I was already looking for a flight home before your mom called me."

The bedroom door swung open, and my mother suddenly appeared.

"Girls!" she gasped out, and then she threw herself into the mass huddle we had going on. She sobbed, not even trying to hide her emotions as she held the four of us together. Then she pulled away, taking my and Beth's hands and extricating us from my father.

"I'm so glad—so glad you're okay," she blubbered as she pulled us over to the couch.

She was about to ask us what happened, I knew it. But if I was going to lie, I needed to know what she already knew. So I beat her to it.

"What happened, Mom? The stuff we found on the news was kind of crazy. What's really going on?"

She shook her head, swallowing hard, her normally confident self confused. "Hundreds of people disappeared the same time you did. I came out of my room and made dinner as usual, and then I called you girls. No one answered, but that wouldn't be a first. I went into the den and the TV was on, broadcasting an emergency alert. I've never seen one like it. It wasn't a weather alert, wasn't an Amber alert or any of those usual ones. This one said to keep your family close because people were vanishing. As soon as I saw it, I got this pit in my stomach, I just knew you girls were gone. I combed through the house, I tried your cell phones, I tried your friends. I told the police, but I'm sure they were backlogged with so many disappearances." She squeezed our hands. "I'm so glad you're home. What do you remember?"

At least she believed our story. It made sense, considering the circumstances. I took the lead. "I don't remember anything. Nothing at all. We were at home, watching TV, and Meredith came over."

I saw my mom's lip turn down at the mention of Meredith, and I crossed my fingers that this wasn't another strike against my friend. "We were just, you know, talking, laughing. And then I woke up in a strange house somewhere else."

"Where?" My mom leaned forward, her hunger for answers reminding me of my journalist friends. "Were there other people with you?"

I hesitated here. I had seen hundreds of other people during the battle with Samantha, but how much could I reveal without making the story tricky? I didn't want to send the police on a wild goose chase after Samantha's army. It was up to me to save them. So I shook my head. "I didn't see anyone. There was a nice man there at the house. He said he found our car stalled in the middle of the street." Partly true. "He said he fixed it and Meredith followed him back to his house. We don't remember any of this, and when we woke up in the morning we just wanted to go home."

My mother's fist closed tightly, her lips pressed together, and I saw the fear in her eyes. Something unusual was happening, something outside of our control. Something paranormal.

She let out a slow breath. "I want to take you to the doctor and make sure you're well."

"Mom, I don't need a doctor. I need to talk to the police."

My mom held my gaze. "You have something that will help them?"

A lump formed in my throat. "Maybe. I'll at least tell them everything I know." For that matter, I probably needed to call my boss.

An hour later I sat in the Lacey Township Police Department, holding a warm mug between my hands as I conversed quietly with Lieutenant Bailey at his desk.

"You know your mom called to report you as missing."

I bobbed my head.

"But you weren't missing, were you. You left to get to the bottom of the symbol."

He wasn't asking, and my head shot up at the mention of the symbol found carved on the bodies of the dead. It flashed through my mind, static electricity raising the hairs on my flesh. "War," I breathed, barely even aware of the word as it left my lips.

Lieutenant Bailey leaned toward me. "What war?"

I turned my gaze on him. He knew I had powers, but he didn't know the whole truth about who I was or what I could do: change how people died. And now I needed him to know just enough to help me.

"There was a battle. Everyone who received the poem was summoned to

15

fight. The ones who answered the call were at the battle, the rest. . . ." My voice trailed off, and I cleared my throat. The rest died before they got there. "I went to fight for them. And I lost."

He frowned at me, his jaw tightening. "We have the cure. If we can get it to the people who were summoned, can we get them back?"

I shook my head. "It's too late for them."

His face paled. "Are they dead?"

"No. But their souls are not in their bodies."

I could see him struggling to believe me, to cast aside his understanding of real life and put his faith in me, a girl who had already proved her unusual abilities over and over again. He couldn't seem to make his reality coincide with mine, however, and instead he changed the subject.

"So when is the next battle and how can we win it? Do you have a location? Where are the people being held?"

Valiant questions. But wrong. "This isn't a war for you to fight." A strange tingling flooded the back of my neck, scooting upward through my scalp all the way to my hairline, and even my voice changed when I spoke. "This is a battle between the ancients. This is my fight."

He didn't say a word when I finish speaking, and I drew back, almost embarrassed by the commanding tone I had taken. He studied his notepad, the pen passing back and forth between the thumbs and index fingers of both hands. Finally he spoke.

"What part do you play in this?"

I smiled. "Finally. The right question." But I didn't answer him. Instead, I leaned forward and said, "There is something you can do to help."

He tilted his head. "Help who?"

"Help me. I'm one of the good guys."

"What do you need?" He stared at me strangely, almost resentfully, as if I were forcing him to do something against his will.

Was I? Was I somehow exerting my will on him?

But whatever it took, right? This war was more important than his free choice. I needed to use whatever measures necessary to ensure his cooperation.

Wait, Jayne. My rational side caught up with my thoughts, and I startled, as if suddenly finding someone else in my head. I stood up and walked a few paces away from him, then took a deep breath to clear my thoughts. The stress was getting to me. Aaron's absence was getting to me.

Aaron. I turned back around and faced Lieutenant Bailey. Stepping closer, I did my very best to look earnest and pleading rather than commanding. "There is a boy in the mental institution nearby. He's been wrongfully accused of a crime so that he would be out of the way during this war. I need him. I need his powers. I need you to get him out for me."

Lieutenant Bailey put down the pen. "There are others like you? With powers?"

He was beginning to understand. "Yes. There are many others. And not all of them are good guys."

He pressed a hand to his forehead and then let it drop. "If I'm not able to free this boy, what happens?"

"Then I can't save all of those souls, and every single person who disappeared from New Jersey, Delaware, and Maryland two days ago will die."

∞

Lieutenant Bailey made me no promises, and I went home unsettled but hopeful he would help me. I didn't think I'd sleep that night, but sleep and I have always gotten along. Barely had I shut my eyes and I was out.

Getting up for school the next day felt like a surreal experience.

My mom almost didn't let us go. She was terrified I would disappear again. Only after I pointed out how the mass exodus had ended did she agree to let us leave.

Not that I was anxious to return. I had better things to do than hang out at school. But what could I do? Our plan was a skeletal outline at best.

Mom wouldn't let me take Beth to school. I think in the back of her mind, she thought if one of us disappeared, at least the other one wouldn't.

Even without needing to drop my sister off at the middle school, I somehow managed to run late. I pulled onto the street beside my school just moments before the tardy bell. To my surprise, I didn't have any problems finding a parking spot in the senior lot. Past experience dictated that if I was late, I was subject to the sophomore gravel pit.

Not today. A prickly feeling scattered across my shoulders. How many of my peers were missing? How many of them were dead?

A few weeks ago when I started having visions of people committing suicide, I realized something was amiss in the world of the Fates. I had gotten used to the visions over the years, but after they showed me how someone would die, it was my chance to change that person's death. Until my sister goddess decided to go on a power trip. She found a different way to alter people's destinies.

That flame of indignation flared up again in my chest, annoyance with Laima for showing up to help me fight Samantha and then bolting right after, giving me no answers and no further guidance. She left Meredith and Beth and me in the care of the sprite — no, the *kaukas* — to try and help us figure things out. Sure, he was friendlier and more talkative than she ever was, but I wanted to get my answers directly from her.

I hurried across the street to the history building and dropped into my psychology class just moments after the tardy bell rang. Meredith was already there, and her eyes tracked to me. She mouthed something as I fell into my seat in front of her, and I didn't catch it all, but I knew the thoughts going through her mind were the same as mine.

Look at the empty seats.

"Jayne!" Coach said, looking genuinely pleased to see me. "We're so happy you could join us."

I nodded and pulled out my notebook, taking a surreptitious glance around the room.

It wasn't as bad as I'd feared, maybe two people missing out of my class of about twenty. Still a decent number, and if Samantha had amassed this many people from all over the tri-state area, her army was much bigger than we had realized.

"How did it go with the police?" Meredith asked me as soon as we escaped class.

"Lieutenant Bailey is going to see what he can do." I hadn't been able to call Meredith because my mom had decided to sleep on the landing beside my and Beth's bedrooms. "He's supposed to get back in touch with me soon."

"Did you tell him everything?"

"No way. Just enough to let him know how desperately we need Trey."

"Like crazy desperate," Meredith muttered.

"Yeah."

We parted at my locker. Every class I went to had people missing, but that wasn't even the weirdest thing. People stared at me. The halls fell silent when I walked by, and whispers started the moment I passed. I wanted to ask them why, but I was suddenly and acutely aware how the only person I really talked to was Meredith. Oh, and Stephen Harris, my boyfriend for most of my junior year. Even though we had broken up, we tried to maintain some kind of friendship.

He was one of the first to go missing. His disappearance was what prompted us to take off for Maryland and find Samantha. We thought if we found her, we would find all of the missing people.

We did. But I couldn't get Stephen back.

I stepped into chemistry and felt Troy's eyes on me as I sat down. I turned around to face Stephen's best friend.

"Troy," I greeted.

"Jayne," he replied, all poker face.

"So have you talked to Stephen?" I asked carefully. I knew the answer, but I wasn't sure how else to get a conversation going.

Troy shook his head, his expression wary. "Have you? He disappeared last week just like loads of other people."

I forced myself to slow my breathing, but it still hurt that I had failed him. "No. I tried to call him, but he didn't answer."

"For me either." Troy studied me carefully. "We thought you disappeared also. But now you're back."

Oh. I sucked in a breath at the realization. People were staring at me, all right—staring at me because I came back.

"Where did you go?" Troy asked, apparently not chalking up my

19

disappearance as coincidence. "You didn't see him?"

I shook my head, concocting a lie on the spur of the moment, something I had become quite good at. "I didn't even realize people were gone. I went to visit Dana in Massachusetts."

"Your name is on the list." He narrowed his eyes. "Your parents reported you missing."

Thanks, Mom. "We had an argument. I didn't tell them where I was going." To strengthen my story, I added, "It's not the first time. I snuck off to New York a few weekends ago without telling them. Maybe Stephen mentioned it to you. He wanted to come with me."

"I think he might have said something," Troy said, looking slightly less suspicious. And now his eyes regarded me differently. "When did you become a rebel? I thought you were a straight shooter."

I lifted my shoulders in a shrug. "I'm not a rebel. Sometimes I just want to do things my parents don't approve of."

Troy gave a snort and rolled his eyes. "You picked a really bad time to do it."

"I know."

The teacher called the classroom to order, and I faced front again, feeling even less settled than I had when I walked in.

CHAPTER THREE

School wasn't even out before Lieutenant Bailey started calling me. I couldn't know for sure it was him because his calls always came to my phone as "unavailable." But then he started leaving messages, and I had no doubts.

"Ms. Lockwood, I've located your friend Mr. Clark, and I have a few more questions for you before we proceed. Please return my call at your earliest convenience."

Now wouldn't be that convenient time, since I was hurrying to class. I listened to his next message.

"Ms. Lockwood, this is Lieutenant Bailey again. We need to take a deposition from you regarding Aaron Chambers, who was apparently last seen in your presence. If you are available this evening to come by the station, please do so. Or return my call and we'll set up an appointment."

Anger shivered along my spine. I couldn't believe it. She'd actually done it! Aaron's mom had turned me in for his disappearance.

I bit down hard enough on my lower lip to draw blood. How was I supposed to reconcile myself with this witch when I hoped to be a permanent part of her son's life someday?

Of course, I thought as an aching sadness filled my chest, that all depended on whether I retrieved Aaron from hell.

But before I could go to Lieutenant Bailey's office and clear my name, I needed to go to work and explain my absence to my boss.

When fourth hour ended, I got in my car and drove across town to the newspaper office of the Lacey-Barnagat Times. I was fortunate enough at the beginning of the semester to be picked for the work-study program so I could spend half of my day at work earning school credit. Since I already knew that journalism was what I wanted to do with the rest of my life, it worked great for me.

I parked my car in front of the office and took the elevator to the third floor. Mr. Edward's door was open, and he was having an in-depth conversation with Kent, one of our reporters with a byline. I paused, giving into my habit of eavesdropping before making my presence known.

"They all seem to have vanished, the whole cult. There have been no more sacrifices, no more suicides, no more disappearances."

"We have to find a lead." I could hear Mr. Edwards pacing his office, which was rather unusual. He generally appeared calm and only mildly interested in current events.

Taking a deep breath, I tapped on the open door and poked my head around the side. "Hello?" I said timidly.

Though I barely knew Kent and didn't expect him to know me, his eyes went wide with recognition, and Mr. Edwards exclaimed, "Jayne!" In an instant he had crossed over to the open door and wrapped me in a very unprofessional hug. My face warmed slightly, but the man was old enough to be my grandfather, and I knew it was with parental affection.

"You're back!" Kent had his notepad out and a pen was down from behind his ear, and I knew anything I said would be used for a story. "Were you with the cult? Did they brainwash you?"

I thought of that moment in the underground parking garage when Samantha appeared with her chanting legions, and my knees nearly buckled. My boss grabbed a chair and settled me into it.

"It's all right, Jayne. You don't have to talk about this if you don't want to."

I shook my head. "I don't want my name in the paper. I don't want people contacting me, trying to figure out where their loved ones are, why I came back when they didn't."

Both of them nodded at me rather eagerly, anxious to hear what I would say.

I took a deep breath. "I don't actually remember anything. I was at home with my sister and my friend. And then there is nothing. When I woke up in the morning, I was in Maryland. My friend apparently drove us out there, and then our car broke down. A farmer found us and took us in. After we woke up and realized where we were, we came home."

Neither of them said anything for a moment, though I could see the wheels spinning.

"So the car breaking down saved you," Kent said slowly. "Otherwise you would be with all of the others who disappeared, and none of them came back."

I shuddered.

"What about this good Samaritan?" Kent continued. "Do you have contact for him?"

"No. I don't even remember his name."

"So where are the others? Did they wake up like you two days ago and realize they weren't at home? Or are they still being brainwashed?"

In other words, were they trying to get home, or did they still not know they were missing? I wished I could say, but I couldn't. So I shrugged.

My boss favored me with a smile. "We are so happy you're back, Jayne. We only lost one other staff member, and it was a rather devastating blow to lose you both."

I lifted my index finger to my mouth and gnawed at the nail. "Anyone I know?"

"I doubt it."

Kent interrupted. "Jayne, can I do a quick little interview with you and print it up? It would be anonymous, of course, but you're the only person we know of who has come back. People want to know, they want to have hope. You can give them that."

I exhaled. "Sure. But I can't stay long, the police want to meet with me also."

They both gave noises of sympathy and understanding, and I looked to Mr. Edwards.

"Tomorrow I would like to work as usual. If I'm still employed here."

"Of course! We always value your input. And next year when you graduate, we'll work around your university classes."

A journalist fresh out of high school. I'd be one of the youngest. But I was getting hands-on learning exposure, more than many people did after four years in college.

I could dwell on that later. I gave a smile. "Thank you. I'll see you tomorrow then."

"And that interview, Jayne?" Kent asked.

I hesitated. "Let me talk to the police first. I'm not sure how much I'm allowed to disclose."

He nodded, making a valiant effort to hide his disappointment.

I hopped back into my car and made the fifteen-minute drive to the police station. The receptionist smiled when she saw me and said, "Here for Lieutenant Bailey, right?"

I bobbed my head, unnerved by her familiarity. I came here too often. She used to give me the third degree every time I wanted to talk to him.

Instead she made a quick phone call to his desk before ushering me around the corner.

Lieutenant Bailey was already making his way down the aisle in my direction, not waiting for me to arrive at his cubicle. "Come on," he said, gesturing me down a hallway and into a room. He closed the door behind us and sat down at the single table, placing his Styrofoam cup on top.

I sat down across from him, trying to convince myself I wasn't a suspect. I'd seen too many cop shows. I pleated my fingers and waited for him to start the conversation.

He put his phone on the table. "I'm going to ask you some questions about Aaron Chambers first. I'm going to record our conversation, so don't say anything you don't want everybody to hear."

I cocked my head, not sure if his warning was exactly kosher. "Aren't you supposed to tell me anything I say can and will be used against me?"

His stern face gave a hint of a smile. "I think you and I are past that."

My shoulders relaxed slightly, and I allowed myself to return his smile. In no way did he think I was responsible for Aaron's disappearance.

Even though I was.

"Are you ready?" At my nod, he hit a red button on his phone. "Deposition of —" He looked at me. "Please state your name."

"Jayne Lockwood," I replied.

"Regarding the disappearance of Aaron Chambers. Jayne, do you know Aaron?"

I started to nod before I remembered I needed to be verbal. "Yes. Aaron is —" I choked for a moment, remembering our break up. "Was my boyfriend. We were very close."

"When did you last see him?"

Lie lie lie. "He came over to my house Sunday evening. His parents wanted him to transfer schools and go back to England. He felt like it would be better for us not to have a long distance relationship, so we broke up."

Lieutenant Bailey was watching me closely. Did he suspect I was hiding things? Probably. "What happened with Mr. Chambers after that?"

"We parted ways. I said goodbye, and he left. I didn't see him again."

"Do you know where he went?"

He followed me to Maryland. "I don't. I assumed he went home to his parents. Although he goes to school an hour away, so maybe he went to be with some friends."

"Did either of you try to contact each other after?"

I had to be careful here. I stared at the wall behind him and replayed the sequence of events in my head, trying to figure out what I could reveal while still holding my story together. "Aaron called me a few times, but it must've been when I was in that odd hypnotic state. I didn't see the calls until two days later when we woke up in Maryland."

"Who is we?"

"My friend Meredith, my sister Beth, and me."

"Aaron's disappearance coincides with several other disappearances in the area, including your own. You didn't see him in Maryland?"

I swallowed hard and forced myself to meet Lieutenant Bailey's gaze. I said with as much conviction as I could, "I don't remember anything from that time."

"Is there anything else you would like to add?"

I shook my head, lowering my eyes and allowing the heat of tears to pool there. "No."

He hit the red button again and sat back. "Now. What are you not telling me?"

"How much should I tell you?"

I saw him considering the question, his eyes looking back and forth between mine. "I ask you a question, and you answer. Truthfully."

I nodded, though my heart beat faster in my neck.

"First question." Again he paused, probably deciding how much he could handle. "Did you see the missing people?"

"Yes." I didn't hesitate, even though I'd just lied in my deposition, and now we both knew it. "They are all in a brainwashed state right now."

"Do you know where they are?"

"No. But even if you found them, you couldn't help them. They are more like zombies under someone else's control."

"How do we save them?"

"I don't know." I pressed my fingers against the table. "I need Trey Clark. We have to reunite the souls with their bodies. We have to overthrow —" I almost said Karta, but I bit it back. The traitor didn't deserve that title.

26

Besides, she wasn't anymore. "Samantha."

"I don't understand what she has to do with their souls."

"She's harvesting them. By using their life energy, she's making herself stronger."

Lieutenant Bailey furrowed his brow and growled, "You're testing the limits of my belief."

"Then don't ask me to tell you," I said. "What you believe or don't believe is inconsequential. This is what's happening." Once again, indignation fired up in my chest. I closed my eyes and gripped the edge of the table.

Images flashed behind my eyelids like fireworks. I stood in a clearing, barefoot, a lightweight cloth blowing around my ankles as dust clogged my lungs. Hot ash drifted between my toes, a noonday sun beating down on me. Trees ringed the clearing in the distance, smoke rising from the forest.

I blinked and the image faded, but for a moment my lungs still felt dry and my toes warm.

"What was that?" I whispered, terrified goosebumps popping up on my skin.

"What?" Lieutenant Bailey leaned closer. "What was what?"

It was some kind of vision, but not like the ones I usually received. This was something different. I stood up. "How are we doing on freeing Trey from the mental institution?"

The lieutenant narrowed his eyes at me but didn't object to my question. "I've actually petitioned a judge to issue a court order for his release. Stating that I need to bring him in for questioning. But that's the best I can do. I can't let him go free, not when he is being held for a crime."

"That he didn't commit," I snarled, all fiery again. Wow. I needed to take a chill pill.

"It's the best I can do," he repeated. "I'll let you know when we get him up to the station so you can talk to him."

I nodded and lowered my eyes so he wouldn't see the defiance in them. If Trey was going to help me, I needed to get him out of police custody.

There was nothing for me to do after the police station but go home. As wrong as it felt.

I tried to distract myself with homework while fighting this sinking feeling in my gut. I heard my sister in her room, singing to music like she hadn't a care. Maybe the world's impending doom didn't plague her like it did me.

Somehow that only made me feel more alone.

And what about that vision I'd had? What did that mean?

The tension in our house hadn't faded by the next morning, and Mom wasn't ready to let go of her reins of power. She drove Beth to school again. I walked into psychology and gave Meredith a lopsided grin before falling into my seat. I waited for her outside the classroom when class ended, and a moment later she fell into step beside me.

"I feel like I'm in limbo," she said.

"Tell me about it," I said. "There are so many things we're supposed to be doing right now, and going to school isn't one of them."

"Any luck getting Trey free?"

"I'm working on it. Lieutenant Bailey thinks he can get him out."

"Well, that's fantastic news! When?"

"I don't know. He'll call me. The question is, what do we do after that?"

Meredith blinked her wide blue eyes behind their wire frames. "I don't understand. You mean, what's the plan?"

I licked my lips and clarified. "I mean, he won't be free. Lieutenant Bailey is going to get him out just so we can question him. It's temporary."

"That's no good!" Meredith cried, attracting the attention of neighboring students. "We need to take him with us! We need Trey to tell us everything he knows about the mystical realm, and we have to help him get his powers back so that he can help us free all of those people, none of which can be accomplished in a twenty-minute interrogation!"

"I know," I said. "So the real question is, how do we help him break out?"

"Break out. Oh. Oh! We have to kidnap him!"

We were across the street now and entering the main wing of the school.

"Something like that. We have to free him, and then we have to run." Whatever my relationship with Lieutenant Bailey was, I knew he wouldn't let it go lightly if I helped one of his prisoners escape. He would hunt me down, if only for the sake of appearances.

"So what are your suggestions?" Meredith lowered her voice, as if she expected the police force to have spies walking around and eavesdropping.

I tapped my finger against my lips. "I have none."

We stood for a moment in the hallway, silent, while students rippled around us as if we were rocks in a river.

"Well, we better come up with something. I don't think this is a plan we want to wing."

"Yeah," I agreed.

We waved goodbye and I headed toward my second-hour class, already scheming different ways of breaking someone out of police custody and wondering where I would get my hands on all of the imaginary gas bombs floating through my ideas.

CHAPTER FOUR

When I walked into work that afternoon, Kent immediately pulled me into the break room.

"Jayne, do you realize how pivotal you are to this situation?" His eyes danced with barely concealed excitement, and he practically breathed fire with anticipation. "You might be the key to all of this."

I looked around for my co-worker Kate, eager for someone to shield me. "I really don't know anything. I don't remember what happened."

"Kent!" Justin, another staff member, poked his head in the room, his hand slapping onto the door frame. "It might be happening again!"

We both looked at him with bewildered expressions.

"What's happening again?" Kent asked, biting before I did.

"Disappearances. Come, check out the hotline."

The hotline was a number the police had set up just for the press, with a stream of constant information, kind of like a verbal newsfeed, mostly with police reports and weather reports. It provided us immediate bulletins without needing to call the police department every ten minutes.

Kent dropped his notepad and pen back into his pocket and they both took off, leaving me virtually forgotten. But I stood up and followed, one anxious finger making its way to my mouth so it could be chewed on.

But the disappearances couldn't be happening again. Samantha's power was gone. Her poem had been nullified.

If there were any more disappearances, they had to be simply coincidental.

The hotline was on speakerphone, with five or six reporters and staff members gathered around it to collect its feed. A missing persons report spouted off, and I did a quick count in my head. Five. Six. Seven.

And then the newsfeed flashed to something else, something happening in the larger world around us. But all I could think was that seven was a lot of people to have suddenly gone missing.

I took a tentative step forward, not wanting to draw attention to myself in case I wasn't supposed to be in here. Nobody noticed me as I stood on tiptoes and peered at the list of names Justin had jotted down. Surreptitiously, I pulled out my trusty flip phone and used the camera function to snap a picture of the list. Then I put the phone in my pocket and snuck back out.

While my official title had been upgraded from intern to junior journalist in August, my duties hadn't changed. My job was to work next to Kate, another junior journalist who was actually in college working on her degree. I would help her with her assignments and her research and any other quick jobs around the office.

But I hadn't seen Kate, and she hadn't tracked me down either. She might not even realize I was back. Which meant, for the moment, I didn't have an assignment.

Except for the one I was giving myself.

I sat down in one of the vacant chairs and did a web search on the first name on the list of missing persons. Tara Elliot. Nothing came up.

I got the same result with persons two and three. But on the fourth name on the list, I found a social media account. The woman, Rebecca Scott, had left a public comment less than a week earlier.

"If you see my husband, please, call me or the police. I already reported him missing, but I know he would never leave me willingly."

She'd also posted a picture of the man.

There were a string of optimistic comments in response, as well as a few negative ones suggesting he had left her intentionally. I pulled up the archives, searching for the list of missing persons the police had put together. They had worked with the news media to put the comprehensive list on news outlets and social media. Public theories of what was happening ran rampant, everything from cults to kidnappings to trafficking.

I hadn't seen the list before now, and my heart squeezed when I realized there were more than six thousand people on it. The list was in alphabetical order, so I only needed to scan down to the S section to verify if this woman's husband was on it.

But first I had to get past the C section. Even knowing it would be there, my throat tightened when I saw Aaron's name.

Aaron Chambers.

I touched the screen. "We're going to get you back," I whispered. "I promise."

Enough of that. The police were doing what they could to get Trey, and I couldn't do anything else until then. I continued scanning for the last name "Scott."

There. Dustin Scott. Turning back to the internet browser, I did a search for Dustin and Rebecca Scott.

Jackpot. It pulled up their engagement announcement from seven years earlier, the only news they had ever made together. Lucky.

Something was coming together in the back of my mind like a tenuous spider web, though I couldn't quite grasp the edges of the sticky strings just yet. I went back to the first name on the list on my phone. Tara Elliott. Just for kicks and giggles, I toggled the archived list. I wasn't surprised when I found another Elliott.

I tried the list on my phone again, comparing the seven newly missing people to the six thousand already missing.

I got five matches on the last names. Five. Out of seven.

What did it mean? How were the new missing people related to the ones who disappeared last week? Had they found copies of the poem lying around the house and only now been affected? The poem didn't mean anything now. Samantha no longer had the power to summon these people.

I sucked in a breath as the sticky web fell across my mind like a net, the tickling thought coalescing into a theory. The new missing people were the significant others of those already gone. More specifically, the women of those already gone.

It was just a theory, but I had a reason behind it. The professor I met with in New York told me how the ancient Latvian people, the druids who still believed in the pagan gods, were originally a matriarchal society, giving higher powers to the goddesses than the gods. But then something changed. New stories had arisen of Saule, the sun-goddess, losing a challenge to Velns, god of the underworld. The price of losing was high: she became his servant, and all women thereafter became subservient to the men.

Professor Kestovely didn't have much more to add to it than that. It was an interesting story, he had said, and explained the more recent trend of venerating the gods before the goddesses.

But to me it was more than a story. Aaron and I had joked about it, but he hadn't forgotten. And when he learned that Samantha wanted to control me through him, he broke up with me first, thus freeing me from being subject to him by mythological laws.

These other women might not have been so lucky. Samantha had their husbands and boyfriends. And that was all she needed.

For moment I felt dizzy, and I bowed my head, taking slow, deep breaths. Children. How many children would be parent-less because of this? Sitting at home wondering where their moms and dads had gone?

"Oh, no. No," I whispered.

Work would have to wait. I needed to get to the police station and share this development. I doubted the police could stop the summoning. Even if the women were incapable of leaving, I didn't know what their state of mind would be.

∞

"Lieutenant Bailey is not here."

"He's—what? He's not?" I stared at the receptionist as if she had spoken in a different language.

She raised her eyebrows and rolled the pen between her fingers. "Did you have an appointment with him?"

"No, but—are you sure?" It was a legitimate question. She'd been mistaken before.

She cleared her throat, a sure sign she was losing her patience with me. "He's off for the next two days."

Somehow it had never occurred to me that Lieutenant Bailey wasn't always at work. He was just a police officer. Right?

Turned out he actually had another life, and today he was living it.

"Would you like to talk to his partner?"

I didn't even know he had a partner. Was it possible the partner knew about me? I needed to talk to someone, and urgently. "Yes. If he's available."

She sat me in a chair in her office, and I waited until she returned. A man I'd often seen speaking with Lieutenant Bailey stepped in. He was portlier, and the crinkle lines around his eyes were stronger, but he looked friendly enough.

"Come with me, Ms. Lockwood," he said.

I followed him back to a cubicle beside Lieutenant Bailey's. I folded my fingers together, my stomach doing similar calisthenics. Was this even a good idea?

He gestured for me to take a seat, and I did. Then he sat in a chair across from me.

"You don't remember me, do you?"

"I've seen you here when I've stopped by."

"I was there that night. You know . . ." He moved his hand across his

34

throat.

"Oh!" I touched my neck, feeling the fabric of the scarf I had knotted there. I always wore one these days to hide my scar. "I'm sorry, I didn't remember."

"I wouldn't expect you to. But we're partners. Where he goes, I go too."

I swallowed hard, remembering again how close I had come to dying that night when the serial killer slit my throat. "Thank you," I said, somewhat sheepishly. Here I had been half prepared not to like the guy.

He settled back in his seat, hooking a thumb through the suspenders over his shirt. "How can I help you?"

I hesitated, still playing with the knot in my scarf. "How much has Lieutenant Bailey told you about me?"

His eyes narrowed, his lips pressing together. "I'm not sure what you mean."

"I just wasn't sure how much he's told you about my lingering trauma," I said, going out on a limb. Lieutenant Bailey would have had to come up with some excuse for my constant reappearance.

He tilted his head, a hint of curiosity in his eyes. "It's normal to take months to recover after an ordeal like yours. And it's not unheard of for the victim to feel an attachment to their rescuer."

I refrained from rolling my eyes. So Lieutenant Bailey had made it out like I had some kind of hero-worship thing going on. Fine. I could work with that. "It's just every time I start to feel scared, I remember he's here, that I can trust the police."

"Of course. We're here to serve."

I kept going. "And I really just needed to talk to him today, just to get that reassurance." Oh, how pathetic I sounded. Did they all think this? Did the whole police force think I came in here for comfort? I ground my teeth together. "Could you just let him know I came by?"

"Sure. But hopefully you feel a little bit better knowing he's not the only one protecting New Jersey."

I forced a smile, not wanting him to feel slighted by my obvious preference for Lieutenant Bailey. "I do feel better." I stood up, shouldering my purse and choking back the bitter taste in my throat. "Thank you."

I managed to keep the scowl off my face until I was safely out the doors of the police department. Poor helpless victim indeed. I yanked out my phone and scrolled through my contacts until I found Lieutenant Bailey's number. I wouldn't be waiting for his partner to let him know I came by.

He answered on the second ring. "Ms. Lockwood." His voice held that same note of caution as his partner's had. "How can I help you?"

"I know why people are still disappearing," I said, almost tripping over my words in my hurry to get them out. "I know who's going to be next."

"You have a name?" He sounded decidedly more interested.

"Not exactly. But I know who it's going to be. Or at least, I'm pretty sure."

"Can you meet me at the station? I can be there in twenty minutes."

I growled under my breath. I had just left the station. But I wanted to be accommodating, and this was important. "I'll be there."

I seated myself down on a bench in front of the police department. I didn't want to go back in and feel the scrutiny of the receptionist and Lieutenant Bailey's partner. They would wonder what I could possibly have to say to Lieutenant Bailey that I couldn't say to them.

So I waited.

A patrol car rolled in nearly half an hour later, and Lieutenant Bailey climbed out. He joined me on the bench and pulled a notepad from his shirt pocket. He looked different dressed in jeans instead of his uniform. I noticed he still had a shirt with a pocket on it, though. Kind of like me, always looking for a place to stock notepads and pens.

A pen was in his hands now also, and he looked at me, fingers visibly twitching. "What do you know?"

He didn't ask me how I knew, probably because he'd rather not find out.

"The people who disappeared yesterday are all related to the people who vanished last week. And they're all women."

His brow furrowed together, pen halting, and he even lifted his eyes from the paper. "What?"

I exhaled and tried to spell it out for him. "The women that were left behind by their spouses, boyfriends, significant others, those are the ones vanishing now. They're going to join the men. They don't need a special poem."

He looked down again, scribbling frantically over his notepad. "Are you sure?"

I shrugged. "Check for yourself."

He looked at me again, his gray eyes somber. "How can we stop this? Who's next? Husbands? Children? Cousins, friends?"

While I suspected the answer was no, I couldn't say for sure. "I don't know." I leaned closer, pressing my fingertips against his knuckles. "I need Trey Clark. And not for just an hour." I said it as clearly and emphatically as I could, hoping when Trey disappeared from the hospital, Lieutenant Bailey would forgive me.

"The judge has granted me an interview with him next week on Tuesday. Three o'clock. But it will be in an interrogation room under surveillance. We'll have to conduct the interview there."

"What good is that?" I said, my anger getting the best of me. "I need him free."

Lieutenant Bailey's gaze remained steady on me. "They won't let him go."

Simmer down, I told myself. I met his gaze coolly. "Tuesday at three o'clock?"

He nodded.

"I'll be there."

CHAPTER FIVE

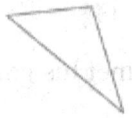

I went straight to Meredith's house after I ended my conversation with Lieutenant Bailey. I told her everything he'd said.

"So what are we going to do?" she asked from where she sat at her computer desk chair, watching me pace the room like a caged lion.

I lifted my arms. "We tried to do this the legal way. I did what I could to get him free. Now I'll just have to break him out."

"The police will know it was you," she said, her eyes trailing me.

"No kidding!" I snapped, the rage boiling again. Criminy. "They didn't leave me any choice. Aaron—"

I didn't say it. Aaron had saved me, and now it was my turn to save him.

"Okay. How do we do this? We can't exactly take him out from under Lieutenant Bailey's nose."

"No. I think he might even expect me to try. He'll have his guard up. We have to do it before he brings Trey to the station. He's expecting me to be there Tuesday for the interview. He won't expect me to take Trey before that."

Meredith nodded. "And how are we going to kidnap him?"

I gave her a tight smile. "Why, my dear Ragana, I'm surprised you even have to ask. You, the one gifted with the powers of persuasion."

Her eyes narrowed. "You want me to manipulate their minds?"

I nodded, my heart giving a nervous little jump. I wasn't asking too much, was I?

She returned my smile. "Looks like I better write some poetry."

Meredith and I spent the next hour plotting what we would do after we got Trey out of the mental hospital. We had no place to hide him, and Lieutenant Bailey was very likely to come knocking on my bedroom door as soon as Trey disappeared. While I hadn't been able to convince the lieutenant that he needed to do everything in his power to free Trey, I was certain I had convinced him of my desperation to get Trey free.

And when he came to my house and discovered I was gone, he would have no doubt. But by then it would be too late.

"Are we doing the right thing?" Meredith asked, looking uneasy.

"I have no idea," I said, some of my frustration leaking into my voice. "All I have to go on is Laima's declaration that Beth and I could save Aaron and all of those people with you and Trey helping us. My only power is to look people in the eye and see how they're going to die. Not very helpful."

"I'm not much better," Meredith said. "We won't have any trouble getting him out of the hospital as long as all of his attendees and nurses read the poem I wrote."

"That's all we're going to need," I said.

"And what about the fact Trey lost his powers? How can you help with that?"

I shook my head. I had no answer.

My mom called a few minutes later, wanting me home. She didn't like me out in the evenings anymore, and no amount of talking would convince her I was safe.

"I'll see you Monday in school," I said, shouldering my bag and heaving a sigh.

Meredith tapped her pen against her lips. "Are we just going to disappear without letting our parents know again?"

My poor mom would have a heart attack. But what else could we do? "Yeah. I guess so."

Meredith didn't look happy about that, but she bobbed her head in acknowledgment.

⚭

I tossed and turned in my bed, thoughts running through my head. Every time I thought of the jail break—well, hospital break—we were planning for Trey, my heart rate increased and the blood pounded in my throat, making the scar on my neck throb.

And then there was Aaron. For a moment I pictured his deep blue eyes, the dimple in his chin, the lazy way he would smile at me as if he knew a secret but wasn't telling.

I banished the image from my mind and squeezed my eyes shut like that would make the ache in my heart go away. Aaron was gone, and it was my fault. And I would not stop until I had him back.

His face was the last thing on my mind when I finally fell asleep, so it should've been no surprise when my dreams led me to the hallway of doors.

"Jayne."

His voice called to me. I'd been here before, and I remembered the way. I hurried to the door at the end, the one from where his voice came.

"Aaron!" I called. "Where are you? I'm coming!"

I touched the tip of my finger to the door knob and immediately clenched my fist and pulled back, expecting it to burn me like last time.

But it didn't. It was cool to the touch. Even so, my palm began to sear. I gasped and flipped my hand over.

There, in the middle of my hand, was the brand I received last time. The star of Auseklis. Only now it glowed red hot, as if a fire burned under my skin.

I stared at it, then I looked at the door knob again. Sure enough, the star was still imprinted there, the same star that last time I had burned into my flesh. Hesitant, already flinching from the expected pain, I pressed the star on my hand to the star on the knob.

The knob twisted without my help, and the door swung inward.

I leaned my head against the door frame and stared down a winding set of stairs as they disappeared into the darkness. A cold feeling rushed up the stairwell, the chill much more than physical, reaching my soul and settling around my heart. I shuddered, wanting to put as much distance between myself and the stairs as possible.

"Jayne."

I closed my eyes. There was no mistaking that voice, the British lilt to my name. I put both hands on either side of the door frame and pushed myself forward.

"Aaron," I said. I wanted to shout, wanted to scream his name into the dark and let his voice guide me to him. But my voice came out in a frightened whisper. I put one foot on the step.

A gush of cold wind blew up at me, blowing my hair away from my face, lifting me up and throwing me backward. I landed on my backside and skidded several feet down the hall. The door swung closed, slamming so hard into the frame that the hallway shook.

"No!" I cried, and then my eyes opened.

I was in my bed, and I was awake. My bedsheets wrapped around my legs, and I took several breaths to calm my racing heart.

I didn't know what the dream meant, but the sense of urgency pummeling through my veins left one thing clear: we needed to put our plan into action now.

∞

The rest of the weekend passed in similar turmoil, with me and Meredith sending surreptitious messages back and forth, half the time panicking and half the time encouraging each other.

"Can I pick Beth up from school today?" I asked my mom at breakfast Monday morning. I willed my hands not to tremble, and I kept my eyes on the grapefruit I dissected. I couldn't let her see my deception.

"Aren't you going to work after school?"

Minor detail. "I thought she could come with me. See what I do." There was a lot of truth to that statement.

"Some other time. I don't want her away from home right now. You either, but I'm trying to give you more freedom."

"Much appreciated," I said, sucking a segment of grapefruit from my spoon. I kept quiet as I ate, trying to figure out how I would get Beth away from my mom's watchful eyes. I would just have to come home and grab her while Meredith hid Trey away somewhere.

Which meant that, by tonight, my mom would know Beth and I had disappeared again. My chest tightened, and the grapefruit in my mouth turned bitter.

"Well, I'll see you later, Mom," I said. Avoiding her eyes, I leaned over to give her a kiss on the cheek. I didn't want to appear overly affectionate, but I couldn't just walk away from her.

"Wait, Jayne." She grabbed my arm, and I paused. Did she suspect? Had I done something to give it away?

"Yes?" I pasted on a fake smile.

Her eyes scanned mine, and it was like looking in a mirror. How we could possibly have the same shade of aquamarine blue was pretty amazing. I held perfectly still lest she read my thoughts.

"Are you okay, honey?"

I widened my fake smile. "Yeah. Of course. Just on my way to school." I held my backpack up by one strap to prove my point.

"I mean, with Aaron's disappearance. You haven't mentioned him once since coming home."

I froze, the smile immobile on my face. Of course she knew he'd vanished. Why did that shock me?

She was still talking, her lips moving as her words droned on, but I only now tuned back in.

" . . . okay to cry, if you want to talk about anything — "

"I'm fine," I said, realizing as I said it that I was using the tone of voice people use when they are exactly not fine. I tried to soften it. "Aaron's fine. Aaron's coming back. I promise, he's going to be fine."

Instead of reassuring her, her eyes welled up with tears. She patted my arm. "Of course, sweetheart."

She could not have had a worse reaction. My throat tightened up, and my eyes burned. "He's not gone. He's just missing. You'll see."

I didn't wait for her response, didn't wait to see more sympathy in her eyes. I simply wrapped my scarf around my neck one more time and rushed out the door.

My heart pounded, the beat sounding like, "Save him. Save him. Save him."

Meredith was waiting for me when I got to my locker, and for the first time since we arrived home from Maryland, something besides despair was written all over her face: anticipation. I returned her smile, feeling the same stirring in my chest. We were doing something.

"Are you ready?" I asked, doing the normal book-switch at my locker.

She bobbed her head. "Ready as I'll ever be. I have the poem here, and I have a back up if I need something more. I tried to make a storm like I did in Maryland, but nothing happened."

"Don't worry about it. I'm sure it will come when you need it." Like I was sure about anything. I closed my locker and faced her. "My mom wouldn't let me pick Beth up from school. So here's the plan. We go to the hospital as soon as visiting hours start at four o'clock. We use your poem to get Trey out and leave before anyone has woken up enough to sic the police on us. Wait." I paused and gave her another look. "The guards will snap out of it, right?"

Meredith looked slightly less certain, but she nodded. "I included a line intended to make the effects of the poem temporary."

"Criminy. If it works, that's nothing short of awesome. You can make all kinds of poems just for temporary effect. It isn't long, is it?"

"Just four lines. I don't plan to stand there reciting sonnets all day. That would just be ridiculous, since they'd fall asleep on their feet from boredom before the effect of the poem ever hit them."

I laughed at that assessment. "So. We need two cars because after we get Trey out, you have to sneak off with him. Don't go home. I'll go to my house just long enough to grab Beth and then meet back up with you."

"We need to have our rendezvous established now."

"Stephen's house," I said without thinking. "His aunt will be at work, he's not there, and it's far enough away from the police station it's not likely to be their first check. And I can get there in just fifteen minutes."

"Trey and I will wait for you there," she promised.

The warning bell rang, and we gathered our books and walked across the street as if we were nothing more than average high school students. But the jittery energy in my veins and the butterflies dancing in my stomach told me otherwise.

And I still had to get through work after this.

When I stepped into my third hour chemistry class, my eyes immediately went to the empty spot next to my seat. I knew Stephen wouldn't be there, but I couldn't help hoping against hope that I would walk into class and everything would be back to normal.

I put my books down at my desk and was about to sit when the whole room went quiet. I hesitated and lifted my head. Even the air had gone still. The noisy chatter of teenagers giggling and gossiping and whispering before class had vanished. I half expected my class to have vanished also, but when I spun around, all of my classmates were there.

Frozen.

They stood unmoving in whatever pose they had been in moments earlier. I lifted my hand to my face and wiggled my fingers. Was I the only one who hadn't frozen? What was going on?

The classroom door opened, and I lifted my head just as Jods stepped through.

I sucked in, fear breathing to life in my gut. I hadn't seen the dark-haired, deeply muscled, demonic god since the confrontation with Samantha.

Was this a vision? Was I imagining him?

No, I was wrong. It wasn't Jods, though they could have been bothers. This one had something different around his eyes and jawline. I stared at him. He wore no shirt over his bronze chest but some kind of sash that looked woven from strands of wheat. A grass skirt finished the ensemble, complete with a fringe of metal beads. He definitely was not my teacher, who I hoped to never see in a skirt. This guy managed to pull it off. A tumble of jet black hair cascaded to his shoulder blades.

What was happening?

"Who are you?" I asked.

He gave a smile, mischievous, dangerous, and inviting all at once. "You don't remember me? I am hurt."

My stomach tightened in recognition when he spoke, and yet I was certain I'd never seen him before.

"Do I know you?" He had to be one of the pantheon, part of the Latvian gods and goddesses. Meredith and I had studied them, trying to memorize who did what, but right now none of them were ringing a bell.

He stepped closer to me, cupping my arm right beneath the elbow. "You and I go way back, Dekla," he said, the warm timbres of his voice like honey to my worried heart. "In time, you'll remember."

Even as he spoke, a memory surfaced in the back of my mind, glossy and trembling like a mirage in the desert sun.

A barren meadow. Barefoot. I was there again, moving steadily forward, one foot in front of the other, a thin tunic wrapping around my ankles like a breeze.

I lifted up my gaze and I was back in my classroom. He stared at me, his eyes penetrating my own.

"What do you want?" I asked.

"The question is, what do you want? I can help you get it."

My eyebrows shot up. These people didn't give something for nothing. Not even Laima, goddess of fate, gave someone a longer life without taking it from someone else.

"What's the price?" I asked.

He leaned close to me, so close I felt the warmth of his breath when he spoke, his lips nearly brushing my forehead. "When you're ready, you'll know the price. And then you will come to me."

A shiver ran down my spine, and I lifted my face, ready with my next question. But the light touch of his hand disappeared from my arm, and he was gone. At the same instant, life returned to the classroom. The cacophony of voices, the slamming of books on tables, the teacher's footsteps scuffing on the floor as he went to his desk. I didn't move, just stood there absorbing every moment and trying to understand what had just happened.

"Jayne?" Mr. Joenks said. "Would you like to sit so we can begin class?"

I nodded and sank into my chair. Just like when I have my visions, time had not passed for everyone else. But unlike my visions, I hadn't been Seeing the future through someone else's eyes. Had I dreamed up the whole thing? Had it just been an extremely realistic daydream?

Something shiny on the corner of the table caught my eye. I slid my hand over and picked up a bead. A metal, strangely shaped, exotic bead.

Exactly like the ones dangling from the man-skirt.

CHAPTER SIX

I was a bit twitchy the rest of the day, practically jumping at shadows and half expecting weird gods and goddesses to appear out of nowhere.

But nothing else even remotely strange happened, and I left campus to head to work without further incident.

I held my breath as I stepped into the office, bracing myself for more bad news. But all was quiet, just the hum of a printer somewhere, keys clacking on a keyboard, and someone talking on the phone. I let out a little exhale of relief. Every time I thought about the jailbreak we were pulling off in a few hours, a hot wave of anxiety washed over me. A nice, non-stressful day at work would do my blood pressure good.

"Hey," I said to Kate as I sat down in the vacant chair beside her. "Where do you need me?"

She swiveled around and placed a stack of papers on my thighs. "We're running a whole section as a memorial to the missing people. These are the remaining family members, and we're interviewing as many as will consent. It's meant to be some kind of tribute, but I think Chief is really looking for a hidden link, something that ties the people together."

I thumbed through the stack. "Did any more people go missing yesterday?"

"I'm not sure. I didn't hear about it. Maybe ask Kent."

I'd rather ask Lieutenant Bailey, but I felt guilty reaching out to him when I was about to directly undermine him. Still, maybe it would make him suspect me less if we had spoken to each other just hours before Trey disappeared from the hospital.

Or maybe not.

"So how are we arranging these interviews?" I asked.

"Cold calling. Try to set up a live interview, at a café or at their house or something. If they refuse, just get a few words off the phone. Any interview you do over the phone is yours." She arched a pencil thin eyebrow, emphasizing the bright green eyeshadow that matched her feather earrings. All Kate needed was a perm to look like she'd stepped out of the eighties.

"Yay me." It was better than nothing.

I set up my stuff at one of the phone cubicles and put on a set of headphones. Immediately the room descended into silence, reminding me so much of my chemistry class right before Mr. Deity walked in that I lifted my head and looked around. No, I was still at work, and everyone was still fluttering around me. Nothing new here.

Why did that disappoint me?

The first person I called was Lieutenant Bailey. He wasn't on my interview list, so I used my phone to get his number.

"Lieutenant Bailey speaking."

"Lieutenant, it's Jayne Lockwood."

"Miss Lockwood. How can I help you?"

I shifted uncomfortably in my hard plastic chair, glancing around to make sure nobody was watching me. "Did you have any luck? With those people in question?"

"I sent patrols out to the households, but that's all I could do. We can't force anyone into custody or lock them in their houses. And I don't know how much good it did, because this morning we were unable to reach several of the women we spoke to yesterday."

A hard knot formed in my stomach. "Did you go check on them?"

"I have men en route. Many of the women had small children at home, and we can't risk the chance of those children being alone." An edge entered his voice when he spoke again. "I thought this was supposed to have stopped."

Did I detect a note of accusation? "It was. But she's got more power than we expected. That's why I need Trey Clark. Not just to talk to him. I need him."

"I'm already breaking protocol allowing you to be present when we interrogate him. It's the best I can do."

I accepted that with a defeated nod. I had no other option, then. But I had to act satisfied with his response. "Tomorrow, then? At three?"

"Yes. I'll see you at the police station."

I let out a little exhale after we hung up, my pulse pounding in my temples. I hated to betray the fragile relationship he and I had created over the past few months. But hopefully the outcome would be positive enough for him to forgive me.

I went through the rest of my calls on autopilot, actually relieved that nobody wanted to speak with me. The closer the clock ticked toward five o'clock and the illicit activity Meredith and I had planned, the more anxious I became.

I knocked on Mr. Edwards' door before I left, my heart already doing the jitterbug. This job meant too much for me to just vanish from it.

Mr. Edwards lifted his head from the dummy sheet, giving the layout his final approval before it went to the proofreaders. I was lucky that wasn't my job. Usually new journalists started there, but anyone with any brains could see after five minutes that I was no good at editing.

"Yes, Jayne? You off for the day?"

I nodded and nibbled on the nail of my index finger, seeking courage and the right words. "I have a little problem."

Mr. Edwards leaned back in his stretchy chair and pleated his fingers. "How can I help you?"

I appreciated the way he phrased the question. "I don't think I've recovered from my ordeal as well as I thought I had. I'm struggling a bit, and I think I need to put my focus on school right now. My grades are falling. My mind is distracted. I can't seem to balance everything."

He nodded. "So you need some time off."

I offered a weak smile. "Can I please? Just a little. I love this job. This is what I want to do."

He held up a hand. "You don't have to say anything else. I understand. Why don't you take off a week or two, get your feet underneath you again? You went through a traumatizing experience. Take some time to recover."

I exhaled, grateful for his understanding and kindness. "I'll call you when I'm ready to come back?" I asked hopefully.

"I've always got a spot for you. You're a talented and hard worker."

"Thank you." I turned and left the hallway, relieved at how smoothly that had gone.

I could only pray breaking Trey out would go as easily.

My fingers danced along the side of my purse as I headed out the door. By this time tomorrow, Meredith, Trey, Beth, and I should all be gone. I hoped Trey knew where we were going, because I didn't.

I spotted Meredith's car as soon as I pulled into the mental hospital. She still sat in the parking lot, and her car rattled with a jarring musical beat. She stared straight ahead, her eyes unseeing and distant.

I parked beside her and rapped lightly on the car window. Even so, I startled her, and she jumped, crashing backward into her seat. Then her gaze latched on me and she smiled meekly before rolling down the window.

"Are you ready?" I asked.

"I think so." She took a deep breath and barreled onward. "I brought the poem, I hope it works. We just have to get him and get out and then shoot away from here. Are you sure the police won't suspect me?"

"Lieutenant Bailey will suspect me right away. I'll have to lay low and act innocent because the moment they check the security footage, he'll be after me."

She bit down on her lower lip. "The security footage. I forgot about that. That's going to cause trouble, isn't it? What should we do?"

"Run fast?" I said. "That's why you're wearing a hat." I gestured to the knit beanie beside her. "I'm not a hacker. I don't know how to fry the system or make the cameras not work."

"Fry the system." Meredith narrowed her eyes. "Maybe I can just get one of the guards to turn them off."

I raised my eyebrows and looked at her with appreciation. "Why are your powers so much cooler than mine?

Barely had I spoken the words before the parking lot and building in front of me disappeared. Instead I stood again on a meadow of burnt grass, debris swirling around my ankles as the wind blew.

And then the hot air and dry wind was gone, leaving me in the parking lot of an insane asylum. Maybe I should take the hint and check myself in.

"What are we waiting for?" Meredith asked.

I shook off the crazy thoughts. "Let's get this show on the road."

She sucked in a little breath and nodded. "All right."

Meredith yanked the beanie over her short brown hair and tucked her glasses into her pocket before climbing out of the car and closing the door, but my mind was stuck on her words. *All right.* That's what Aaron used to say to me. Every time he called me or every time he saw me, his first words to me were always, "All right." I nearly doubled over at the strong desire to get him back.

"You okay?" Meredith asked, reaching for my arm.

I shrugged her off and straightened, more resolute than ever. "I'm good. Come on."

I spotted the security cameras as we neared the building, and one finger jumped to my mouth automatically, where I anxiously chewed on the nail. I, at least, would be easily identified. "We need to split up. Lieutenant Bailey will try to track who I came in with. He needs to think I did this alone."

"I have an idea."

"What?" I stopped just out of view of the camera pointing toward the reception area. The receiving desk was in front of us, and a security guard leaned against it, chatting with the receptionist behind it.

"Go ahead and check in as planned. Go to Trey's room. I'll meet you there."

"What are you going to do?" My heart began to pound harder.

"Make our getaway easier. Just go."

I eyed her warily as I approached the reception, but Meredith hung back in the parking lot. I turned my back on her and pushed through the front doors. "Excuse me," I said to the lady.

"Yes?" she said. The security guard moved away, probably disappointed his flirting session had ended and he had to man his post. He was one more person Meredith and I would have to get past with Trey in tow. My pulse quickened to double time.

"I'm here to see Trey Clark," I said, already fishing through my purse for my driver's license. I remembered that from last time.

She waited until I handed over my identification before saying, "I'll need your cell phone as well."

I froze. Had she done that last time? I couldn't remember. "Really? I kind of need my phone."

She didn't even bat an eye. "You can have it back after your visitation."

I glanced behind me. The security guard lingered by the door, a bored expression on his face. I didn't see Meredith in the parking lot, but I knew she had to be nearby.

"Okay." I sighed and handed over my flip phone.

She used my driver's license to write my name down, the tangible proof that I'd been here. There was no way out of this now.

She handed a clipboard to me with a pen. "Sign here."

52

I did.

She put my phone in a drawer and tapped a call button. "I need a nurse to escort a visitor."

We stood in an aggravated silence waiting, and then an attendee arrived. The receptionist handed her a set of keys.

"She's going to see Trey Clark. Room five-seven-three."

The woman eyed me with interest, and I wondered if Trey already had a reputation here. "Follow me."

My heart rattled around in my head as she walked down the hall. What now? We were supposed to get Trey out, but without Meredith, I wasn't sure how to do that. We couldn't escape out a window, and this lady was gonna stand by the bedroom door and watch everything we said.

We took an elevator up a few floors and then went down another hallway. She unlocked the door to his room, not bothering to knock or give any other kind of warning before she pushed it open. I hoped he wouldn't be changing.

He wasn't. He sat at a desk with an open paperback in front of him, looking extremely bored. His face lit up when he saw me, his gray-green eyes flashing. "Jayne!" A smile pressed against his lips. "You came back."

I nodded, anxious to reveal our plan but knowing I couldn't yet. "Why are you still here?"

Trey shrugged. It didn't look like anyone had bothered to cut his red hair lately, and it nearly brushed his shoulders. "Beats me. Somebody important wants me here, is all I can think. I've passed every test they've given me, and even my previous history doesn't account for me staying here this long."

I cocked my head. "Previous history?" I repeated. "Have you been in trouble before?"

He lifted one corner of his lip. "I've been in trouble ever since I was born."

I stared at him, trying to pry his meaning from his mind. "Have there been others like me you tried to help? Others who have caused trouble for you?"

He leaned toward me, and I mimicked his movement. "You are the first goddess to awaken and summon me in my lifetime. I was born to protect you. But there are those who know what I am. They follow me."

I knew the words weren't meant to be accusatory, but it made me feel guilty. "I'm so sorry."

"You're sorry?" He shook his head. "I led them to you."

I glanced toward the door. Where was Meredith? My fingers itched to take out my phone and text her, but I didn't have it.

"But you came to tell me something, right? Did you meet Karta? Was there a battle?"

I focused on him, remembering that he didn't know anything that had happened. "Yes," I said slowly. "I confronted her. And I lost. She took all of their souls into herself and disappeared."

Trey closed his eyes, and I read the sadness etched on his face. "I was afraid of that. I felt the shift in dynamics. But I am helpless here, as imprisoned by my body as I am by this building."

I looked at the runes engraved on his wrist, the ones that had appeared to lock his powers away. "I need your help."

He lifted one eyebrow sardonically. "I'm afraid I'm a little indisposed at the moment."

"One more minute," the attendant said from the hallway.

"Meredith, where are you?" I groaned under my breath.

"Meredith?"

"Never mind." There was still no sign of her.

"Time's up." The woman stepped into the room.

I looked at Trey and let out a slow exhale, my heart heavy in my chest. It was now. We would just have to make a run for it.

His eyes were glued to my face, and I knew he read something there.

"We're getting out of here," I mouthed. "Follow my lead."

He didn't question me, didn't ask me to repeat myself, didn't wonder aloud what my plan was. He just stood up, trusting me.

I turned around, flashing a smile at the attendant. "Okay." I walked out of the room with her behind me, but as she put her hand on the knob to pull the door closed, I pretended to trip. I jammed one foot into the doorway and sprawled face-down on the floor. She stumbled over me with a little cry, letting go of the door knob and grabbing the wall to right herself.

My eyes shot to Trey, but he didn't need to be told twice. He bolted through the open door and joined me in the hallway.

"The elevators!" I said.

But the woman was already scrambling to her feet and unhooking a walkie-talkie from her belt.

"Inmate on the loose! Secure fifth floor!"

Criminy. Where was Meredith and her almighty plan? Both of us bolted for the elevator at the far end of the hallway. But it opened before we got there, and two security guards stepped out. Neither was the one we'd seen downstairs, but I couldn't worry about his whereabouts right now.

"Stairs," Trey said, already heading toward them.

The security guards were faster. They darted ahead of him, blocking the way.

Static electricity built up in the air around us, making the hair on my arms stand up straight. I glanced around, looking for the source.

The security guards stopped in their tracks. One put his hand up to his face as if shielding himself from something, and the other one took two steps toward us with the slow movements of someone walking through water. Without thinking, I thrust my hands outward, and they both came to a halt before scooting backward. The woman charged at us, but I swiveled my arm her direction, and she also scooted back.

I stared at my outstretched fingers, feeling my eyes bulge in disbelief. What was I, a Jedi also?

The woman yelled, pressing the button on her walkie-talkie again, and anger surged through me. How dare she try to stop us? Didn't she know who we were?

The stairwell opened behind the security guards, and Meredith dashed into the hall. She froze, eyes taking in the way we stood. "Jayne?"

"Just hold them long enough for us to get out," Trey said, and he ran to Meredith's side.

Just hold them? I could end them. I was a goddess of fate, and I had that power. I held the fate to their mortal existence in the tips of my fingers.

"Jayne!"

Trey shouted from the stairwell, and an icy feeling like cold water rushed through my brain and down my neck. I released the guards, who slumped forward as if holding still had taken all their energy. I darted past them before they could recover. Meredith shot me a look, but I was already racing after Trey. She stayed behind a moment longer, but before I could worry about her, she dashed into the stairwell, letting the door bang behind her.

What just happened? I'd analyze that later. Right now we needed to get out of here.

Nobody blocked our way at the entrance. Even the receptionist was missing. I stopped just long enough at the desk to sign out and grab my phone.

"Hurry, hurry, I don't know how long the spell will last!" Meredith said. She held the door to the parking lot open for me, and I barreled past.

Trey paused outside. "Where now, my knights in shining armor?"

Meredith grabbed Trey's arm and met my eyes. "He's with me, right?"

I nodded, my heart still working overtime. "I'll head straight home and wait for your signal. What happened back there? Where were you?"

"I got distracted by the guard," she said. "I managed to get him to turn off the cameras, but my spell worked a little too well. He couldn't remember where they were. I don't know how long he'll be out of it. But at least all the police will see is you walking into the building. There's no sign of me. Go home and claim innocence when they call. You saw Trey, but he was fine when you left."

"They won't believe that," I said. And that didn't begin to answer what happened in the hallway.

"It doesn't really matter what they believe, they won't be able to prove you did anything."

"What about the guards who saw me? And the nurse? Where did the receptionist go?"

56

An expression mixing guilt and pride flashed across her face. "The receptionist is taking a nap. And the guards and nurse who saw you have short-term amnesia. All poetically induced."

We'd reached our vehicles, and I unlocked mine quickly. "Okay, that's impressive," I admitted. "But you still took too long. I was about to freak out."

"Looked like you had it under control when I got there."

"Dekla," Trey said.

I inclined my head toward him, some instinctive part of me responding to my Latvian name.

He stood with the passenger door to Meredith's car open, already half inside. "Jayne." He softened his tone. "You're starting to remember. That's good. That's what will save us. But we have to teach you to remain in control."

Yeah, whatever that meant. Things were definitely wicked strange right now.

CHAPTER SEVEN

❋

I drove as fast as I dared, not wanting to get pulled over and find out that there was a warrant out for my arrest. I made it home without incident and breathed a sigh of relief when there were no patrol cars in my driveway.

"Mom! I'm home," I called as I burst through the front door.

She appeared from the den. "I expected you an hour ago."

"Sorry. I went by the mental hospital to say hi to a friend. And then I had a craving for sugar, so I stopped at the gas station." I pulled a handful of candy out of my purse, pleased that I had made just such a stop yesterday.

Mom only look mildly pacified. "I don't want you going out right now, Jayne. It's such a crazy climate."

"Is that Jayne?" Beth appeared at the landing. She flashed me a smile, and my heart did a little somersault, remembering that in a matter of minutes, she and I had to break away. I needed to tell her what was going on, but how could I—

My phone rang, and an ominous feeling prickled up the back of my neck. I pulled the phone out and scanned the Caller ID.

Unavailable.

It had to be Lieutenant Bailey. Did I answer it? I could pretend like I didn't hear it.

No. It would be better to let him know I was safely at home. I flipped it open, putting on my most casual voice.

"Hello?"

"Is this Jayne Lockwood?"

Definitely Lieutenant Bailey. "Yes."

"Miss Lockwood, there's been an interesting development at the mental hospital. Your friend Trey Clark has gone missing. You wouldn't know anything about that, would you?"

I pressed the palm of my hand into my chest, getting into character. "Missing?" I gasped. "I just visited him an hour ago!" I saw my mom moving in closer, concern emanating from her aura.

"And nothing seemed odd when you were there?" he said.

Lieutenant Bailey didn't mention seeing me on the security footage or on the check-in sheet, but he also didn't act surprised that I had been there, which meant he'd already known. And hadn't said anything.

I could feel the battle lines being drawn. He'd already laid a trap for me.

"No, nothing. I told him I would see him tomorrow. You're sure he's gone?" I winced at my question. Maybe too much.

"Yes, he's gone. Moments after you were seen entering the building. I find it strange that he would vanish right after seeing you, especially when you were so adamant about needing him."

My face warmed at his insinuations, correct as they were. But he wasn't done.

"Even more oddly, all of the camera feeds went dead shortly after you arrived. And every personnel in the building acts confused. Nobody remembers anything. It's like the whole past hour didn't even happen."

He was all but outright accusing me. He knew I had some kind of power, and he knew I'd been there. But he had no proof.

"That's so odd!" I said, continuing with my act. "How are you going to find him? My time with him was so short, I didn't get to ask him what I wanted!"

"Oh, don't worry, we'll find him." His voice was icy now. "Before the feed went dead, the parking lot camera caught another girl who arrived close to the same time as you. We saw you talking to her before you went inside. Who was it?"

My blood ran cold. Parking lot camera? Criminy. We'd missed that one. And he wasn't really asking; he knew. Judging from his voice, our truce was over. I could lie and say I didn't know her, buy us some time. But when the lie was discovered—and I knew it would be—I would lose all credibility with the police department.

I swallowed hard. "Oh, that was Meredith. We didn't come together. But we both knew Trey from school. She knew I was going to visit him and decided to also."

"So she must've gone in to see him after you."

I could practically see the gears turning inside his head, putting this new piece of information together and casting the net of suspicion over Meredith. "Yeah, I think so," I said, gulping.

"Wait a minute. Her name rings a bell. Isn't she the one that wrote the poem that caused all this trouble?"

Criminy. Criminy, Criminy. "Yeah. But it wasn't her fault, remember?" I was breaking a sweat. I couldn't text her while I was on my phone, but there was no telling what he was doing while he was on his. I ran up the landing to Beth's bedroom, pushing past her as she watched me from the doorway.

"What are you doing?" she asked as I rummaged through the things on her dresser.

I pointed to the phone in my hand and pointed to her and snapped my fingers. She just stared at me.

"That's what you said," Lieutenant Bailey said. "And I believed you. But she's the one who disappeared with you in Maryland."

I mouthed at Beth, "Now!" and jammed my finger into the back of my phone. Suddenly she got it. She pulled her own phone, covered in beautiful rhinestones, out of her back pocket. How could she stand to sit on that thing?

I took the phone from her, punching in Meredith's number while I answered Lieutenant Bailey. "No, I trust her. She's one of my best friends." Then I focused on Beth's phone and typed, *Get Trey out of town now.*

"You've made it very clear there are forces at work that I don't understand. But I'm going to get to the bottom of this, with or without your help. I'll be in touch."

The line disconnected, and I shoved my flip phone into my pocket. Using Beth's phone, I called Meredith.

"Jayne, is that you?" she said as soon as she answered.

"You've got to go," I said without preamble. "The police tracked an image on the security camera to you. They're probably on their way to your house right now!" I could feel Beth's eyes on me, drinking in every detail. "Get out of there!"

"I'm not there, Jayne. We're at Stephen's house."

I'd forgotten we made that plan. I relaxed slightly, picturing them on Stephen's couch and chatting with his aunt. Which would be weird, since Stephen was one of the people who had disappeared. "What are you doing?"

"Sitting in the driveway."

Even weirder.

But Meredith wasn't done talking. "You're the one who needs to get out, Jayne. The police will probably be at your house soon."

I shook my head. "Lieutenant Bailey didn't say that."

"You think he would warn you?"

Good point. This was going so much deeper than I wanted it to. "Drive out to Southampton Township and find a gas station. Text me the location and then get out and start walking. Turn your phone off and don't turn it on. Leave it behind if it's a temptation. I'll pick you up."

The car engine revved as she spoke. "And we're supposed to, what, walk until you show up? How long will you be?"

I looked at my sister. "I'm right behind you."

Beth spoke the moment I handed the phone back. "What is it? Where are we going?"

"Meredith and I busted Trey out and the police are on our tail. We've got to go before we're all arrested and lose any chance of defeating Samantha."

"And what do we tell Mom?" Beth whispered.

"Tell me what?"

My body stiffened at the sound of my mother's voice. She'd been hanging around our rooms like a shadow lately, and I'd forgotten about her. I turned around, totally unsure of how to get out of this one.

"Beth and I are going for a quick drive. I need to get something, and I want her opinion."

Could I be any more nonspecific? Mom's eyes narrowed.

"It's getting late. I don't want you girls going anywhere."

Late? It wasn't even seven. "We won't be long," I lied.

Mom shook her head. "I don't think so. Whatever it is you need, I can get it in the morning."

"I need Beth," I said, digging my heels in. "You're not letting her ride to school with me anymore, so I only have the evenings to be with her."

My mom hesitated, and I could see her wanting to allow us our sisterly bonding time. Then she brightened. "Why don't I come with you?"

So not what I was going for. I looked to Beth for help.

"Jayne's on a mission to save the world," Beth said. "If you don't let us go, all those people who went missing are going to die."

I gawked at Beth, not sure if I should agree with her or try to laugh it off.

"Not to mention, Jayne got in trouble with the police," Beth added. "If we don't leave now, she's going to be arrested and the world as we know it will come to an end."

"What?" Mom gasped out. She looked a little faint, and I reached out a hand to steady her arm.

"Beth's just being silly," I said with a nervous laugh. "Just joking around. It's this role-playing thing we do."

Beth gave an aggravated sigh. "No, it's not, Mom, but we were afraid the truth would be too much for you, so we've been hiding it. Jayne and I are both goddesses."

Now I knew my mom would think we were crazy.

"Okay, Beth, let's try to keep this little game just between me and you, okay?" I said, doing my best to sound patronizing rather than scared.

But my mom looked terrified. Her eyes darted from me to my sister and then landed on me. "Does she really believe what she's saying?" she asked, her voice high and nervous.

Now I felt guilty. I remembered my parents' reactions when I told them about my visions when I was younger. It hadn't gone well, and knowing they didn't believe me, knowing they were concerned for my sanity when they put me in various therapies and under medications, put a huge wedge of betrayal between us. Could I do that to Beth?

"Jayne!" Beth cried, tears welling in her eyes.

My mom's phone rang before I got the chance to respond. Distracted, her gaze still on me, Mom pressed the green button and held the phone up to her ear. "Hello?"

I could almost make out the words coming through the speaker, but not quite. Just tiny little micro noises. But my mom's face tensed, and her eyes refocused.

"Yes, Jayne's here with me. No, she hasn't gone anywhere. No, not that I know of." Now her eyes locked on mine, something like steely determination in them. I gulped.

"Absolutely, Officer. She's not going anywhere."

I sighed and closed my eyes. Great. Just great.

She hung up the phone and slid it into her front pocket. "I'm afraid I need answers from you, Jayne, and I need the truth. That was the police. For some reason, they think you might've been involved with helping a mental patient escape his hospital today. They wanted me to make sure you don't go anywhere. What's going on?"

I looked again at Beth, but she glared at me, her eyes red. Well, to heck with it. The cat was out of the bag anyway.

"Beth told you the truth," I said, concentrating hard to maintain eye contact with my mother. "We're on a special mission to free the missing people. But if we don't leave now, the police will detain us and we'll be stuck here. If that happens, all those people will die."

Mom's face flushed, and her eyes narrowed. "This isn't a joke, Jayne!" she snapped. "What's going on?"

We were out of time. Either I convinced her now, or Beth and I walked out of the house in deliberate disobedience. I stepped forward and put my hands on her shoulders.

"Do you remember the visions I used to get about people dying?"

Fear flickered in her eyes, that same fear I'd seen years ago when she thought her child was losing her mind. "Yes. But that was a long time ago, just nightmares, and the medicine made them stop."

I tightened my grip, trying to impart my sincerity. "No, Mom. The medicine did nothing. I pretended like they stopped so everyone would leave me alone. I still have them. But now I know why."

Her lips parted, and the word escaped as if she couldn't help herself. "Why?"

"Because when I see a death, sometimes I have the power to stop it. That's why—" I hesitated, then plunged onward, exposing all in the hope she would let us go. "That's why we vanished with everyone else. We weren't hypnotized; we were trying to save them. We failed."

She shook her head, pity and compassion swirling in her eyes. "Oh, Jayne, honey. It's not something you can fix! You're just a child—"

I cut her off. "Mom. I'm not having delusions of grandeur. It's my job. My mission. And Aaron—" Her eyes had wandered away from mine, toward Beth, but now they tracked back to me. "They took Aaron, Mom. And I'll do anything to get him back. Which means I have to go now."

"I don't understand—" she began.

"You don't have to," I interrupted. "What you have to do is trust me. You never have. I'm taking a chance telling you the truth now."

I held her eyes, and finally I saw a flicker of shame in her gaze. I softened my voice. "When this is all over, if you want to know every morbid

64

detail, I'll tell you everything. But right now you have to let me and Beth go, or we can't save them. We'll walk out of here without your permission if that's what we have to do." I removed my hands from her shoulders. "Beth, let's go."

We stepped past Mom, Beth casting uncertain glances over her shoulder until we exited the landing. Then she faced forward, and we took the stairs two at a time as we ran for the door.

"Beth! Jayne!" My mom appeared at the landing, clutching the railing.

I stopped with my hand on the doorknob. "We won't stay," I warned.

She exhaled. "Be careful. Will you call me?"

I flashed her a smile. "Soon as we can. Oh, Mom. In the top drawer of my dresser is a file folder. A green one. Take it. If the police search my room, I don't want them to find it. You can read it. But keep it in your room."

She nodded. "I love you both."

"Same," I said, and I pushed the door open, leading the way to my car.

The file listed every vision I'd ever had and the outcome. If the green file folder didn't convince her, nothing would.

☾☽

I watched all of the cars behind me as we drove out of town, my heart in my throat. Any moment I expected to see the flashing red and blue lights of a police car, and then I didn't know how we would get out of this. But nobody appeared.

Beth didn't say much, though I was certain she had plenty of questions about our activity. More specifically, she was probably dying to know what happened with Trey and Meredith. But I still wasn't quite sure how I felt about her revealing the truth to Mom, and I think she knew that, so she kept quiet.

I spotted Meredith's car about half a mile from the gas station, pulled over to the side of the road like she'd stopped to pick blackberries. She and Trey couldn't be much farther.

I found them nearly two miles later and parked in front of them. A moment later, the back doors of my car opened and they popped inside.

"Wow, you guys were really booking it," I said. "Made it nearly two

65

miles."

"Wasn't much else to do," Meredith said.

"I was just trying to keep ahead of her incessant chatter," Trey said, grabbing the handle above the door and settling behind Beth. "Does she ever stop?"

Meredith crossed her arms over her chest, a gesture I saw from the rear view mirror. "I get talkative when I'm nervous."

She was always talkative, but I decided it wasn't time to point that out. "Any cops?"

She shook her head and readjusted her glasses as they tried to fly off. "No. That doesn't mean they're not on their way."

"No kidding." I put my foot to the gas and took off down the country road. "They'll be looking for me also. Once the police figure out I left town, they'll be all over me."

"And your car," Meredith added.

Beth shifted slightly in her seat. "Can't you get them off our back? Don't you have a connection at the police department?"

I made a hissing sound with my tongue and pressed my finger into the steering wheel. "Burned it."

"To the ground," Meredith said.

I shot her a glare in the mirror. "You're not helping."

"Just saying it like it is."

"So what do we do about the car?" Beth asked.

Trey cleared his throat and leaned forward, catching my eye. "How much do you remember, Jayne?"

"I don't remember anything."

"Nothing?" He raised one amber eyebrow over his light eyes. "Then how are you able to manipulate people?"

"What are you talking about?" I focused on the road. "Meredith is the one who can manipulate people."

"Oh, so all of the security guards at the hospital just randomly decided to lean up against the wall?" Meredith said.

I sputtered. "I don't really know what happened there."

"You haven't had any memories? Seen yourself in other places? Doing other things?" He said each word emphatically, and I felt his eyes boring holes into the side of my head.

The meadow. The ash. "I haven't been controlling anyone. I don't remember anything."

"Then we'll still run into problems," Trey said, settling back. "If Jayne could remember, we could easily fend off any authorities. But she can't."

The accusation hung heavy in the car, as if all of this had somehow become my fault.

"We still have Meredith," I said defensively. "She can recite a limerick and everyone jumps to do her bidding."

"They become mindless clowns. Their lives aren't altered, just their actions."

I furrowed my brow. "And there's something I'm supposed to be able to do about that?"

"Yes. As soon as you start remembering."

"Hey, it's not as if I have any say in the matter!" I said.

"Sure it is. You're not letting go of yourself."

"Let go of myself? That's not really an option!"

"What are you afraid of? That you won't be you anymore?"

Instantly memories of the anger and condescending attitude I'd felt in the hospital washed over me. "Yes, that's exactly what I'm afraid of!"

"You can't be in opposition to yourself!" Trey said, raising his voice. "You're only making it worse!"

"I'm not sure what we're solving here," Meredith said, interrupting us. "Jayne doesn't know what she's supposed to do, we don't know what it will affect, and we still have to figure out what to do with this car."

Trey gave a sigh and rolled his eyes. "You girls are way over-thinking things. Meredith pulled out some cash from the ATM at the gas station. We'll just take an Uber or taxi from here on out."

Either he watched way too many spy movies, or this wasn't the first time he'd had to do this. "Take an Uber to where? I don't have any idea where we're going."

"To Wooded Acres, Delaware."

"Where?" I raised an eyebrow. "Why the heck are we going there?"

"To see my grandfather." A smile pulled at Trey's lips, crinkling the corners of his eyes. "He trained me. Maybe he can help me get my powers back. And then we can train you."

CHAPTER EIGHT

We drove my car south for another two and a half hours. All of our phones were off, but I couldn't help thinking of what was going on back home. How had my mom handled the police? Had she looked at the green folder?

"Meredith, do you think your dad and brother are okay?" I asked her, chewing on the nail of my pinky.

Meredith gave a short laugh. "Not to worry. I wrote my dad a little forgetful poem so that every time he thinks of me, he knows I told him I was going somewhere but he can't remember where. He won't worry."

Beth swiveled in her seat. "For the love of witches. You cast a spell on him!"

Meredith's cheeks flushed pink, but she looked rather pleased. "I'm getting kind of good at it."

I tensed as we drove past a cop car. I wasn't speeding, but still he rolled slowly out of a side street. My heart raced, and I gripped the steering wheel tighter. He wasn't really following me, was he?

We continued down a two-lane highway for a stretch, me not daring to go a single mile over the speed limit, him on my bumper. Silence descended over the car as the others noticed him. I couldn't think what would happen if he pulled me over, if he'd recognized my car.

We came to a dotted yellow line, and suddenly he put on speed and passed me, zipping into the other lane to cut back in front of me and take off down the empty highway at least twenty miles an hour faster than I was going.

I let out an unsteady breath, finally relinquishing my death grip on the steering wheel.

"It's time to ditch this car," Trey said. "Find a town."

"Right," I said. "Like I know where one is? Usually I print a map before I leave the house!"

Beth giggled. "She doesn't even have a smart phone."

Ouch. Just because I had a car payment and she didn't. "And a lot of good yours does us right now!" I said, smacking her forehead. "We can't turn on our phones. One of you use your weird powers and figure out where we are on the map."

"I don't think any of us have that power," Meredith said, a little timidly.

"I was being sarcastic," I grumbled.

Trey appeared nonplussed by my tirade. "All of these highways go through cities. We'll find one."

As irritating as it was, Trey was right. Twenty minutes later, the speed limit slowed from sixty-five to forty-five to twenty-five as we drove through a sleepy little town.

Trey directed me to park at a grocery store. I did.

"Now what? With no phone, how are we supposed to get an Uber?"

"We ask someone for help. Have you never had to do that before?" Trey smirked at me before getting out of the car and closing the door.

"You're kind of snappy, you know," Meredith said, as if I had requested a personal evaluation on my behavior.

"Really? Snappy? I think I have the right to be."

"Let's just get out of the car," Beth said to Meredith, and the sense that the two of them had teamed up against me raised my hackles.

"Hey," I said, getting out also. I followed them as they approached Trey where he stood talking to a man who had just left the store. "This hasn't exactly been the most ideal field trip for me. The police hate me now, my boyfriend's still missing, I'm waiting for this psycho dude to decide he's got powers and can protect me, and I'm losing my identity! Which part of this am I supposed to be okay with?"

Trey handed the man's phone back along with a wad of cash. "Thanks so much, man. Our Uber will be here in five minutes."

"No problem," the man said. He pocketed the cash and walked away.

Trey turned his attention on us and flashed a smile. "It's not Jayne's fault. She's changing and doesn't know how to deal with it."

Beth raised an eyebrow like only a sister can and said snarkily, "Like, she's going through puberty?"

I glared at her, but Trey almost managed to keep a straight face when he said, "Something like that."

Neither one of them was helping the situation. I crossed my arms over my chest with a humph and stomped back to the car.

They left me there to stew alone until the Uber pulled into the store parking lot. Then Meredith called my name, and we all climbed into the back.

None of us said a word as the driver headed to the address Trey had previously given him. I had no idea what everyone else was thinking, but I was lost in my own world. Something strange was going on with me, and I didn't like it at all.

It was nearly forty-five minutes later that the Uber deposited us at an old farmhouse. Pasture stretched out around it with a line of trees in the distance, probably indicating a stream farther on. By the time the Uber driver left, a few dogs had come out to greet us, long tails wagging slowly as they surveyed us.

"Come on," Trey said. "Let's get inside and say hello."

"He's not expecting us, is he?" None of us were using our phones, so I knew no one had contacted him that way.

"No," Trey said with a snort. "We don't have some special telepathic means of communication."

He said it so derisively that I immediately felt stupid for wondering. "Of course not," I said. "We're the most normal group of teenagers you could ever find, with no unusual abilities. Telepathic communication would just be outside the realm of possibilities."

Meredith laughed, which did give me a smug validation. But then she said, "Will he be happy to see us?"

I turned my attention back to the matter at hand.

Trey shrugged. "We won't find out till we go in."

Not exactly reassuring.

By the time we got to the farmhouse, the screen door had opened to reveal an old man. And I do mean old. He kept one hand on the porch door, and I could see how it trembled. The other hand was in his pocket. His eyes, watery and rheumatic, stayed on us as we approached. His expression was blank, and I wished I was telepathic. I had no clue what he was thinking. I hoped he would welcome us and not turn right around and call the police.

"Hey, Grandpa!" Trey called out, his voice louder than usual. "I hope you don't mind a visit."

"I wasn't expecting one," the man said, the words taking their time to exit his mouth, like each one held weight and importance.

"Yeah," Trey said. "Kind of an emergency. I have some questions. About our family traits."

We had reached the porch now, and his grandfather's watery gaze moved from Trey to focus directly on me. I gulped. He knew who I was. His eyes froze me, holding me still for an eternal minute.

"Come on in, then," he said finally, opening the door wider. "It's past suppertime, but I can heat something up."

I didn't realize I was hungry until he said that. We'd run out the door in a hurry, and I'd been stressing. I was coming down from my adrenaline rush.

We stepped inside, Meredith and my sister and I huddling close together. A living room with a hearth greeted us, a small breakfast nook and kitchen to the right before a staircase climbed to the second floor. The furnishings were simple and rustic, an old couch and a polished table with benches. "This is a nice place you have here," I said with an attempt at a smile.

He chuckled as he closed the door and shuffled behind us, shepherding us into a dining room. "Been in the family for generations. Almost as long as we've been associated with your kind."

I didn't know what to say to that, so I was silent as he turned on the gas range and warmed up a pot of beans. He put a chunk of corn bread into four different bowls, scooped beans next to it, and passed it around. I had never eaten such simple fair, but it was incredibly satisfying.

"You live here alone?" Meredith asked after she finished her food, a touch of concern in her voice.

"Have for the past seven years, since my Lillian passed on. But farm work is good work for the soul, and I'm satisfied." He turned his eyes from Meredith to Trey. "What's going on, son? Last I heard from your mama, you'd been locked up."

Some emotion flared behind Trey's eyes. But he kept his voice calm. "I was discovered. The *vadatajs* planted false evidence and used their influence to get me locked away."

"Vadateyesh what?" Beth whispered to me. "What's that?"

"The goblins," I whispered, then waved my hand to shush her.

"I could have used your help," Trey continued, eyes steady on his grandfather.

The man leaned back in his chair, studying Trey. "You know I am nothing but an old man now. I can't help you. But you should have been able to help yourself."

Trey thrust his arm out and pushed back the sleeve of his long T-shirt, revealing the braided chain branded across his arm. "They took it from me."

73

His grandfather's face softened. "I didn't know."

"You could've checked on me," Trey bit out.

I shifted uncomfortably, feeling like I'd been caught unawares in a domestic dispute. I glanced around the kitchen, wondering if I could flee up the stairs.

"The last time I tried to help you, you told me to stop interfering. You told me you could handle it."

"Well, I was wrong!" Trey snapped. "I'm nothing but a headstrong adolescent teenager! You should know better than to listen to me!"

A wry smile spread across the lips of his grandfather, and the old man chuckled. He slapped one hand against the wooden table and gave a hearty laugh.

A twin smile appeared on Trey's face. And then they were both laughing, while I exchanged a very confused look with Meredith. The two of them laughed while I sipped my water, trying to be patient.

Finally his grandfather spoke again. "I'm sorry it's been hard for you."

Trey nodded, the last trace of a smile fading from his lips. "Can you help me get my powers back?"

"You know I can't. But she can." He nodded, turning his gaze on me. And despite his age, his eyes suddenly seemed sharp and penetrating.

Trey made an impatient noise. "She doesn't remember anything yet."

"She's lying."

I gave a start. His eyes hadn't left my face, and obviously he could see much more of me than I was comfortable with.

Trey turned to me also. "So you have been remembering!"

I swallowed hard, feeling as if I were under attack. "I don't know what you're talking about."

"She's scared," the old man said, and I felt a rush of irrational anger that he should speak for me. "Until she gets her emotions under control, she won't be able to help you."

"Okay, so." Trey waved his hand at his grandfather and then at me. "Train her."

He shook his head. "I can't."

74

Trey scrunched up his brow in confusion. "Of course you can. That's what you did last time."

"Last time I was Auseklis. This time you are. You must train her, and she will set you free."

"How can I train her if I don't have any powers?" The irritation rose in Trey's voice.

"What about the other one?" Now Grandfather looked at Beth. "Does she remember anything?"

I'd had enough of this talking about us without talking to us. "Hey, we're right here. What do you need to train me to do? And what is it I'm supposed to be remembering?"

"Yeah, I'm a little confused too," Meredith said, dragging herself into the conversation as if she were somehow relevant here. "What does Jayne do besides learn how people are going to die? And why was she forcing the guards to stand up against the wall?"

I growled deep in my throat, shooting daggers at Meredith, annoyed she'd brought that up.

"And why is she growling at me?" Meredith added. "Is there somewhere in the rules that Dekla becomes a werewolf also?"

Beth giggled, her only contribution.

"Trey, let me show you to your rooms and help you get settled down for the night," his grandfather said. "And then your friend and I have things to discuss."

"Jayne," I said. "My name is Jayne. And I'm not his friend."

The old man raised an eyebrow, and Trey kicked my foot under the table. "Jayne!" he hissed.

But it was my little sister who said, "For the love of sugar, Jayne. Could you be any pricklier?"

Judging from the set of Trey's lip, he was thinking about laughing again, and I couldn't have that. I stood up, pushing my chair into the table. "Let's get this over with."

CHAPTER NINE

I learned that Trey's grandfather's name was Rory. Rory put Meredith and Beth in the same room but gave me a room to myself. Their room only had two beds in it, but I still thought it odd not to be with them. I worried he was trying to separate us, or worse, that they didn't want to be with me.

Rory found some cozy flannel pajamas that must've belonged to his wife. I wrapped myself up in them and sat down on the bed, tucking my knees up to my chin and rocking back and forth. Why did I feel so completely out of my element?

Someone knocked on my door, and I straightened up. "Come in."

The door opened, and Rory poked in his bushy white head. "Can you come out to the living room for a moment?"

I nodded and untucked my legs, then followed him down the stairs to the rustic wood living room beside the kitchen. A floral couch from the eighties sat in front of the empty hearth. It was the only seat, and since Trey already sat there, I sat down on the bricks of the fireplace.

"Well, Jayne," Rory said, entering the living room to stand behind the couch. "I'm sure you have some questions. I know you're very scared right now. But let me just tell you, you need to stop fighting it."

I frowned at him. "Stop fighting what?"

"And stop acting like nothing is happening," Trey added.

I narrowed my eyes at him, but that was my best defense. I turned my attention back to Rory. "So Trey said you can train me?"

"I'm sorry for the confusion, but I can't. As I said at supper."

"But Trey said you've done it before."

"Yes, I've trained my Dekla. But you are not her and I have not been assigned to protect you. I don't even have powers anymore. Trey is your protector, and he is the only one who can train you."

I sent an accusing glare at Trey. "Why did you say he could help us? Why'd you even bring us here?"

"Whoa there." Trey held up his hands. "First of all, I'm super grateful you got me out of that place, but you're the one who didn't have a plan, not me. I'm coming up with one the best I can. I didn't know Grandpa can't train you. We needed somewhere to go, anyway, and here we're still in your jurisdiction."

My jurisdiction? Before I could ask, Rory spoke.

"And don't write me off as useless just yet," he said, his lips turning upward. "I can help Trey. And then he can train you."

I let out a slow exhale and unclenched fists I hadn't realized I'd clenched. "Sorry."

"It's all right. You're not yourself right now. Quite literally."

And that was bugging me also. "Why? What's happening with me?"

Although I directed my question at Rory, he turned his placid gaze to Trey and said nothing.

Tray cleared his throat. "First of all, I'm new at this also, right? I didn't come into my powers until you got yours, and I'm still trying to figure things out. But I've at least been learning the lore since I was a kid. Now Dekla, when she handed her powers out to mortals, in a sense it was like she handed her DNA to another person. Also her experiences, her memories, even sometimes her feelings. And each time one Dekla comes to the end of her life and passes that thread on to another person, she passes down her memories and experiences also."

"Why?" I couldn't see the sense of that. My chest tightened, and I fought panic. "I'll just get so confused about who I am."

Trey shook his head. "Only at first. This is what you've been asking for, Jayne. Discernment. Answers. You've been asking how to make the best decision, how to judge. You'll have a thousand years of experience behind you once you get all their memories."

It was too much to wrap my mind around, and I was glad I was sitting down. "Everyone's memories?" My hands gripped the bricks beneath me, and I felt a little sick to my stomach.

"Not everyone's," Rory said, jumping in. Maybe he saw my panic. "Just the direct line you come from. Remember that Dekla spread her powers out among many mortals. There are hundreds of other Deklas scattered across the globe. You're not an omniscient god who can see what's happening with everyone everywhere at all times."

"And how many people have there been in my line since Dekla handed over these powers?"

Trey shrugged. "There's no way for me to have a real answer for that, you know? Just depends how many people died and passed it on. The host doesn't have to die until she's ready, so some of the Deklas may have lived for a very long time."

Rory interrupted. "It doesn't really matter. At first it might feel like they're taking over, all these memories, but you'll adjust. They're not going to affect who you are. But you'll be able to tap into them, like opening a book or asking a friend a question. It's only overwhelming right now because the memories are coming and going, the personalities are bumping into yours, and you have no place to put them, you have no classification for them."

I shuddered, desperate to believe that I wouldn't be haunted by these dead people's memories. "Okay. So how can I make this happen faster? And then is that it? I'll have all the answers I need?"

"It will happen faster when you stop being afraid of it. But we can also move it along with training," Rory said.

"Why do I need training if I'm going to learn from their experiences?"

The two of them exchanged a look that almost seemed smug.

"You don't have a clue how powerful you can be, do you?" Trey said. "You're a goddess of fate. You don't just see how people are going to die. You can change how they're going to live."

I rolled my wrist. "Yeah, it sounds like I've got so much power, but actually I don't do any of that. All I can do is give suggestions to Laima, and she decides whether or not to take my advice."

Trey shook his head. "That's only until you master your powers. Do you really think she wants to be the go-between forever?"

I kind of thought Laima preferred to micromanage all of her mini-goddesses. I tilted my head, intrigued by the prospect of something different. "So what, then? Eventually I'll have the final say?"

"You'll have so much more than that," Trey said. "You can alter someone's destiny. You can change the course of their life, not just their death."

His words sent a shiver down my spine. Really? I wasn't just a specter of doom? The idea had so much hope and expectation in it that my throat closed off. "How?"

"You have to learn to summon."

Images filled my mind of dead bodies rising from the ground to do my bidding. That didn't make sense.

"Summon your visions. You should be able to look at someone and summon a vision of their death at will, and then you can expand the vision to give you information about their life. You'll see the choices they have, the pivotal ones that could change the course of their future."

I could only stare at him as past visions flashed through my head.

Hannah. If she hadn't gone to that bar, she might not have died by the hand of a serial killer. Harold. Could he have woken up earlier and saved his little sister from the fire? "I could've made a difference before now, you know," I said with a snarl. "Someone should've been there with me the moment I started having visions, guiding me through this process!"

Trey shook his head. "You're forgetting you weren't Dekla yet. Those visions were preparation for what was coming. You couldn't change anything."

His words hit me like a punch to the stomach. I sucked in a breath. Aaron. The vision I'd had of him, of his future, his death. "But I supplicated Laima on behalf of some of them." My hands trembled to think that vision might still come true. "Are you saying it was for nothing? She won't change those deaths because I wasn't actually Dekla yet?"

Trey moved from the sofa and crouched in front of me, taking my hands. "Of course it wasn't for nothing. Are you listening to anything I'm saying? You're Dekla now. You can see someone's future at will and ask to change it. And eventually, when you understand your power, when you have confidence in your abilities, you won't even have to ask Laima."

I nodded, swallowing back the rush of nervous emotion that flooded me. "What about my sister? She needs the same kind of training, right?"

"Yes, but she's not ready yet," Rory said.

"Why not? She just got her powers. Now is the perfect time to help her understand all of this."

"How many visions has she had?" Rory asked.

"One."

"That's why. She's only had one vision. She hasn't started receiving the memories."

"She never even went through the preparation process," Trey said. "It was kind of a spur of the moment thing."

Rory nodded. "If she were to learn to summon now, it could permanently hamper her ability to make fair judgments."

"But I'm not going anywhere," Trey said with a wink at me. "I'll be here to help train her whenever she's ready."

I gave him a look of surprise. "You? You'll train her too?"

"It's not the first time in history that Dekla and Karta are once again actual sisters," Rory said. "It does facilitate things. You share a protector, you share a ragana. You also have a more intuitive bond with each other and can communicate directly. Ideally, the sister goddesses would always be real sisters."

"Okay. Okay." I nodded, beginning to understand just how much I didn't know about my role. "So I have a lot to learn. But I need to do it quickly if we're going to free all of those souls and win this war against Samantha."

Rory's expression darkened. "Quickly indeed. Because until you learn to summon and access your memories, you are weak. And Samantha grows stronger every day. If she destroys you before you have named a successor, the thread of Dekla that lies within you dies."

I stared at him in horror. "Has that happened before?"

"Absolutely. Through the centuries, we have lost many."

"There is one other small problem," Trey said. "I can train you, but I still don't have my powers. And until you master yours, you can't help me. Which puts us in a great catch twenty-two, because I can't help you if I don't have any powers."

I lifted my chin. "Sounds like I'm pretty powerful by myself. What exactly are you supposed to do for me?"

He smirked at me. "You'll never make it to the underworld to rescue Aaron without me."

The blood drained from my face. "The underworld?"

Trey's smirk faded into a sympathetic expression. "If we're going to get him back, we have to wheel and deal with the devil."

∞

"Concentrate." Trey's voice whispered in my ear as we sat on a park bench an hour from his grandfather's farm. I stared at the boy in front of me, willing him to look me in the eyes so I could summon a vision of his death.

How twisted was that?

"Compel him," Trey said. "You can influence him. But remember." He

81

softened his voice. "You can't take away his free will."

Right. Influence him but don't control him. Compel him but don't force him. It was enough to make my head swim.

"Look at me," I whispered, trying to send out mental pleadings. "I'm here. Lift your head."

The boy paused on the swing set, cocking his head so that one ear bent closer to me. My heart rate quickened. Had he heard me? I held my breath, urging him to continue the movement.

The slightest whiff of lemon reached my nostrils just as the bench jolted beneath me, startling me. I swiveled sideways, and Trey groaned, "Meredith."

"Sorry," Meredith said, her voice chipper and unworried. "What is it, exactly, I'm supposed to be doing here? It's not like I'm going to go practice my cloud-forming over the kids in the sandbox. Or did you want me to use my voodoo to make people look at Jayne?"

She wiggled her fingers, and I sent her an annoyed look. "I almost had it all by myself," I said.

Now I had missed my chance. The boy's mother took his hand and pulled him from the swing, and together they started for the parking lot. I stared hard at his retreating figure.

And then he stopped in mid-motion and turned around, meeting my eyes across the park.

I inhaled deeply, seeking the lemon scent that always indicated a vision, waiting for my soul to get swept up in his death.

Nothing happened.

He turned back around and continued with his mother to the parking lot. I groaned and thrust my head into my hands.

"It didn't work!"

"You can't expect it to work the first time. You did great, actually! He must've sensed you, he must've felt your presence."

Meredith unwrapped a candy bar. "Which is really quite creepy, if you think about it. People can sense the specter of death looming over them? You realize you're the person people have nightmares about?"

"And, time to get your story straight," Trey said. "She's not death. She's not the grim reaper. Jayne can see how people die, not collect their souls."

"My bad." Meredith held the candy bar out to me, offering a bite, and I accepted. "Who's got that grim job? Get it? Grim job?" Her laugh was so ridiculous I couldn't help smiling.

"Whatever. You're laughing now, but you won't be when you meet him," Trey said.

That cut off Meredith's mirth. Her eyes went large behind her glasses, which made her look very comical as her cheeks puffed up around the peanut butter and caramel bar. "Meet him?" she squealed.

"Yep."

"You mean there really is a guy who's a skeleton wearing a big black robe and cutting people's lives short?"

"He doesn't actually look like that, but yeah, he works with the goddesses of fate. Jods usually has the role of severing the mortal string, but he's joined Samantha in her rebellion. Grandpa said when that happens, another god has to step up, so it's probably fallen on his brother Jumis. He's had to help out before. Jumis waits for the fates to pronounce that a life is over, and then he seals the death and collects the soul."

"If he doesn't look like an evil skeleton dude, what does he look like?" Meredith asked.

The image popped into my mind of a tall man with brown skin and amazing abs. Straight dark hair, black eyes, and beads on his grass skirt. "Like a very tan Thor," I said.

Meredith raised an eyebrow. "Is that wishful thinking?"

Trey stared hard at me. "How did you know that? Was that a memory?"

I shook my head, my heart hammering in my throat. "I had a vision. A real-time one. He came to see me at school."

"What did he offer you?"

I focused my gaze on Trey. Up until that moment, I had almost thought I'd imagined the vision. But Trey's question was too specific. "How did you know he offered me something?"

Trey dropped his eyes, suddenly seeming unwilling to meet my gaze.

The toe of his shoe dipped into the sandy dirt around the bench. "That's what the gods do. They always try to strike a bargain to get what they want."

"What could he hope to get from me?"

Trey shrugged. "Who knows? The gods love messing with mortals. We're like a reality show slash soap opera to them."

Another young mom walked into the park, pushing a stroller with two children inside it. Trey elbowed Meredith.

"This is why you're here."

"Right. I almost forgot." Meredith hopped off the bench and approached the mom. She stepped over like she was going to ask a question, but I knew the next words out of her mouth would be the couplet she'd memorized. The one created to make the woman forget she ever saw the three of us here in the park.

"Why can't I have her power?" I grumbled.

Trey turned to me. "Remember, Jayne, if it weren't for your succession, you would be dead."

It was true. I didn't often think about it, but when Adele saw my death, I was just another victim of the Lacey Township serial killer. She interceded on my behalf to change my death, but Laima said it was my own choice to be in the path of danger.

That left Adele no other option. If she wanted my life to be saved, she would have to pass her powers on to me.

I squinted my eyes at Trey. "Wait a minute. Adele still had to ask Laima's permission to change my destiny. Why couldn't she do it without any help?"

Trey returned my perplexed gaze. "Because she never mastered the former Deklas."

"Did you know her?"

He shook his head. "My grandfather did."

My mouth fell open as I finally put the pieces together. "He was her protector." At Trey's nod, I continued, "So he was her trainer?"

"He tried to be. She was already at an advanced age when she inherited the powers, and it wasn't easy for her to learn how to deal with the other memories."

"How old was she when she became Dekla?"

"I don't know, exactly. Mid thirties, I think."

I remembered the notes I had read, her memories, the vision she'd had of her son. But that meant . . . "She was old when she died. Like in her eighties. So in all fifty years, she never mastered it?"

Trey's eyes were steady on mine. "She was much older. Remember, Dekla is immortal until she gives up her powers."

I pictured his grandfather back at the farmhouse, the white hair, trembling hands, the watery eyes. "How old was she?"

Trey shrugged. "My grandfather was a little older than me when she came into her power and he was assigned to her. As long as you are Dekla, you'll age, but you will not die."

And Aaron. He would age, and he would die. Without me. Suddenly I understood why each Dekla had chosen to pass on her powers. It was better to die and let someone take over than live forever without your loved ones.

I swallowed hard. "But in all that time, Adele never mastered the memories? What makes you think I will?"

His eyes never left my face. He put his hands on my shoulders, and I felt the weight, the pressure. But I also felt the reassurance. "You have a lot more going for you. You're young. Your sister is also your sister goddess. You have Ragana. And you're motivated. If you don't master this, you can't give me my powers back. And if you don't get me my powers back, I can't help you save your boyfriend."

"Boyfriend" felt like such a shallow way to describe mine and Aaron's relationship. It went so much farther. And technically he wasn't even my boyfriend, since we'd broken up. "Are you saying I have to master my powers before we can even begin a rescue mission?"

A smile crossed Trey's face. "Now you know why I'm in such a hurry."

"But that could take years! Adele never did it in over fifty!"

He used his grip on my shoulders to give me a shake. "You're not her. You're going to master this in just a few weeks. So long as you stop fighting it."

I closed my eyes, took a deep breath, and let it out slowly. Opening them, I gave a determined nod. "Okay. I'm ready to try again."

CHAPTER TEN

We spent hours at the park. I mentally encouraged every child who walked in to turn and look at me, but other than that first one, not a single one did.

"You know what I don't understand?" Meredith said.

We had walked over to the food truck to purchase street tacos. She used a napkin to mop up the grease collecting in her hand.

Trey turned to her with an air of annoyance. "What is it this time that you don't understand, Meredith?"

She scowled at him. "I don't appreciate your tone. You're awfully condescending toward me, as if you think you're better than me because you're the protector of a goddess and I'm neither a goddess nor a protector.

But I am something, and I'm here for Jayne just like you are. So I think you should treat me with a little more respect."

I arched an eyebrow at Meredith's impassioned speech. She'd obviously spent some time thinking about this, though I hadn't known Trey's jibes bothered her.

A pink hue spread across his cheeks, emphasizing his freckles, and he had the good grace to look chagrined. "Sorry. Sometimes I'm a little sarcastic."

She waved off his excuse. "Sarcasm is fine. You're more like patronizing. But I get it. You didn't mean anything by it and you're going to do better, right?" She didn't wait for him to pledge his promise before continuing. "What I don't understand is how Jayne was able to manipulate those guards at the mental clinic. You said she doesn't have control over adults, which they clearly were." She crossed her arms over her chest. "That's what I don't get."

I turned my perplexed expression from Meredith to Trey, waiting to see what he would come up with.

"See, now, there are some problems with your conclusions because you seem to think this is an exact science. It's not. There was a lot of overlap thousands of years ago, with each helping the other out when necessary. Their roles have evolved over time to help those who inherited the power have somewhere to focus. Samantha wasn't just manipulating adults; she got a lot of teenagers on her side, too. But that's getting into a whole bunch of historical background that won't help you right now. Let's just concentrate on one thing at a time."

"But there must be some absolutes." Maybe I just desperately needed a rulebook. "What can I do and what can I not do?"

"You cannot order someone to do something against their will. That requires a different power and manipulation."

"I can do that," Meredith piped up.

Trey closed his eyes for a moment as if summoning patience, then said, "Yes, you can. You are not bound by the same rules she is."

"But Samantha did it," I said.

"And she lost her position as Karta because of it."

"So those men that I threw against the wall," I said, fighting back a thread of worry. "They didn't exactly choose to do that. Am I in danger of losing my position?"

"First of all, you've got some leeway while you're trying to control your memories. Second of all, they still had a choice. They could have resisted you. What you unknowingly did, though, was frighten them so badly that they felt like they had no choice. In their minds, falling against the wall and making a path for you was the only option."

I could feel the deep wrinkles in my brow. "That sounds an awful lot like manipulating them."

"I'll admit the difference is negligible. A lot of it has to do with your intent. For you, at the mental hospital, it was an accident. You didn't know what you were doing and definitely weren't trying to control them."

"Yes, I was," I said before I could stop myself. "That's exactly what I was trying to do. I was angry at them for getting in my way and I wanted to stop them."

"No, you didn't," Trey said. "That's where you're wrong. It wasn't you wanting those things. You'd given into the ambitions of a different Dekla and haven't learned how to tell the difference yet."

He got that right. I threw away the trash from my street taco. "Let's try again." I had to make this work. Aaron was counting on me. He just didn't know it.

We stayed out for several more hours. I finally got another kid to turn around and meet my eyes, but no matter how much I tried, I could not get any sort of impression off him. And he quickly lost interest in me and returned to the teeter totter.

"I'm failing," I groaned, shoving my hands through my hair.

"I think it's time to take a break. Let's head back to my grandpa's house."

The three of us piled into the single bench seat of Rory's vintage truck. Meredith squeezed into the middle between us since she was the smallest. I leaned my head against the window.

"I'm never going to get this."

"Yes, you are," Trey said. "It's just not going to happen in a day."

I didn't answer, feeling too depressed to have any kind of positive outlook. I closed my eyes and let the hypnotic sounds of the road rolling underneath the tires lull me into a restful state. I barely heard Meredith whisper, "She's going to get this, right?"

Trey's response was just as quiet. "She has to. There's no other option. Everything relies on her."

Criminy. The pressure was on. And it didn't sound as if either of them really believed in me.

∞

Beth was sitting on the porch swing watching when Trey turned the truck onto the gravel drive, kicking up dust behind us.

"For the love of cats!" she said, hardly waiting for the truck to come to a stop before she pulled open the passenger door. "I thought you'd never get home. Do you know how bored I've been? There's no TV here. No books. I didn't even bring my homework. And I can't use my phone."

I blinked at her, silhouetted by the setting sun, and empathized with her situation. "So what did you do all day?"

"I slept for most of it! I did spend some time at the barn playing with the kittens."

"Well, that sounds like fun."

"For all of twenty minutes!" She eyed Meredith and Trey as they came to join me. "How did it go?"

"Great," Meredith said. "I'm getting much better at reciting my couplet. It worked on everyone! I'm excited to try something more next time. Like maybe convince people they need to stick ten dollar bills in our hats."

"She wasn't even asking about you," Trey said. "We could care less how good you are at rhyming. Besides, you should be able to recite a word or two and have the same effect."

"Hey! Remember that talk we had about being condescending? I've come a long ways. A month ago I had to write a poem to have any effect. And what did you do today? You sat there and coached Jayne, who managed to accomplish nothing under your tutelage. Sounds like one of us had a more effective day than the other."

With that Meredith pranced away, leaving me open-mouthed.

"Well, the witch part comes naturally," Trey said.

I punched him in the arm. "She's one of the nicest people I've ever met! You're the one who's being a jerk. I've never seen her treat anyone that way."

"Isn't she the one who got us into this mess? Giving her poem to Samantha?"

"Yeah, but it's your stinking fault! You were supposed to be protecting me, protecting us, not falling prey to some demons who could twist your power away from you. How can you protect us if you can't even protect yourself?"

"First of all, my job is not to protect her, it's to protect you."

I interrupted him. "Then you better add Meredith to your job description. Because if you can't protect her, I will fail." With that, I turned on my heel and pranced after Meredith.

Dinner was a quiet affair. Rory asked a lot of questions about how the training went, but he didn't seem surprised or disappointed by our answers. Maybe he hadn't expected it to go well.

Meredith and Trey were civil with each other to the point of being humorous, all "can you pass the salt, please?" and "yes, here you go" and "thank you very much." She turned subtly in her chair to give Trey the cold shoulder. It was enough to make me excuse myself to the outdoors. Or maybe I just needed to be alone for a moment.

I sat on the porch step next to a large sheep dog and watched the sunset. There really wasn't anything to do once the sun went down. None of the things I usually did for entertainment were available. There was no story to investigate, no sports to watch, no obituaries to peruse. Why hadn't I ever taken up running? I could jog for hours through these fields and not see the same corn stalk twice.

Somewhere my boyfriend's soul languished while his body was doing what? Lying dormant in a warehouse? Fighting a battle with swords and shields against immortal beings who refused to bow down to Samantha's power trip?

The war against the mortals hadn't started yet. We would've heard about people dying, strange weather, unexplained phenomenon . . . right? I only had guesses right now. I had no idea what we were facing.

My eyelids were heavy with the need to sleep, and my troubled spirit felt sluggish and uneasy. I pushed the screen door open to the house and murmured a good night to those present before escaping to my room.

Sleep claimed me almost immediately. Once again the stairwell appeared in front of me. The door was already wide open, and I didn't waste any time. I needed to get to the bottom. I walked down the steps, trying to stifle the fear that lifted goosebumps on my arms. The steps started out even and smooth like hardwood stairs. As I descended, they became rougher, uneven, steeper and bumpier, like rough-hewn stone left to chip and break away by the elements of wind and rain. Moisture saturated the air around me, clinging to my skin and hair, condensing to droplets and pinging onto the floor from an unseen height.

The whole stairwell smelled musty and dank, ominous and creepy, but still I descended. One hand clung to the wall beside me, for balance and leverage and to make sure I didn't pitch headfirst into the darkness.

Blackness. Because I could see nothing in front of me. But still I kept going. Down. Down. Down.

"Jayne."

His voice whispered up, up to me, no louder than a breath, making my heart pound harder.

"Jayne." Louder this time, yet strained, as if he carried a heavy burden.

"Aaron," I whispered back, willing my voice to travel to his ears and his heart. "I'm coming."

You'll never be able to save him.

The words were not spoken out loud, yet they rang through my mind like someone had shouted. They were not threatening, but a warning. I drew to a halt in my downward progression. Doubt crept up my spine, shivering into my thoughts while the speaker gripped my mind.

You will only lose yourself also. Turn back while you still can.

The voice was in my head again. I wasn't alone here on the stairs. Someone else knew I was here.

I pivoted on my heel, turning to go back up the stairs, when I felt the warmth filling the palm of my hand, radiating all the way to my elbow. I snatched my hand away from the wall and flipped it over to see the brand, the star of Auseklis, glowing brightly.

"I'm here with you."

I lifted my head and saw Trey standing above me on the stairs.

"You will succeed." He extended a hand, and I placed mine in his, never so relieved to see him. "I am with you. I will protect you. When it is time, we will go together."

The stairwell shimmered like someone dipping their toe into a clear pond, and then he vanished along with the moisture, the musty air, and Aaron's voice. I felt the absence like a blanket being pulled away in the cold night, and I shivered, curling into myself. I opened my eyes. I was on my bed, wrapped tightly around myself, dressed in the flannel pajamas of Rory's deceased wife.

My bedroom door opened, and I lifted my head as an orange glow bobbed into the room. The glow called to me, urged me to get out of bed and claim it. I narrowed my eyes. Was I still dreaming? Legs descended from the fiery ball, and then it grew arms and a head, until the brilliance disappeared and all that was left was a man.

A very familiar man, with dark skin and jet black hair and well-defined pecs.

"Who are you?" I asked, pushing myself into a sitting position, even though I suspected I knew the answer.

A smile tugged at his lips, warm and inviting. "You don't remember me? After all the life times we've shared?"

A memory whispered through me, and I almost knew him. And yet, I didn't at all.

"I can help you remember," he said. He held his hand out and opened his fist, revealing the same brilliant ball of fire in the palm of his hand. "Here are your past lives. Your memories."

I stared into the flickering fire, captivated by the arcs and flares. I lifted my eyes back to his, saw the reflection of the flame in their depths. "Am I still dreaming?"

"Are you?" That same smile played about his lips. He closed his fingers, concealing the little ball of flame. It seemed to take a little piece of me with it, and I gave a sigh of longing.

He stepped closer to me. "All those memories. They're all right there. Waiting for you."

"And after I get them, I'll be able to summon visions? I can free Trey?"

"You already know how. You've just forgotten."

It seemed so easy. And yet, something about him made me suspicious. "Is there any other way for me to get them?"

He gave a snort of impatience and thrust his hand into his pocket. "Yes. But how long will you wait? Six months? Five years? A decade? A word of advice: don't. The gods don't have too long."

I opened my mouth to ask him what he meant, but suddenly I was swept once again to that desolated clearing. I walked along barefoot, the wind swirling around my ankles, burnt grass crinkling beneath my feet. But this time, I wasn't alone. For the first time, I heard the sounds around me. Shouting, screaming. The unmistakable clang of weapon on weapon. I lifted my chin, my heart beating fiercely, my breath ragged in my throat. I saw them in front of me, mere mortals, fighting in a war that wasn't theirs. Fighting in a war that could forever silence their lives. My power as a goddess of fate couldn't save them as they met untimely ends, swords cutting off the thread of their existences. Not even my own brothers and sisters were infallible. One after another, brands appeared on their wrists, trapping them without their powers, leaving them as vulnerable as the mortals.

How could we save them? How? I turned my tear-streaked face to my sister, beautiful even as the tragedy twisted her features, blue eyes shining with grief.

"It's time," Laima said.

It was time. Our desperate hour had arrived.

I blinked again and took in the familiar surroundings of the farmhouse bedroom. My eyes shot around the room, seeking the man who had been there before my vision.

There was no one. My door was closed. Outside my window, dawn was just beginning to break. I settled back on my pillow and stared at the ceiling. How much of last night had been real? How many of those visions were simply dreams? All of them?

I squeezed my eyes shut. What did it all mean?

CHAPTER ELEVEN

I was awake now. With nothing else to do, I changed back into my clothes and wrinkled my nose at the rank smell of body odor. I needed a shower and new clothes. I couldn't wear this outfit forever.

I tiptoed down the stairs and discovered I wasn't the only one up. Rory had already gathered the eggs. He pulled the skillet off a rack and set it on top of the gas stove, but I intercepted him before he could start cooking.

"Let me. You don't have to just serve us the whole time."

"I don't mind. It reminds me of what my role used to be." But he stepped to the side, putting a lump of butter next to the pan along with the freshly gathered eggs.

Trey popped into the kitchen next, his red hair spiking up, wearing a button-up shirt under a pair of overalls. "Look at you, miss farmhand."

"What are you supposed to be, the farmer's son?" Meredith came into the room also, her hair still in yesterday's ponytail but not nearly so neat.

"You should write a poem about how the farmer's son wakes up better looking than the farmer's daughter."

Meredith joined me at the stove, pulling down plates so I could spread eggs onto them. "If that's supposed to be an insult, you're gonna have to try harder. Because I ain't the farmer's daughter."

"What are your plans today?" Rory asked Trey, interrupting their verbal sparring.

"I need to take Jayne out to practice."

Meredith sat down at the table, passing out plates of eggs and forks. "So you can continue to prove what a horrible teacher you are?"

"Hey," Trey protested, "she actually got two kids to turn around and meet her eyes yesterday."

"Hardly because of you," Meredith said. "If I stared at the back of someone's head long enough, they'd probably turn around and look at me also."

"Because you would give them the heebie-jeebies."

I raised the spatula I'd been using to cook. "I have a request. I need new clothes."

Beth stumbled in, somehow totally cute in her frumpy pajamas. Her straightened hair had long since returned to its natural curl, and she gave a huge yawn. "Did somebody say clothes? I need some. I reek."

Meredith sniffed her shirt and made a face. "We all do."

"You can say that again," Trey said. He avoided Meredith's fork as it tried to stab his arm and brought his empty plate to the sink. "Thanks for breakfast, Jayne. We can find somewhere for you to get clothes and practice at the same time."

"But I'm definitely coming today!" Beth said, piling her plate high with more scrambled eggs. "Can we buy some bagels?"

I looked at Trey. "I have a debit card. We can use it."

"And give away your location? I raided my piggy bank last night. We're set."

"You kept a secret stash at your grandpa's house?" Meredith said, arching an eyebrow.

He looked at her coolly. "At my house. I grew up here. I moved in with my mom in Jersey only to be close to Jayne."

I blinked in surprised, startled to realize how much I had uprooted his life before I'd even met him. "We'll pay you back, I promise."

He shrugged. "I'm not worried about it. It'll be fine."

"Well, in that case." Beth stuffed the last bit of her eggs into her mouth. "Let me go wash my face and I'm ready to go."

"Guess I'll change into what I wore yesterday," Meredith said with a sigh.

I took the skillet over to the sink and began to wash it. Trey followed me, hovering near my elbow. "I wanted to talk to you, Jayne."

He sounded so serious, not like the Trey I'd come to know over the past few days. I put the skillet down and faced him. "What about?"

He licked his lips and slipped his hands into his pockets. He actually looked nervous. "That dream you had last night."

It was a good thing I had put the skillet down, or I would've just dropped it on my foot. Or his foot, if I was lucky. Knowing me, I wouldn't be. "Dream?" Which crazy night time experience of mine was he referencing?

His hand came out and took my wrist, flipping it over so it was palm up. His fingers traced the brand of his star, barely visible in the sunlight pouring in through the window. "How many times have you been to those stairs?"

I gave a startled gasp and jerked my hand back. "Were you—how did you know? Is it real?"

He met my eyes. "It's real. It's the way to the underworld. I want to know how you got there."

I shook my head. "I don't know. Aaron. I heard Aaron calling me. All I've done is follow his voice."

Trey's eyes narrowed. "How many times?" he repeated.

I tried to remember. "Three times, maybe."

He stared at me, gnawing on his lower lip. "We have to speed things along. You have to get your memories back before you go into the underworld. You're doing this without me, and that's not how it's supposed to be done. But I don't think you have any control over it."

"I don't. But the first time, when I opened the door—that's when your star appeared."

He took my hand again, studying my palm. He touched the center of the star, and immediately a heat pressed outward from my palm, a light traveling from my flesh to his finger. He pulled his hand back and stared at his finger in wonder.

"What?" I whispered, unable to tear my eyes from the expression on his face.

"I felt it. My powers." He stared again at my hand. "It's like you've got them. Somehow, that's made it so that you can begin the descent without me." He flexed his wrist, the brand of chains on his arm bulging. "It won't be enough, though. I need to physically be at your side to protect you." He lifted his eyes to mine again. "What else did you see?"

The god-dude. I saw him. He made me promises and spoke in riddles about us that I did not understand.

I didn't say any of that. I was afraid of what Trey might say. Was it shameful for me to consider the guy's offer to get my memories back and free Aaron? Or was it better to reject him and avoid whatever deal it might be?

"Jayne?" Trey's sharp tone shook me from my thoughts.

"Nothing," I said, remembering his question.

He didn't believe me. I saw it in the way he eyed me. But he shrugged it off. "Let's get the others and get out of here."

⚭

By the end of the day, all I felt was frustration. The bag of clothes I purchased from the discount store didn't make me feel any better. We had wandered around the store for hours, making small talk while quietly trailing any family with small children. I'd had no more success than the day before, with a total of two meeting my eyes. And I couldn't even be sure if it was intentionally looking at me or just happening to glance my direction.

We all squished into the cab of Rory's truck when it got closer to dinnertime. We were totally crunched now that there were four of us. I ignored Meredith and Trey bickering over which radio station to listen to. Instead I rolled my window down and tried to get a reaction from the few people we saw outside. I'd been concentrating so hard and for so long that my brain hurt, literally drilling away at the inside of my skull.

Somewhere within my purse, my phone dinged. Three faces swiveled my direction, expressions varying from surprise to accusation.

I gave them my best wide-eyed, innocent look. "I swear, I turned my phone off!"

Meredith let out a huff. "If the police are looking for us, they'll be able to track your GPS."

Beth's shoulders tightened beside me. "You mean they could be tracking us right now?" she asked.

I yanked the offending phone out of my purse, ready to twist it into pieces with my bare hands. But then I froze. The exterior screen on my flip phone was gray. No digital display or any indication of power showed.

"I don't think my phone's on," I said slowly.

"But you got a message. Right?" Trey said.

I flipped the phone open. A message glowed on the dark screen, even though every sign indicated that my phone was off. My stomach give a little tumble even as I read the words.

Samantha is harvesting the powers of the fates so she can defeat the other gods. You must stop her.

That was it. But I knew who it was from. My fingers flew over the keypad, hoping the two-way messaging system worked even with my phone being off. *How do we stop her? Where do we go?*

She is hunting you. Do not use your powers. Follow her trail.

Trail? What trail?

"What is it?" Trey asked.

I looked up and realized he had stopped the car. We had pulled over to the side of the road while I read through the texts. "I'm not sure. It's a message from Laima, but I'm not sure how to follow through. She said we have to stop Samantha. That we can find her by following her trail."

Beth wrinkled her nose. "What sort of trail is Samantha leaving?"

My eyes met Trey's, and the answer that came to my mind left goosebumps on my skin. "Death and destruction."

Trey faced the highway again and gunned the engine, jerking the car back onto the road.

"Where we going?" I asked, mildly freaked out by his demeanor.

"Somewhere we can watch the news. We need to see what kind of trail Samantha is leaving."

I wasn't sure exactly where Trey had in mind for finding a TV, but I sure didn't expect him to drive back out into the country and turn down a long dirt road.

"They have a satellite farm out here among the cows?" Meredith asked wryly. "Dish Network, maybe?"

"So funny." Trey turned a sharp corner, gravel spitting behind us, and a beautiful plantation-style farmhouse rose out of the scenery in front of us. It was pristine, elegant, and noble, nothing like anything else we'd seen around here.

Trey ground to a halt in front of it, already undoing his seatbelt and climbing out of the car before I'd fully appreciated our stop. Meredith followed Trey while Beth and I got out my side.

"What, does his mistress live here?" Beth said.

"Mistress with lots of money," I replied, waiting for the front door to open and some immaculate Latvian princess to walk out.

Trey smirked. "The only kind worth having." He climbed the steps and rang the bell.

Meredith grumbled something that sounded suspiciously like, "Male pig," but before anyone could ask her to clarify, the door opened.

"Trey! No one told us you were in town!"

The woman who wrapped her arms around him was about the age of his mother. But she was much rounder and healthier looking, in contrast to the thin waif of a woman Meredith and I had met in Trey's crumbling house a few weeks earlier.

"Please tell me that's not his mistress," Beth breathed.

Meredith snorted. "Mistress? That guy is going to be lucky to get one woman."

Completely unaware of the topic of our conversation, Trey turned around and gestured to the woman. "This is my aunt Tessa. Tessa, these are some of my friends from school. They're doing a living farms research project and get to stay at Grandpa's place for a bit."

Smooth. Lies fell from his lips even easier than they fell from mine.

Tessa reacted excitedly while I glared at Trey. We could've been staying here, in high comfort, instead of wallowing about his grandpa's place?

Tessa ushered us into her house and quickly sat us down with glasses of ice cold lemonade. Trey settled onto the couch in the living room and obligingly answered every question she threw at him.

"I've barely heard a word from your mom since she moved to New Jersey. How do you like that private school Grandpa put you in?"

Trey leaned forward and picked up the remote control on the end table beside him. "I didn't like it so much and it was really expensive. I'm at a regular public school now."

Tessa blinked. "But Grandpa worked so hard to get you in there."

"I know. I feel bad about that, but it wasn't for me."

"He was suspended," Meredith said with a sweet smile. "For killing ducks."

Trey shifted his body and glowered at her. "I did not. That's not why."

"Why, then?" she hummed.

"That's okay. You don't have to explain." Tessa inspected us, and I know she was thinking that we didn't look like private school material anyway. Not with our discount store clothing. "Well, as long as you're happy. You've got friends. Anyone special?" Her eyes lingered on me.

"Nope." His lips popped on the final P. "Just going to school and staying out of trouble."

"Or that's the plan," Meredith said.

Trey's eyes narrowed, but he didn't look at her this time. He aimed the controller at the TV and pounded the On button as if he could inflict pain on it. That didn't deter Tessa, who kept right on talking over the cacophony of

102

voices that filled the room.

"And your mama?" Tessa's voice softened. "She never texts or calls. Doesn't answer my letters."

"Sorry." Trey kept his eyes on the television, acting disinterested in the conversation. Maybe he really was? He flipped through channels until he landed on the news. "I don't know why she won't talk to you."

The conversation dwindled, and I wondered what more wasn't being said.

"Well, you're here, and that's all that matters!" Tessa was back to happy. "How long are you staying? Let's have you and Grandpa over for dinner!"

"Does Grandpa come over often?" Trey asked. He caught me looking at him and inclined his head toward the television. Right. I was supposed to be paying attention to that.

"Often enough," Tessa replied. "Usually on Sundays after church. Sure would be nice to have you and your mama come up once a month, at least."

Trey shrugged and shot me another pointed look. I made a very conscious effort to stare at the television. So far the telecaster was going on about a problem with the traffic lights causing huge congestion in the small towns. So fascinating.

Trey was giving some excuse for why he and his mom never came over when the news report abruptly changed, catching my attention.

"Three more bodies have been identified as people who went missing from the tri-city area last week. This brings the total number of dead to eight so far."

I lifted to my feet, guilt lancing through me like a hot knife, splitting my chest wide open and making me ache. I didn't even hear what else she said. "They're dying," I gasped out.

Tessa looked over at me. She pulled her mouth down, sadness in her eyes. "It's awful, isn't it? All of those people. Randomly abandoning their homes, their families, and now they're showing up dead. Theory is maybe they got some kind of contagious disease and are slowly dying by the wayside."

"Like zombies." Beth shuddered. "It's like the real walking dead."

I had used the same words when talking with Lieutenant Bailey. It almost fit, except these weren't zombies. They were people, and Samantha had trapped their souls.

Tessa was still talking, inviting us and Rory over for dinner, though Trey's eyes hadn't left my face.

"Thanks, Aunt Tessa," he said, rising and giving her a hug. "Maybe we'll come over this week. I think it's time for us to go now, though."

I wrapped my arms around my torso, shivering slightly. "Yes. We've got to go."

Laima's intention had been for us to discover Samantha's trail and follow her, but something had occurred inside me. I was angry, and indignant, and some fiery and ferocious emotion swelled through me.

War had happened before, and I had lost people to it.

Not this time. Not on my watch.

CHAPTER TWELVE

We left at daybreak. All four of us shoved into the cab of Rory's pick up, armed with his debit card and what was left of Trey's cash. We had a general direction, thanks to the bodies left behind by Samantha, but none of us really knew where we were going or what we were going to fight, and the uncertainty weighed on us.

We stopped to get gas and Beth went inside to buy a map. Meredith stayed inside the car, but I sidled up next to Trey.

"There's something else Laima said," I murmured. "I didn't want to say it in front of everyone."

"What?" He didn't even glance at me as he stuck the nozzle in the back of the truck.

"She said Samantha's hunting me. And that I shouldn't use my powers."

Now he looked at me. "She said that?"

"Yes." I chewed on my lower lip. "What does that mean?"

He squinted and lifted his gaze skyward. "I'm not sure. But the powers part is a moot point. First of all, you can't summon, and second of all, we're about to leave your geographical area."

"My geographical area? What do you mean?"

He redirected his attention at me. "Why do you think Karta and Dekla split their souls into hundreds of pieces? So they could spread themselves out across the earth, that's why. And each companionship covers a certain region."

"Oh," I said, starting to understand. "So my region is the tri-state area?"

"Yep. Once you leave this area, you won't smell any uncertain deaths. The people won't be your responsibility. Now, if you could summon, you could still summon a vision from any child and cast judgment. But you can't, so." He shrugged.

"What good am I, then? Why are we even going?"

"Because Laima told us to."

Well, didn't that just solve everything.

We climbed back into the truck and got going again. Beth acted as the navigator, using the atlas we'd bought at a gas station.

"I can't believe this is how people used to get around," Meredith said, inspecting the backside of the map as Beth folded it at odd angles so she could focus on the roads. "It's a wonder people made it anywhere."

"Before smart phones, people used to be smart," Trey said.

Meredith clicked her tongue. "I was waiting to see what acerbic response you would have for me."

"Whoa, acerbic. I hope you didn't hurt yourself coming up with that one."

I wanted to wallop both of them upside the head for being so ridiculous. But before I could say anything, something tugged so hard on my belly that I sat up straight and grabbed the door handle.

All three of them swiveled to look at me.

"What's wrong?" my sister asked.

I shook my head. "I don't know. I just felt something weird in my stomach."

Trey turned left into the intersection, and I cried out as something yanked on my insides, like a shepherd's hook gripping me by the small intestine. It pulled me against the passenger door.

"Stop the car, stop the car!" I said.

Trey pulled over and squealed to a halt, his eyes large and concerned as they turned to me. "What is it, Jayne?"

I doubled over. An urgency to move filled my brain, like the instinct to duck when a fist flies at you. My hand fumbled for the lock on the door, and then I pushed it open and tumbled out of the car.

"Jayne!" Trey called after me, alarm in his voice.

But I was heedless to him, speed-walking back the way we'd come as quickly as I could until the ache in my stomach lessened. I let out a careful breath of relief and slowed my pace, feeling normal again. As long as I didn't stop moving forward.

Meredith was at my side in an instant, her hands jumping up and down frantically as if she wasn't quite sure what to do with herself. "Jayne? What's wrong?"

"That's not the way."

"Well, you just tell us which way to go. Let's get back in the car, though, okay? We'll make better time behind the wheel than on foot."

That made sense. I nodded. "I'll wait here."

She shot me a dubious look but ran back to the truck. I watched her and Trey argue through the driver's side window, and then she got in and he turned the truck around. Look like she'd won that one.

Trey pulled onto the shoulder of the road beside me and waited while I climbed back in. "Where to?" he asked me carefully, as if afraid the wrong words or tone might set me off into hysterics.

"Just go back to the intersection we drove through and keep going straight."

Trey obliged me, shooting me suspicious looks the whole time. I relaxed as we drove west on the highway, until that same sensation began to tug at me twenty minutes later. I sat up and paid attention as we neared another junction.

"Go left," I said.

Trey followed the highway in a southwestern direction, and I nodded as the tugging relaxed.

"Yes, that's good."

"Where are we going?" he asked.

"I haven't the slightest."

Trey looked slightly irritated, his brows knitting close together. "Then why are we following your directions? How do I know you're not being tricked by something?"

I gave him my own suspicious glare. "You mean there are elements out there that will try to trick me?"

"It's happened to me before."

Was that how he lost his powers? I did my best to insert lasers into my glare. "And how am I supposed to know the difference?"

"That's why we're training you. And why you've got me."

I growled impatiently. "And right now? How do I know I'm not leading you into a trap?"

"You guys are not reassuring me," Beth said.

"Do you think something is manipulating her?" Meredith asked.

"Obvious. Question is, is this someone on our side or their side?" He glanced at me, and I returned his stare.

"If you have a better plan, by all means, feel free to share."

He didn't. Trey merely grunted and turned his eyes back to the road.

Beth clicked on the radio and searched through stations, probably looking for the news. When she didn't find anything, she settled on a country song.

"Oh, please no," Meredith groaned. She reached for the dial, but Trey smacked her hand away.

"Hey! Some of us like this music!"

"This is not music." She reached for the dial again, and again Trey knocked her hand away.

"You touch me one more time," Meredith said, "and you lose a tooth."

"My truck, I'm driving. I decide."

"Oh yeah? Is that how this goes? The king of the car rules the road?"

Beth giggled, and we looked at her.

"Sorry," she said. "But you guys fight like these two little kids I used to babysit."

Meredith's face flushed crimson, and even Trey looked chagrined.

"Sorry," he muttered.

"Oh, don't stop on my account," Beth said, her eyes sparkling. "I think it's quite funny. And there's not much else to entertain me."

Knowing they were the source of Beth's amusement did the trick. Neither Meredith nor Trey said another word to each other, although the music feud raged on in silence, both of them switching the station whenever they got the chance.

We drove past a fast food chain and my stomach give such a hard jerk that I twisted around in my seat, staring out the window.

"Hungry, Jayne?" Trey asked, laughter in his voice.

Hunger didn't begin to describe the sensation in my gut. I pressed both hands against the back window, staring out. "Turn around."

"Are you serious?" Beth asked.

"Just turn around!" I snapped, little tremors erupting from my fingers.

"I think she's serious," Meredith said.

"For the love of hamburgers," Beth mumbled.

Trey had already done a u-ey and was heading back to the fast food restaurant.

The tension in my stomach dissipated, and I let out a little breath, quite annoyed with whatever was doing this to me.

Trey parked the truck, and I climbed out first. Now that we'd arrived, I eyed the restaurant with trepidation. Did I really want to find out what had brought me here?

"I guess it is dinner time," Meredith said. "Although I think you could've found a better way to tell us than to order us to turn around, Jayne."

Before I could defend myself, the door to the fast food restaurant opened, and two women came out. One was tall and thick, looking like a cross between a backliner and a viking with her short blond hair and square jaw. The other was slim and tiny, diminutive in stature with long black hair and porcelain skin.

They walked straight toward us with quick, deliberate steps. The four of us stood at attention, watching their approach. I didn't know them, but I didn't feel afraid. In fact, the warm tingling that started up in my navel could only be described as anticipation.

They stopped in front of us, and we stood in silence for a moment before Meredith spoke.

"Who are you?"

The shorter one focused her dark eyes on Meredith and said, "They have a ragana."

Her tone held a mixture of envy and admiration.

"That must be why they've been chosen for this," her companion said in a much lower voice.

Trey shifted slightly. "We seem to have missed something here. What's going on?"

Their eyes focused on him, and then the tall one bent her head and they whispered to each other. I couldn't hear what they said, but I thought I caught the word, "Auseklis."

The tall one stepped forward, her pantsuit swaying gracefully with her movements. She extended her hand to Trey, towering over him like an Amazonian warrior. "I'm Melissa." Trey clasped her hand in his, and she nodded at the girl behind her. "That's Amy. We are Dekla and Karta. You have entered into our territory."

I sucked in a gasp, my hand fluttering around my mouth.

The short one — Amy — focused her eyes on me. A smile played about her lips, and she said, "You are Dekla." She stepped forward and took my hand in both of hers. Her skin was soft, and only now that I was closer did I realize she was much older than I had first thought. I had originally guessed her to be in her late twenties, but the smile wrinkles around her eyes made me think I was off by about two decades. Remembering how slowly we aged, I realized I could still be wrong.

"So am I," she said, releasing my hand and stepping back. "Dekla, I mean."

"You've been waiting for us," I said, my eyes looking back and forth between the two of them.

"Amy called you here," Melissa said, lifting that square jaw. The short blond hair fell back from her face.

"Anybody hungry?" Trey said, re-directing all eyes to him. "I think we better go inside to get our questions answered."

"And I thought you were only thinking of your stomach," Meredith said.

"Sometime I use my head," Trey said casually.

"You'll never cease to amaze me," Meredith replied.

Melissa and Amy had already turned back toward the fast food joint, completely disinterested in anything else we had to say. I hurried to catch up with them, Beth on my heels. I thought we would sit down at a table and immediately begin to ask our questions, but instead they got in line behind the counter.

Right. We still had to eat.

"Get it to go," Melissa said. "We can't stay here."

I watched her and Amy move in front of us, tilting their heads toward each other as they spoke. They moved in a kind of rhythm, with the grace of dance partners familiar enough with each other and the dance to know the next step without asking. They placed their order and then went over to a side booth to wait.

"What are you getting?" Beth asked.

I studied the menu. "I'll just take a grilled cheese sandwich." Food was not foremost on my mind right now. My eyes kept looking at the two women, sitting at a booth now, and I was desperate to pepper them with my questions.

"Me too," Beth said.

I placed the order for both of us, indicating Trey with my finger as the guy who would be paying. Then I joined Amy and Melissa at the table.

"So how did you know I was coming?" I said, barely waiting for my rump to touch the bench before I started asking.

"Laima told us," Melissa said. "She asked us to set up a location and let you know."

I scooted over as Meredith pushed in next to me. "So Laima texted you?"

Amy nodded, holding up her smart phone. "But she didn't give us a way to contact you, which meant we had to be creative." The two of them exchanged a smile.

"You have some kind of physical hold over me?"

"No. I called you. One goddess to another."

Melissa leaned forward. "If you were a mere mortal, Amy could just tweak your destiny so you would decide to come and eat here."

My head swiveled to Amy. "You have the power to summon visions at will? So you've already mastered your former selves?"

Amy twirled a strand of her long black hair around her finger. "I can summon visions. And I can call on memories when I need them."

My eyes switched to Melissa. "And you?"

Melissa shrugged. "It's taking me longer, but I've almost mastered them."

"With no help?"

I hadn't noticed Trey drop into the booth on the other side of Meredith until he spoke.

"We had help." Amy's lips formed into a tight line. "We had an Auseklis."

"Had?" Trey leaned in closer. "What happened to him?"

"She took him." Amy's eyes smoldered.

"Who?" I demanded, even though I suspected the answer.

"Samantha." Melissa spat the word out like venom. "She took his powers. Amy and I barely escaped with ours intact."

I leaned back in my seat, a cold chill washing from the top of my head to the tips of my toes. "You were in danger?"

Amy focused her dark eyes on me, brimming with sadness. "She's seeking out as many from the lines of Karta and Dekla as she can. Since joining her powers with Jods, she's no longer restricted by geographical lines or age. She's not bound by a moral code to not manipulate. She could force us to relinquish our powers to her. We relied on Kevin—our Auseklis—to protect us. Without him, we are more vulnerable."

"How did she get to you?" I asked, my skin prickling. "Did you seek her out? Confront her?"

"No," Melissa said in that gravelly voice of hers. "Laima told us to lie low and wait for you. But Samantha felt one of us change a future and tracked us. We are not allowed to use our powers now."

"She's hunting us," I whispered. I glanced around the restaurant and fought the urge to crawl under the table. "But you used them to get me here."

"Out of necessity," Amy said.

"Then we shouldn't stay here."

"We won't stay long," Melissa said. "By the time she gets here, we'll be gone."

I didn't feel their confidence. I took a deep breath and tried to shake it off. The food hadn't arrived yet, but the desire to fly away raced through my veins.

Like I could fly.

Focus, Jayne. I furrowed my brow, bringing my brain power back to the issue at hand. "But can't you help your Auseklis get his powers back?"

Melissa shook her head.

I sent Trey an accusing look. We'd rescued him because he said he could help us. But what if there was no way to do that?

Before I could lift my voice, Melissa said, "She killed him."

That cut me off short. "She did?"

"Well, one of her soldiers," Amy said tightly. "He was too old to defend himself without his powers."

"How did she take them?"

"She changed his destiny," Amy answered. "It became his fate to die."

"So he just what—gave up?"

113

"Pretty much. He gave her his powers. And then he died."

The temperature seemed to have dropped by ten degrees. I wrapped my arms around myself, unable to meet Trey's eyes. Was that his fate, as well?

"That's not gonna happen to us, Jayne," Trey said, his voice firm. "Your situation and your abilities are different."

"Yes," Amy said. "You are stronger. That's why you've been chosen to lead us."

I jerked back, startled. "What?"

Melissa spread her hands wide. "It's like he said. You're unique. Your sister goddess is your actual sister. You still have your Auseklis."

"But she can't even control her power. How is she supposed to lead anyone?" Trey said, the derision ripe in his voice.

I frowned at him. "A lot of good you are as my Auseklis. You don't have powers either."

"Guess we make quite a pair," he said with a smirk.

"And you have a ragana," Amy said, locking eyes with Meredith. There was no mistaking the envy on her face now.

"If we'd had a ragana . . ." Melissa sighed.

"What do you guys do all day?" Beth asked. "Do you have jobs? Families?"

Amy laughed, a high, tinkling, playful sound. "Of course we have jobs and families. And real lives. But we communicate with each other always. Rarely does the day go by without a vision. And right now, Laima wants us by each other's side. We've answered her call, just as you have."

The server arrived with our food, and Amy stood, collecting the napkins and utensil wrappers. "We should go now."

Amy ushered us out the door, putting our food in our hands and prodding us along.

"Where are we going?" I asked, digging my sandwich out of the foil wrapper.

"We reserved a hotel room for you. Go, rest. We'll call you tonight."

"We don't have phones," Meredith said. "We turned them off."

Melissa pulled hers out of her purse and handed it to Meredith. "Use mine."

"Jayne still needs training," Trey said. "Can you teach her to summon?"

"And me?" Beth asked.

Trey unlocked his truck, and I climbed in and then hung out the window while the others climbed up beside me.

"We know a safe place where we can practice with our powers," Amy said. "We'll be in touch."

"Others are here," Melissa said. "Laima has called our sisters. More will be coming."

Trey started up his truck. "Good. We're going to need them."

The skin around Amy's eyes tightened, and she looked older now, more tired. "It won't be enough."

CHAPTER THIRTEEN

Trey nervously paced in the small hotel room Amy and Melissa had arranged for us. Meredith and Beth had gone to the ice machine, and it was just me, pretending to be interested in the television while the strange boy beside me marched around the room.

"Can you just sit down?" I said. "It's not like you're accomplishing anything."

He ignored my request, shoving one hand through his red hair while he marched. "Gathering Deklas and Kartas in one place, it makes us an easy target for Samantha."

"What's she going to do, launch her torpedoes at us? Besides, Melissa said none of us are staying in the same hotel."

That didn't stop Trey's pacing. "Will it be enough? How many Deklas are coming? It gives her a chance to—" Trey cut himself off.

I frowned at him. "Gives her a chance to what?"

He shook his head. "Nothing, it's nothing."

The hotel room door clicked open, and Meredith and Beth walked in with a full bucket of ice and several soft drinks nestled inside. Beth settled beside me on the bed we would be sharing while Meredith sank down onto the other. Front desk had brought a rollaway bed for Trey, but he still hadn't opened it or set it up.

"So what happens now?" Beth asked, focusing her attention on me.

I shrugged. "We just wait." I glanced at the cell phone Melissa had let us borrow.

Trey uttered a low growl of frustration. "We are worthless to them. The only one here who can do anything is Meredith, who still has to spout off poetry to get her powers to work!"

"Thanks," Meredith muttered. "Feeling really useful now."

"You?" Beth turned a lifted eyebrow in Meredith's direction. "He pretty much just said the rest of us are good for nothing."

Trey threw his arms into the air and walked out of the room.

"Should one of us go after him?" Beth asked.

"Let him stew," I said. "Whatever is going on is way over our heads. He knows it."

Meredith flipped on the television and sifted through channels until she found the news. I didn't want to watch, but I couldn't turn my eyes away from the thought that we might get updated information. Luckily the newscaster's biggest concern seemed to be the early migration of butterflies, and I lay back, letting my mind drift into a hypnotic state of relaxation.

I turned across the pillow and said to Meredith, "Do you have your poem ready?"

She bobbed her head, though she looked uncertain. "I don't know if it will work on Samantha."

I splayed one hand wide. "I don't see why not. Your spells work on me."

"Yes, well, I don't know exactly what she is anymore."

"I guess the best we can do is try. But there's still the problem of her minions. The army of people she has under her command. You can try the poem on them."

Meredith didn't look any more reassured. "And how human are they?"

She brought up a relevant concern, but I brushed it off. We couldn't be plagued by our doubts. "They're still human. It will work." It had to work, because the alternative . . . I began to understand Trey's frustration.

Where had he gone, anyway? At any moment Melissa might call, and I didn't want to have to track him down.

Beth stood up and wandered to the hotel window. "A storm is brewing," she murmured, staring out over the horizon.

Meredith and I joined her, and we stared at the mass of swirling dark clouds centralized over a location a few blocks away. I wrapped my arms around my torso, squeezing my elbows.

The hotel door opened at the same time that Melissa's cell phone rang. The three of us turned as one from the window as Trey picked up the phone. "Hello?" he said.

Amy's voice carried through the line. But she sounded panicked, anxious, and Trey's expression tightened as he listened. He hung up without answering, then looked at the three of us.

"There's no time for training. We have to go now."

"So that's the bat signal," Meredith said.

No training? Now? "What are we supposed to do?" My voice came out high-pitched, and I gestured out the window behind me. "What are we walking into?" Premonition crept along my spine like the skinny, hairy legs of a spider.

"She's going to try to turn us all," Meredith said.

Trey tilted his head, his cold eyes on me. "You are the goddess of fate. You tell me what we're walking into. You're the one who can smell death."

"And on that optimistic peptalk." Meredith shot a glare at Trey. "Nothing like a vote of confidence to get our spirits rallied. Let's go. They're waiting."

Trey didn't say anything, just lowered his head and followed us out of the room. But I knew his silence wasn't an apology. He fully expected us to die or lose our powers and become Samantha's minions or something like that.

I grabbed his arm as we followed after Meredith. "What did you mean back there? Am I supposed to See something here?"

He shook me off, frustration evident in his entire demeanor. "How am I supposed to know? This is my first rodeo too. I didn't think it would be my last."

"Hey. It's not my fault you lost your powers. That was you not being on your guard. And now you blame me for not being able to save you when you're the one who's supposed be protecting me? So just chill your boots."

He stared at me for a moment, and then his face cracked into a grin. "Chill my boots? Where did you come up with that one?"

My face warmed. "I don't know, you just seem like someone who would wear boots. Living out here in Hicksville."

"We're in Kentucky now. I don't live here. But this is definitely Hicksville." His hand landed on my shoulder, and some of the tightness eased out of his mouth. "Do what you can out there. Maybe we can reverse this." He let go and followed after the other two.

"The people of Kentucky might take exception to that observation," I muttered. But I didn't feel any better. Somehow Trey's attempt at reassurance had only made me feel worse.

I pounded the palm of my fist against my temple. "Remember, Jayne! Put yourself together! All of yourselves!"

"Jayne!" Beth called, and I quickened my pace to reach her.

I was the last one into the truck, which meant I was by the door, again.

"It stinks in here," Meredith said. "Like sweat and boys."

"Don't look at me," Trey said, starting the engine. "I don't sweat. That's on you."

"I suppose next you're gonna tell me you're not a boy?" Meredith raised her eyebrows.

Trey opened his mouth to respond, but Beth burst out laughing, and he

119

promptly closed it.

A phone dinged somewhere, and I turned my attention to Beth as she held up Melissa's smart phone.

"She just sent me a dropped pin."

"Great," Trey said, eyes forward. "Guide me there."

I bit down anxiously on my thumbnail.

The weather changed as we got closer. The clouds above us looked like a funnel tunnel in reverse, dark gray and twisting.

"How does she control the elements like that?" Beth asked, peering out the window.

"She can't," Trey said. "It's probably Velu Mate. She's Velns' mother, the goddess of the dead. That vortex is a portal to the world of the unliving."

Trey's grandpa's truck came to a stuttering halt, and a chilling sense of déjà vu went through me.

"Just like last time," Meredith murmured.

Unlike last time, we weren't going to sit here like ducks waiting to be attacked. I pushed open the car door and climbed out. The others followed my lead.

Beth still held the phone out in front of her. "It's this way."

No business park this time, no concrete warehouse or parking garage. This time, it was a city park. A running trail wound around the perimeter of the green grassy field, a baseball diamond in the center. And standing at home plate was none other than Samantha. She wore jeans and a pink tank top, looking more human and normal than the first time I'd met her. But somehow, with her black hair billowing away from her face and her hands out at her sides, she fit the perfect stereotype of an evil witch.

Or maybe that fit the hunched old woman beside her, face hidden by a hooded cloak, spindly fingers moving around each other as if caressing an invisible ball. Something about her terrified me, and my feet ground to a halt.

Trey hands clenched and unclenched, and he practically bounced on his heels. "This isn't right. Why would they stand out there for all of us to see? Taunting us, wanting us to go out there."

I struggled for breath, not wanting them to see my fear.

120

"It's a Dementor," Beth whispered, and Meredith turned to her.

"Eyes of light, heart of gold, you are ready for this fight," she said.

Her words prompted an immediate reaction, dispelling the fear as if a flashlight had sliced through the darkness. I inhaled and straightened my shoulders.

"Jayne, Beth."

My head swiveled around at the sound of our names. Amy and Melissa approached and stopped a few feet behind us.

"What now?" I asked.

"The others are coming," Amy said.

Melissa pointed behind. I turned around and saw about a dozen people moving closer to us.

"We got five other goddess pairs," Amy said. "Two of them have their own ragana, and three of them have an Auseklis." She cast a quick glance at me and Beth. "You are the only two with both."

I studied the motley group of people as they approached us. Mostly female, of course, and older. These groups had much more experience than me.

Amy looked at me. "Do you want to take the lead?"

"What? Me?" I shook my head. "No! I don't have any idea what to do here!"

Amy smiled, though it was tinged with sadness, like everything she did. "Follow my example."

She turned around and walked toward the baseball diamond, where Samantha hadn't moved except to drop her arms. There was a flash of light, and suddenly Jods appeared beside her. I gave a start. He looked so similar to the other one, the one who kept coming to me. Except where the other one wore grassy reeds over one shoulder, this one exposed his muscular torso with only a woven man-skirt around his hips.

The rest of us fell into place behind Amy. The wind picked up as we approached, whipping Amy's hair behind her head and tugging at her flowing blouse.

"Samantha," Amy shouted as we approached within hearing range, "it's time to give up. Relinquish your hold on the souls and renounce this power quest, and you will be returned to a mortal life."

Samantha burst out laughing, her voice far louder than it should have been from the distance. "Is that something you think you can grant me? You have no power over me."

Amy continued unfazed. "If you don't relinquish them, we will be forced to destroy you. You have broken the laws of nature, and Jumis will not claim your soul for the underworld. There will be nothing left of you."

The storm darkened overhead, thunder rumbling, and Jods put his hand on Samantha's shoulder. She visibly straightened, and I narrowed my eyes. Perhaps I had misunderstood the dynamics. It didn't look like he was taking orders anymore.

"You have no power over me," Samantha repeated, a twisted smile pulling across her lips. "I'm surprised you dare face me again. I will suck your power from you just like I did your manservant."

"We have back up this time!" Melissa shouted. "And he wasn't a manservant!"

One of the women to the right of me pulled back and moved her hands together. Between her palms lightning flickered and then grew, forming an electric ball.

"What is she doing and how is she doing that?" I gasped.

"She's their ragana," Trey said. "They don't just manipulate emotions."

"You mean I can do that?" Meredith asked, her eyes wide.

Trey didn't get the chance to respond, or maybe he was never going to, but at that moment the woman pulled her arm back and released the lightning ball.

A wreath of light and smoke wrapped itself across the baseball field, nearly obscuring Samantha and Jods and the old croan. Jods held out a hand, and the light coalesced into a streak before flying into his outstretched palm.

Samantha shouted, "You didn't really think you could take us out that way, did you? We are not mere mortals." Even from where I stood, I could see the sneer on her face. "But they are."

She gestured behind her just as the smoke cleared, revealing thousands of people standing ramrod straight on the baseball diamond, crammed together in tight rows about a hundred across. Before I could even wrap my mind around who they were or what they were doing, Jods released the lightning ball. He stepped out of the way, and the ball crashed into the mob of people behind them.

Several bodies collapsed in the first two rows of people, and panic and fear ripped through my limbs. "No!" I screamed, lunging forward. Shock rippled through me. She was slaying her own army. Trey grabbed my arm, stopping my motion.

One of the women beside me whirled around to the ragana. "Don't attack again, you might hit the humans!"

"Bring them to me," Samantha said, her face contorting with an evil grimace.

Immediately her army of soldiers began marching toward us. I sucked in deep breaths, my eyes scanning for Aaron. This couldn't be happening.

"What are we supposed to do? We can't hurt them!" I said, tears thick in my throat.

"We have to get to Samantha." Trey took my hand and gave it a squeeze. "I can protect you, but you've got to free my powers."

"How?" I said, remembering our attempt in Maryland to defeat Samantha, feeling the utter helplessness as she claimed Aaron's soul for her own purposes.

"Last time your sister wasn't Karta. Last time you hadn't started remembering the past lives. Last time Meredith didn't have control of her power."

He had a point. A lot had changed since last time. But one thing hadn't. I couldn't give him his powers back.

Trey let go of my hand. "Defend yourself," he said, and I turned to see the advancing army upon us.

"I'll try my poems," Meredith said, stepping forward.

"I'm not trained in hand to hand combat!" I cried. Since when was this in the job description?

But it must be. The others on both sides were already fighting, arms and legs moving in synchronized battle moves. The only things lacking were swords and shields. Beth and I hung back, unsure of what to do.

Trey leapt in front of us, fists swinging as he knocked a man aside. My throat clenched. He was only human right now, but he was still doing his best to protect us.

"Do something!" he yelled at me, even as one of Samantha's soldiers punched him in the face. It was a woman, and I cried out as Trey grabbed her hair at the back of her neck and knocked her to the ground with a punch to her temple.

"Is she dead?" I couldn't tear my eyes away from her crumpled form. This was a woman who never should've been here. It wasn't her fate to be in this army.

"Jayne!" Trey's nose was bleeding, and a guy had his arm trapped. "Which side do you want to win here?"

I jumped into the foray. My doubts hushed as prime fear and instinct took over. I pulled my arm back and clocked the guy in the face with my elbow.

The first time I'd ever punched someone was Samantha when we'd fought in Maryland. The same jarring pain shot through my forearm. Before I could fully appreciate it, the man let go of Trey and reached out both hands for me.

Without hesitating, I dropped into a crouch. I thrust my head into his stomach, wrapped my arms around the backs of his legs, and threw him.

I threw him.

What the heck? I looked at Trey, wide-eyed, and he shot me a grin. "Didn't anyone tell you you're a goddess?"

"What?" I gasped out. Someone approached in my peripheral vision, and my hand formed into a fist and lifted, smacking them in the nose faster than I could blink.

Before I could examine my new abilities, a bolt of lightning shot straight out of the whirling storm clouds above us. When it hit the ground, half a dozen small creatures burst out of it and ran in our direction.

Trey swore and said, *"Vadatajs."*

"What are those?" Beth squealed. She hadn't moved, but stood pale-faced and frozen.

"The goblins," Meredith said behind me. "Little troublemakers."

And trouble they were. One of them raced right up to Meredith and bit her ankle. She let out a shriek and collapsed, wrapping her hands around the bite.

"It's just a flesh wound, the goblins can't hurt you," Trey said, directing my attention back to him. "Stay in the fight."

"But they can," Amy said.

I hadn't noticed her circling our direction as she and the other members of our side fought their own battles. Now I tried to see who she meant, and the sight sent a cold dread to my belly.

Several other beings had appeared on the field, large and shaped like men, but with the heads of something like a dog. They stepped forward, thrusting some kind of staff into the ground with every step. The staff was tipped with what looked like a very wicked pitchfork.

"What are they?" I asked.

Amy's eyes narrowed and her lips pinched together. "Cynocephalus. Men with the heads of jackals. The jackal represents their true selves. They made bargains with evil and are no longer men."

Trey turned around and threw his arms around me, hauling me backward. "She's right. They can hurt you." He gave me a shove, sending me stumbling away from the fight, before he turned back around and ran for Beth.

CHAPTER FOURTEEN

T rey grabbed Beth and dragged her toward me. Meredith was still on the ground, her hands around her ankle, eyes trained on the approaching demons. Beth joined me, taking my hand.

To my right, the other ragana threw another lightning ball. It blew up in the middle of the field, knocking over five or six humans, several goblins, and one demon. One.

"Get in the truck!" Trey shouted at me and Beth, then he ran back into the battle.

"Do as he says!" I said to Beth.

"Jayne!"

The deep male voice jolted me in my tracks. I turned around, scanning the fallen bodies before I saw a man approaching me. Armor covered every inch of his exposed flesh, a tall staff in his hand. Why was I so ill-prepared? Where was my staff?

"Jayne!" he called again, and this time something familiar in his voice had me catching my breath.

I shaded my eyes and took a step closer, my heart in my throat. Could it be Aaron? Had he regained the use of his senses?

In a moment he was beside me, chest heaving. I lifted up my hands, ready to yank his helmet from his face. But he did it first, revealing the wavy brown locks and sharp green eyes.

Not Aaron. I pushed aside a sharp stab of disappointment and focused on the boy in front of me. "Stephen! You're okay!" I reached for him, but he pushed my arms down.

"Oh, I'm better than okay, Jayne. But this scene here—" He gestured to the makeshift battlefield behind him. "This doesn't have to happen. All she wants is for you to join her. All of you. She needs your power, she needs your strength to accomplish her plan."

"She? You mean Samantha?"

"Yes, Samantha!" he said with an eye roll. "Why are you standing in her way? She only wants what's best for humanity!"

How could he make Samantha's plan sound so reasonable? What had she told him? "I can't, Stephen. Innocent people are dying." I tried pleading, imploring to his emotional side. "Why don't you help me? We can end this if we stop her!"

"No, you don't understand. Things will be better. People won't die when they shouldn't. My parents—" He shook his head, but his countenance fairly beamed. "She can fix it."

"Fix it?" I whispered.

"Their deaths."

My hope sank like a stone in the ocean. "Is that what she told you? It's not true. Nothing can change that now."

Fury flashed across his face, transforming Stephen's handsome features into something dark and sinister. "You're wrong. You don't know anything.

The god of the dead has already agreed. And if you stand in the way, I swear, Jayne, if you do something to keep it from happening, I will take you down myself."

The friendship, the gentleness, the relationship we'd built over the past year was completely gone. I did not know this boy in front of me. My lip trembled and I blinked back tears, forcing myself to remember the bigger picture. "Where is Aaron?"

Something like disbelief crossed his face. "Still interested in him? He's nothing now. He was too weak."

My hurt turned to panic, and I lunged forward and grabbed Stephen's arm. "What do you mean, he was too weak?" What had she done with him?

Stephen tried to shake me off, a sneer on his face. "He's just one of the masses. He wasn't strong enough to keep his identity when Samantha took his soul. He has no position."

Spots danced in front of my vision, and I tightened my grip on his arm. "Did she take your soul, too?"

"I gave it to her!" His eyes flashed. "And she let me keep my connection to it. I'm stronger now. More than any other human in her army." Anger twisted his features, darkness burning in his eyes. "She said you're one of them, the ones that try to control us. The ones that say we have to die before our time. Did you know, Jayne?"

For a moment, it seemed the battle around us stopped. Everything went silent, and it was just me and Stephen facing off.

"Know what?" I whispered.

"That my parents were going to die."

How was I supposed to answer that? I stared at Stephen, for the first time feeling afraid.

And suddenly Trey was at my side, bringing with him the rush of the battle, the screams, the clanging of weapons and the thundering of feet. He panted from the effort of holding Meredith, who clung with her arms around his neck, face turned into his chest.

"What are you still doing here? We have to get to my truck. Now." He spotted Stephen then and came between us, his jaw tightening.

"Go, Stephen," I said, not wanting Trey to toss Meredith to the dirt and fight him. "Tell Samantha we won't join her."

Stephen jerked backward as if someone had yanked on his head, and then he shot me a final glare. "You've picked your side. Remember that." He turned and raced back toward the baseball diamond.

"Into the car!" Trey said.

"Where's my sister?" I asked.

"In the car!" Trey snapped. "I'm putting Meredith inside and I expect you to be there also!" He started to turn away and then froze, eyes landing on something on the battlefield.

I spun around, seeking whatever had startled him.

"Jayne," Trey said, "Let's go."

Something in his tone commanded me to leave with him, but it only fueled my desire to know what he'd seen. Stephen had already retreated, and I considered myself lucky he hadn't taken me captive. In fact, only the jackal-men and perhaps a hundred mortals remained. And one man who marched in front of them.

"Jayne!" Trey shouted, his voice panicky now. "I can't wait for you. I have to help Meredith. Let him be!"

I think I stopped breathing. My heart might've even stopped beating. I wasn't sure why the sight of that soldier should cause such a reaction, but my body spasmed, leaning toward him even from this distance. And my mind caught up a moment later, recognizing the gait, the movement of the soldier. Not to mention the sweater and pressed pants.

"Aaron," I whispered.

His hand moved to his belt, and then he withdrew a sword. Behind him, the jackals and minions did the same.

Swords? Really?

Around us, everyone was in full retreat. But I didn't move. I wasn't leaving Aaron here.

"Jayne!" Trey returned to my side, empty-handed this time, his face haggard. Wind picked up, tugging on my curls, whipping across my face. "We've got to go!"

I stood my ground. "It's Aaron." I gestured toward the battlefield, not expecting Trey to understand; he'd never even met him. "If I can just talk to him, I might be able to get through to him."

Trey grabbed me above the elbow and jerked me backward. "It's a trap! Samantha sent him to get to you! We have to go!"

I yanked my arm away and gave him a shove. "Then go! Aaron gave himself up for me. He won't hurt me now!" I faced forward, ignoring Trey. But I felt him step up beside me.

"Jayne, he's not in there," he said in a voice so quiet I shouldn't have been able to hear him. "You and I both know the only way to get him back is to go to the underworld. And we can't until I get my powers. You see that sword in his hands?"

I couldn't help looking at it as Aaron and his army approached.

Trey continued. "That's not a toy. It's not designed to kill you. It's designed to strip you of your powers. To shackle you, just like I have been."

His words sent a shiver through me. Somehow that sounded even worse than dying.

Aaron picked up speed and then broke into a run, his sword lifted high over his head. I turned around, defeat bitter in the back of my throat, accepting Trey's pronouncement.

We ran for the truck. A whirlwind rose up from the dirt, whipping the debris into a frenzy. Leaves and branches flew around us, blinding me. A limb hit me in the side of the head, and I staggered, tripping over my feet and stumbling to the ground. Heart pounding in my throat, I flipped myself over to see the armored demons mere feet from me, Aaron leading the way.

"Aaron!" I cried. His only response was to raise the sword, and my stomach twisted so hard I thought I would puke. Trey was right. He wasn't Aaron anymore. I propelled myself backward on my hands as fast as I could, but he moved faster, the sword swiping down at me.

From out of nowhere Beth appeared, throwing her arms out to shield me. I screamed as his sword came down on her forearm, horrified that I would see him chop it off.

Beth arched her back, her mouth falling open in wordless agony, but her arm did not come off. Instead her whole body pulsed with a blue, flashing light before Aaron pulled his sword back.

Arms went under my armpits and hauled me to my feet. Somehow the pick-up truck was right beside me, and I barely registered Meredith behind the wheel before Trey tossed me into the bed of the truck.

"Beth!" I cried. "What about Beth?"

"I'll get her," Trey huffed.

He just left her? Indignation burned through me, but Trey was already gone, too far away to hear my rage. Two seconds later he was back, depositing my sister into a heap next to me in the back of the cab.

"Go!" he shouted at Meredith through the open window. He hovered over Beth and me, his body like a human shield.

Meredith didn't hesitate. The gas pedal slammed down so hard the tires spun as the truck kicked into reverse, sending the three of us crashing against the cab. Then she spun it in a circle and we fishtailed away from the park. I peered over the side to watch Aaron and his legions disappear in the dust.

A man walking on the distant battlefield captured my attention. My gaze was riveted on his tassel skirt, grass tunic, and washboard abs, striding among the fallen. He stopped next to each body, holding his hand above the face. I thought I saw something travel from the mouth to the palm of his hand before he moved onto the next.

"What's he doing?" I whispered.

Trey didn't seem to hear me. "I knew this was a bad idea," he huffed as we booked it out of the park. "Gathering all of us in one spot, making us more vulnerable. We look like a joke, not even somebody a half—" His language went downhill from there, but I could barely flinch at the words he used.

Everything had gone so, so wrong.

There was no plan for an organized retreat, and all of the vehicles scattered in different directions. Maybe Meredith and Trey had talked, though, because she seemed to know where to go.

Either that, or she had decided for herself. Meredith slammed the truck to a halt outside a corner pharmacy.

"Stay," Trey said, hurdling out of the car.

I cradled my sister in my arms, who was unconscious. Her skin still radiated a blue glow which seemed to be soaking into her, leaving behind small blue lines that made her look like a broken porcelain doll glued back together. Blue runes marred her wrist, much like the ones on Trey's.

"What's wrong with her?" I cried out, fear thick in my voice.

"She'll be okay." That was all Trey left me with as he went to the front of the car. He opened the car door and spoke with Meredith, then turned and jogged into the pharmacy. She leaned her head back against the seat and closed her eyes.

Beth groaned, and I turned my attention back to her, relief warming my heart. She was alive.

A moment later Trey pulled down the ramp on the bed of the truck. "I want to get you guys inside the car. Here, I'll take Beth, you go sit by Meredith."

I nodded numbly, overwhelmed and confused. Meredith sat in the middle now, and I saw an open first aid kit on the driver's seat, with what looked like a roll of gauze wrapped around Meredith's ankle. Tears had dried into dirty tracks on her face. She looked haunted and wooden. I touched her thigh as I squeezed in next to her.

"You okay?" I whispered.

She swiveled her head to look at me, her eyes glistening. "My poems didn't work. It didn't affect the soldiers at all. Trey's right. We're a joke. We were created for a task we're not even capable of doing."

My throat closed as she voiced the feelings of failure I'd been fighting. Why had Laima chosen us for this? Why were we not able to utilize our powers the way we needed to?

The passenger side door swung open, and Trey laid Beth next to me. Her head flopped over onto my shoulder, and I held her against me as he shut the door. A moment later Trey was in the driver's seat.

"Where the thing bit you, is it okay?" I asked Meredith. "Will she be okay?" I shifted in my seat and directed my last question at Trey, relying on him as the only person who could give us answers.

"She'll be fine," he said, his tone softer. "It's a wound, but it's not going to infect her bloodstream and turn her into dust or anything."

I looped an arm around Beth and clung to the door handle, feeling slightly dizzy. "Is that a possibility?"

"Depending what bites you, yes."

Meredith cleared her throat. "The other raganas were throwing balls of fire and lightning, making a storm or wind to crash against the demons, and I couldn't even muster a breeze."

"You panicked out there," Trey said.

She whirled on him, her nostrils flaring. "I didn't know what to do! Nobody has taught me anything! I didn't even know I could make lightning balls!"

"I wasn't accusing you," Trey said, raising his voice. "I'm just stating it like it was. We were not prepared. We all panicked."

Even though his eyes didn't leave the road, I felt the accusation.

Whatever I was supposed to be doing, I had better figure it out fast. "Did the people die?" I asked. "The ones hit with the lightning balls?"

Trey took a moment before answering. "Yes."

My throat constricted, and tears burned behind my eyes. "What about their souls?"

"They've been claimed and escorted to the underworld." Trey glanced at me, and I remembered the dream we'd shared where I was going down, down, down. To the underworld.

"What happens down there?" I asked.

"They'll be sorted and judged. Then they'll receive their eternal reward."

I felt sick. "Will their actions count against them?"

Trey squinted, his eyes focused on the road again. "I'm not really sure. Since they were forced to act against their will, I'm not sure how accountable they are for their actions."

"So maybe they can be redeemed," I said.

"Maybe. But even if their souls are redeemed, they won't come back to life. Their bodies are dead."

133

Trey drove us back to the hotel, where I put an arm around Meredith and helped her out of the car. We stumbled down the hall to our room without a word. As soon as I got the door open, Meredith pushed away from me and collapsed on the bed, face-down. Trey carried Beth inside, and I helped him lay her down beside Meredith.

"Are we safe here?" I murmured, wrapping my arms around myself.

Trey sank onto the other bed and shrugged his shoulders. "As safe as we can be, I guess. Samantha doesn't know where we are. As far as I know, she doesn't have the ability to sense us out unless you or Beth use your powers."

I nodded, only mildly reassured. "We need a bigger army."

Trey gave a short laugh, and Meredith rolled over slightly to watch the conversation.

"We don't have an army," he said. "Period. We need to step up our game plan."

Meredith sat up. "Can you help me?"

We both looked at her, and Trey hesitated. "I don't know how. I've never known a ragana. I'm not sure what your powers are. But it seems to be coming naturally to you. The way you're manipulating people—"

"And when we encountered Samantha in Maryland," I added, "you summoned the storm to save me from her."

Meredith looked down at her hands and turned them over. "But I couldn't do anything out there." She lifted her head and looked at Trey. "I'm not losing my powers, am I?"

Trey shook his head. "No, but we are all linked to Jayne. The stronger she is, the stronger we are."

Again, the guilt rippled through me. Everything circled back to me. My mind flashed back on the battle, on Aaron. On my own failures. I looked over at Beth, where she lay unconscious on the bed. The blue had faded from her skin, leaving only black lines.

"What happened to her?" I whispered.

Trey met my eyes, his gaze exhausted. "They took her powers. The sword broke her."

My throat closed up. "Broke her?" I squeaked.

Trey nodded. "When she became Karta, she changed, merging her mortal self with the immortal powers. Without that part of her being, she's not whole."

My heart broke at those words, and I looked at my little sister. What had I done? Everything I had feared about dragging her into this was coming true. "She was better off never knowing."

Trey's fingers closed around my wrist, forcing me to look at him again. "That's not true. We need her just like we need you."

"But what good am I? I can't get her powers back. I can't even get yours back." I choked back a sob.

Trey shook his head. "She's different. She's your sister, both by blood and by legacy. You'll be able to get her powers back."

"How?" I practically screamed question.

"You forget you have a ragana."

Meredith sat up on the bed, wiping her eyes and looking steely. "I guess I better figure out how to be one." She pushed off the bed and limped to the door.

"Where you going?" I asked.

"To do what I'm good at. Research. I saw a business station in the lobby. Maybe I can find us some answers."

I didn't want Meredith to go alone, but I was not leaving Beth. I looked at Trey, and he read the question in my eyes.

"I'll go with her," he said with a sigh. "Don't leave this room. We won't be gone long."

CHAPTER FIFTEEN

Meredith and Trey were still out in the lobby doing research when Beth finally lifted her head and pulled herself into a sitting position.

"What happened?" she whispered. She looked down at her arms and the criss-crossed, jagged lines. She flipped her arms over and studied them.

My throat closed. "How do you feel?"

She pressed a hand to her stomach. "I'm okay. Hungry."

Of course. We could remedy that. I picked up the hotel phone and quickly placed an order for pizza from a brochure next to the television. Hopefully Trey had enough cash to cover it.

When I turned around, Beth's large brown eyes were staring at me, unshed tears shimmering in their depths. "What happened?" she repeated. "I remember the *vadatajs*. Aaron." Her eyes flashed to my face, but I held myself impassive. "I thought he was going to kill you."

"So you jumped in front of me." My sister hadn't hesitated to take the blow for me. My own eyes grew hot. "We owe you everything."

"But I'm not dead. What happened?"

I let out a slow breath, my insides churning at my part in allowing this to happen. I'd overestimated Aaron's ability to conquer the enchantment. "The swords weren't meant to kill. They have a different ability: to take away our powers."

"My powers are gone?" Beth whispered. "I'm not Karta anymore?"

She hadn't been Karta for more than a few weeks, but I could see how much the loss devastated her. "You're still Karta," I said fiercely. "And we're going to find a way for you to get your powers and put you back together."

Her eyes went back to her arms, fingers trailing over the fissures on her skin. "Because I'm broken."

This time I could not contradict her.

The hotel room door opened, and Trey came in, brandishing two boxes of pizza. Meredith followed behind him.

"You're an angel," he said to me, dropping the pizza next to the television and opening the top box.

"That's funny. I've always been told I'm a goddess."

Trey laughed, and I cracked a smile.

Meredith put a note pad on the bed next to me. I noticed she favored her left leg as she walked, but otherwise she didn't complain.

"How's the ankle?" I asked, picking up the notepad.

"It burns like someone wrapped a hot coal against my skin, but Trey said that's normal for being bit by a goblin." She smirked. "Not everyone can claim that."

No, I supposed they couldn't. I looked at the notepad in my hand. "What's this?"

"These are symbols, hieroglyphics that I researched. I want you to look them over, tell me if you recognize any."

"Or have a reaction to any," Trey amended.

A reaction. Like I had when I saw the symbol for war that was being engraved into the skin of every one of Samantha's victims. As soon I saw the symbol, I knew what it meant, instinctively.

I looked at the notepad with renewed interest. "What are we hoping to find?"

Meredith glanced at my sister. "Something to bring back her powers."

I stared hard at the notepad, almost as if it were one of those 3-D images buried in print and I needed to look crossways and upside down to make it appear. "Nothing."

"Try them one at a time," Trey suggested.

"Okay." I took Meredith's pen and proceeded to draw the symbols one by one on the preceding papers. I heard Trey turn on the television, and I knew he was looking for the news, but I focused on my work.

I finished drawing the third symbol and flipped the page over to begin the next one. The imprint of the image burned into my eyes, and I knew what it was. "Creator."

"What?" Meredith had a slice of pizza in her hands, and when she leaned near me, the smell of basil and tomato sauce and spicy pepperoni rolled my own hunger to the forefront. I dropped the pen and paper on the bed, going for the pizza.

"She said creator," Trey said.

Meredith hunched over the notepad. "Does Samantha have one of these symbols on her somewhere?"

Trey looked grim. "She might. It would increase her power."

I came back over, pizza in hand. "If I carve this symbol into my skin, will it make me the creator?"

"It could. If you had an army of souls to convert. Which you don't."

"What a ray of sunshine you are," I muttered.

"We could call the lesser gods to join us," Meredith said. "Even the *kaukas*. Have something more on our side."

Trey nodded. "We might have to. Samantha and Jods are already calling gods to their side. Velns is guiding them, and now his mother is involved."

He nodded at the notepad. "What else can you figure out?"

I copied down a few more symbols. "Messenger," I said, tapping another.

"Keep going. We need more than that."

"Water. Fire. Thunder. Wisdom. Healing."

No one commented on the new symbols I had deciphered, and I was so absorbed in my task that it took me a moment before I realized they were lost in the news.

"A random lighting storm apparently caused the deaths of over a dozen people at Stadium Park today," a reporter was saying. The camera panned over the grim site, and I looked away, tuning it out.

"She's expanding her range," Meredith whispered a moment later.

I lifted my head again. This time the image showed thousands of people gathered around the police station in Louisville, Kentucky, protesting, demanding to know where their family members had gone. I pushed off the bed and moved closer.

"More people are disappearing? But how? How is she summoning without a poem?" I asked.

Trey shook his head, his lips compressed into a thin line. "She doesn't need a silly poem anymore. We know she's taken the powers of at least one goddess of fate."

"But she can't, what, just make people do things, can she?" Meredith said.

"Yep."

I felt that burning rage well up in my chest again, an emotion I'd come to recognize as not my own. That didn't make it any less real. "Why are the humans so weak? Their minds are so feeble, so easy to control."

"She's just altering their destinies like you do," Trey said.

"Except she's doing a much better job of it," I snapped. I picked up the pen and broke it in half and threw the pieces across the room. "I'm going out. I need a breather."

Nobody stopped me, and for some reason that made me even angrier. But as I huffed down the hallway, the door opened and Meredith hobbled after me. I couldn't stay angry at the sight of her limping, so I slowed just enough to let her catch up.

She held the notepad in her hands. "This symbol, right here, the last one you said. Is it used for healing?"

I glanced at it, pretending to be less interested than I was. "Maybe. I don't know what I'm supposed to do with it, though."

Meredith's eyes glinted. "I think I might." She handed me an unbroken pen, and I wondered where she was keeping her stash. "Draw it on me."

I drew the symbol on her arm, two C-shapes facing opposite directions and intersecting at the back. Meredith placed her other hand over it and whispered under her breath. She lifted her hands, but the wound looked the same.

"What were you hoping to happen?" I asked.

"Well, I thought maybe I could use the symbol to heal my ankle. I wrote a few lines to a poem designed to make the body heal quickly, but I don't feel any different."

"Are you sure? Let's take a look." I caught some of her excitement. This could be our first breakthrough in days.

We wandered over to the hotel lobby, and she sat on the couch. She bit down on her lower lip and whimpered when I started to remove the bandage.

"That's not a good sign," I said, my heart sinking. I turned her leg so I could unroll the gauze.

"Stop, stop, stop!" she cried, putting her hand on mine.

"Maybe we did it wrong. Maybe I have to put the symbol next to your injury," I said. It couldn't hurt to try, anyway. I was desperate for this to work.

"Go ahead."

I unwrapped enough of Meredith's bandage to reveal a ghastly wound, as if a wild animal had sunk its teeth into her flesh and ripped the skin. How was she even walking on this? My hands shook as I drew the symbol next to the weeping wound. I had to make this better.

I finished making the symbol, and Meredith put her hands on it, again whispering the words.

Nothing happened. I sank back on my heels. "What are we doing wrong?"

"It must be the wrong symbol."

"That has to be it." I tempered my disappointment with a weak smile. "Let's go back to the room. We can experiment with the others."

∞

None of the other symbols had any better result. Meredith grew more frustrated with each one.

"I must have the wrong words!" she said. She snatched the notepad from me, sweat beading on her forehead. She muttered to herself as she scribbled lines and scratched them out.

"You need a break," Trey said. He opened a bottle of painkillers and handed her two. "Take these and rest."

She glared at him. "I don't need a break." But she swallowed back the pills, making a face as she did so.

I kept quiet, but the guilt grew and festered inside of me. I knew the failure wasn't with Meredith; it was me.

Amy called on Melissa's phone to check on us. She spoke to Trey briefly, and he passed along the message.

"She says not to feel bad. We weren't prepared because we didn't know what to expect. It won't happen again."

I said nothing. But all I could think was that whether it happened again or not depended entirely on me.

"Did we lose anyone on our side?" Beth asked. The lines had faded into her skin, and she had some color back after eating food. But I couldn't look at her without thinking of how I'd failed her.

"A few," Trey said. He turned the TV off. "Everyone get some rest. Tomorrow we'll strategize."

I crawled beneath the covers next to Beth and faced the bathroom wall, pretending to be asleep. I heard Trey and Meredith murmuring as he redressed her bandage. The cot squeaked as Trey climbed onto it, and the room drifted into silence.

Only when I was sure everyone was asleep did I allow myself to give in to my emotions.

I tried to be quiet when I cried, but my body shook as my tears soaked the hotel pillow. I must've woken Beth, because she curled up behind me and stroked my hair.

We had come all this way only to face defeat. With all of those souls at her disposal, Samantha had only to snap her fingers and refuel her power, while person after person crumpled beneath her will. All because of me.

Beth's hand stilled in my hair, and I knew she'd fallen back to sleep.

The hotel window opened with a sigh, and I rolled over to face it. I didn't even know those windows could open. And then an orange glow suffused through a moment before the dark god of the underworld stepped in.

"I know you now," I said.

"You only think you do," he corrected. "You don't remember. You saw me out there on the battlefield and think you understand."

"Then enlighten me. I saw a god who followed in Samantha's tracks, happily collecting the souls of the fallen."

"You forget those bodies have no souls. Their souls are already trapped in the underworld. I followed along to seal the deal when their mortal bodies died."

I turned away from him, in no mood to discuss the finer details of his treacherous role.

"I don't want their souls, Dekla. I'm not their collector. I'm simply the escort. But they are dying, and needlessly. I told you I could help you. But you haven't asked yet."

I lifted my eyes back to his, fear whispering down my spine. The solution was within reach of my fingertips, and all I had to do was take it. But at what cost? I was afraid to know.

He opened his hand, again revealing the little orange ball, flames arcing and shooting off it. It called to me. My fingers reached for it so quickly he barely closed his hand in time.

"You want it," he stated.

My eyes couldn't tear themselves from his fingers. "It's mine."

"Yes, yes, it is. But you lost it. What do you say in this culture? Finders keepers."

On the other bed, Meredith stirred, and both of us looked at her. My eyes went to Trey next, passed out face-down on the rollaway bed.

We must have had the same thoughts, because the god of the underworld said, "I'm tired of meeting this way. Let's take our conversation elsewhere."

I didn't argue with him. I slid out of bed, glad that Trey's presence obligated us to wear long pajama bottoms and T-shirts for sleepwear. I followed him to the door of the hotel room and out into the hallway. He glided across the carpet while my footsteps padded behind, reminding me of my mortality and his elevated state.

"Not for long," he said.

I started slightly. "Are you reading my mind?"

"I see you, Dekla. I always have."

The verb left much to be interpreted, but I thought I understood what he meant. I pressed my lips together, wondering how I could keep myself more guarded.

The hotel clerk wasn't at the desk, and we sat down on the couch in the lobby, quite alone.

"The battle didn't go so well for you today, did it?" he said conversationally, studying his fingernails.

I swallowed hard. "I don't know how to save them."

"You will when you remember."

"How?" I knew that my memories were key somehow, but I didn't understand. "Is it like a magic button I press, and all of a sudden we'll win the battles? Free the souls?"

A smile played at his lips. "It's slightly more complicated than that, but you know that." The ball of flames appeared in his palm again, and he toyed with it as if it were nothing more than a marble. "I could give this to you right now. And you would have everything you need."

I tore my eyes away from the glowing light that called me. "Who are

143

you?"

"Dekla." His words were like a caress, a feather rushing across my skin, and I shuddered at the goosebumps that popped out on my arms. "You know who I am."

I met his eyes, searching them, and images came to my mind. Collecting the souls on the battlefield. Guiding them down to the underworld. Death. But more than that. Using the same power from the cycle of life to bring forth fruit from the land, grains and produce to feed the people.

A name came to me, and recognition. I knew him, so well that it baffled me. "Jumis."

His hand reached out as if to touch mine, but I pulled back.

"So you remember." His eyes flickered as if the fire were in them now. "What did you see?"

A ribbon of dread was unfurling in my stomach as I began to realize the bond that must have existed between me and him in a past life. "I am not the Dekla you remember. I am Jayne."

"Oh, I know who you are. I know more about you than you do. The part of you that is Dekla is stronger than any I've felt in a thousand years. And when you remember everything, you'll feel the connection between us." He opened his hand again, revealing the glowing orb, taunting me.

I needed that. I could feel the power calling to something inside of me. My body trembled with the desire to pluck it from his hand. I sucked in a breath and allowed my fingers to step nearer, close enough to feel the heat radiating from the orb. Almost I could glean its energy. "Is there any other way?"

"As we discussed. Are you closer to accessing your memories?"

I wasn't, and I knew he knew it. "What do I have to do to get that from you?"

His hands closed over the ball. I snatched my hand back, embarrassed at my obvious need.

"What do you require of me?" I met his gaze.

"Fulfill the promise you made to me. Take your rightful place beside me. We belong together, fate and life. Be my wife, like you consented to be."

Talk about a turn off. Desire for the little fireball was replaced by indignation. "I never made such a promise to you!"

"Dekla did. And you are becoming her, completely. You are not the only one who sees the future." He leaned closer to me, his eyes swirling with hunger. "Renew your vows, fulfill your promise, and I will give you back your memories."

I shook my head. "I'll do it the long way, thanks."

He raised an eyebrow. "I would reconsider if I were you. Every moment you wait, souls are lost. Every moment that Auseklis is powerless is a moment you are unprotected, a moment when you might lose the mortal Aaron forever."

Aaron. My heart give a little tumble, and the pain tore through me again when I pictured his soulless eyes, the man on the battlefield who held no regard for me. But if I agreed to be Jumis' wife, I would lose Aaron in a different way.

I shut my eyes, remembering the vision I had of Aaron when we first met. The vision where he was married to his ex-girlfriend. Not me.

What if it was never meant to be me?

A scream rang out, rattling down the hallway. I bolted, racing for our room. The scream came again, verifying my suspicions that it came from within. Only as I got there did I remember I had not brought my key. I pushed on the door and slammed my palm against it.

Before I could hit the door again, Jumis was there, his eyes on me as he calmly pushed it open. I tumbled inside.

Meredith sat upright in her double bed, sobbing, tears rolling down her face as her words spilled out in a garbled mess. Trey knelt beside her, hands on her knees, staring intently into her face as she spoke. Beth hovered nearby, chewing nervously on her fingernails she watched them.

I stepped closer, catching Meredith's words.

"She was winning. Somehow she convinced more of the gods to join her side, and people were dying. Hundreds. Thousands. Regular humans being used as pawns on both sides, fighting each other vicariously for the gods."

I raised my eyes to the door where Jumis stood. Nobody else had noticed him, but his expression was somber, his eyes locked with mine.

"You are not the only one who sees the future," he said, repeating what he had told me earlier. "Ragana has always been a mystic and a seer. There is a way to stop this. But only you can do it."

I glanced toward my friends to see if they would comment, but their faces were still glued on Meredith. Had time frozen again? Had they even heard Jumis?

I looked at the doorway, but the door was shut. And he was gone.

CHAPTER SIXTEEN

I hardly slept the rest of the night. My thoughts tumbled over themselves, from Jumis' offer to Meredith's nightmare to Aaron nearly cutting me down and back to Jumis' offer. Then there was Beth, the loss of her powers, Meredith, Stephen's hatred for me, and my parents, who must be worried sick about us. I tossed and turned, my eyes itchy with the need to sleep. But for once, sleep wouldn't come.

I finally managed to rest a few hours before dawn, and I opened my eyes when I heard Meredith whimpering. Trey sat on the bed next to her, holding her foot in one hand while the other hand unwrapped her bandage. He spotted me when I stood up.

"Bring me that plastic bag on the nightstand, would you?" he said.

I grabbed it up and brought it over, then watched as Trey dug out medicine. He applied a salve and re-bandaged her wound.

"You're sure there's no poison or anything in the bite?" Meredith asked. "I'm not going to turn into a demon now, am I?"

"They weren't werewolves," Trey said shortly. But as he stood up and moved away, I caught his concerned expression. "I'll grab some breakfast for us."

I followed him to the lobby, where the continental breakfast was displayed in all its glory. "Is there something going on with her that you're not telling us?"

Trey loaded a plate with yogurt, some danishes still in plastic wrappers, and a few oranges. "She should have been able to heal herself." He cast me a look. "It would be really helpful if you would come into your powers."

"You think I don't know that," I said. I took a deep breath, pushing down the rage.

"Maybe you should let it out."

I gave Trey a surprised look. "What?"

"Stop trying to suppress it. Give into the anger. It might free the memories of your former selves."

Was it possible? Could that be another way? The relief that hit me was so profound I nearly collapsed, grabbing the counter for support. To think I had seriously been considering Jumis' offer.

When I straightened up, I found Trey's eyes on me.

"What are you thinking?" he said.

I scowled. How was it he had the ability to read me like a book? "Nothing. I'm just glad I have another option."

"Another option?" he said, something dangerous in his voice. If he weren't holding a plate of food, I think he would've grabbed me. "Have you been talking to that god again?"

"It's not like I call him to chat. He just kind of appears. He came yesterday. He offered me all of my memories, all of my power at once."

Trey's eyes met mine, his pupils dilating. "Why? Why would he offer you that? That's a great gift." But instead of sounding grateful, he sounded suspicious.

I shrugged it off. "It doesn't matter, because now I'm just gonna try to get really angry. Like the Incredible Hulk, and my powers will come out."

Trey couldn't help cracking a smile. "If you turn green, nothing in this world will stop me from putting your picture all over social media. And I only said it might work."

"Ha." I grabbed a few cartons of milk. "I'll take it."

We trailed back to the room together, our spirits slightly higher.

Meredith sat at the desk next to the television, and she brandished Melissa's phone at us as we came in. "Melissa called. She and Amy want to meet."

"Yesterday did not go well at all," Amy said, shaking her head.

We were in the courtyard of a massive cathedral. It felt wrong, almost deceitful, to be using such a building for protection, but Amy said it was one place Samantha and her entourage couldn't penetrate. She also said it would shield our powers, something essential, since we'd need to use them.

"We know," I said. "We're trying to figure out what to do."

"Laima said you would lead us. She said you were the key to winning this." The accusation was heavy in Melissa's voice, and I shifted uncomfortably.

"Maybe she should've coached me a little more before she put me in the position of leadership," I said. "Now even my sister has lost her powers. Any advantage I had is gone." I look down at the flip-phone in my hands, off since the day we left home. I knew if she wanted to, though, Laima could contact me. I'd gotten so used to being frustrated with her that I barely registered any emotion at all.

"But I should be able to do what the other raganas out there were doing," Meredith said. "I need someone to teach me."

Melissa shook head. "We can't teach you, and we don't have a ragana. But you've learned how to manipulate people, right?"

Meredith's cheeks flushed. "It's kind of the reason we're in this mess."

"So it's really no different. You just have to manipulate the elements

149

instead."

She cocked her head. "The elements have feelings?"

Amy laughed, a high, pleasant sound, and even Melissa smiled.

"A thing doesn't need feelings to be manipulated. If you hold a magnifying glass under the sun over a piece of wood, the wood catches on fire. You manipulated the sun's rays," Melissa said.

"And you didn't even hurt it's feelings," Amy giggled.

Meredith didn't crack a smile, but I saw the thoughtful look in her eyes. She pushed her glasses up and swiveled on the bench, facing the trees. "I've done this before without meaning to."

"Of course. We've all done things without meaning to. And now you have to mean to."

Meredith took a deep breath, and then she recited a couplet she must've barely composed in her head. "Dust and dirt and leaves on trees, gather in the winds for me to see."

It wasn't even subtle. The dirt around Meredith's feet swelled up to a whirlwind, getting stronger as leaves in the air joined it, creating a little tornado right in front of her.

We both gasped, and Amy applauded. "See? You've got it."

"What about the symbols?" I put the ones on the table that I deciphered. "Is there something here that can help my sister?"

"Or Meredith's ankle?" Trey added.

Amy and Melissa looked at each other, their expressions solemn. And then Amy faced me.

"I know someone who can help."

Twenty minutes later, a tiny white civic pulled into the parking lot in front of the cathedral. A woman got out, probably around my mother's age.

"Who is that?" I asked.

Melissa stepped forward to join her. She cradled the woman's elbow in one hand as they came closer to us.

"Her name is Norma," Amy said.

Norma reached us, and I saw from her bloodshot eyes that she was crying. I also saw from their solemnity and depth that no matter her appearance, she was much older than my mother.

"Norma? Are you okay?" I asked, shooting a bewildered glance at Meredith. What was this lady doing here?

"Where is Karta?" she asked, sidestepping my question.

Melissa jerked her head at Beth, and Beth spoke up.

"I'm her. Or was."

Norma sat beside her and took her hands. "I'm sorry for your loss."

I looked at Melissa and then at Trey. "Is she a ragana?"

Norma surprised me by answering. "I am a Karta. And my sister is gone."

Of course she would give me an answer that begged more questions. I turned to Trey as the only person I could rely on to give me real responses. But it was Amy who spoke up.

"Yesterday in the battle, Samantha took Norma's sister goddess prisoner. She stripped her of her powers and made her a part of Samantha's army. Now she has one more portion of the powers of Dekla."

"That's her end game," Trey said. "She wants the power of the goddesses."

"Why didn't she take me?" Beth asked.

"Because she didn't take your powers," Trey said, a light burning in his eyes like he'd just clicked several puzzle pieces together. "The sword did. Your powers were lost, not stolen."

I was dying to ask him what he'd figured out, but Norma interrupted me. Still holding tightly to Beth's hands, she made eye contact with Amy. "Are you sure this is the only way?"

Amy nodded. "Your pairing has fallen and you are weakened. The best way to keep Samantha from taking your power as Karta is to give it to Beth."

I jolted. "Wait. What are you doing?"

Amy turned to me. "Beth needs to reclaim her power, but she needs power to get power. Norma is willing to give up her powers so Beth can find her lost piece."

This alarmed me. I wanted my sister to be Karta again, but I didn't want Norma to die for it. I put my hand on top of Norma's. "Let's rethink this."

"Won't you die if you pass on the powers?" Meredith added, echoing my own fears.

Norma's eyes softened. "I will cease to be immortal, yes, but I won't keel over and die instantly. I will simply start to age naturally."

"But Adele had to die before I could become Dekla," I said, still unsure.

"Your sister already is Karta. I'm not giving her my title. Just my powers."

Amy nodded. "Do it."

"The ragana has to do this," Norma said.

"Me?" Meredith squeaked. "How?"

"Come." Norma took Meredith's hand and used her finger to trace a shape on her palm. "Now say the words that will take my powers and give them to Beth. It's your intention that matters, more than the words."

"What if it doesn't work?"

"Just try it."

Meredith whispered too quietly for me to hear. Norma closed her eyes, took a deep breath, and froze.

I didn't see anything, but I felt it. Something like a shimmer in the air, like thermal energy, and then Norma's shoulders relaxed and she exhaled, bobbing her head forward.

At the same time, Beth sat up taller. She opened her eyes, and they looked more lucid. But the cracks in her skin hadn't disappeared.

Amy put a hand on her shoulder. "Now you have the power of Karta, but not the same power as before. We have to call it back to you."

She gestured to Melissa, who stepped forward and took Beth's hand.

"You and I hold two pieces of Karta's soul," Melissa said. "You need to reach out and find the piece that belongs to you. Close your eyes."

Beth did so.

"This is how I called you to us," Amy said softly next to my ear. "I felt you when you entered our territory. Then I found your energy and pulled you to us."

"Like you changed my fate?" I whispered, my eyes on my sister.

"No. I didn't need to. I just put a physical call on your energy. You could have resisted." She smiled. "But it wouldn't have been pleasant."

"Reach out with your mind," Melissa said, coaching Beth. "I know you didn't have your power for very long, but it should feel familiar. Like a part of you. Find it."

"There," Beth breathed. "I found it. But the energy is weak."

Melissa looked at Meredith. "She found it. Now we need you to reunite them."

"Same as before." Norma used Meredith's finger to trace a symbol again. "Call it to her."

"Undo the break and whole her make," Meredith whispered, barely audible this time.

"It's working," Amy said.

I could only stare in fascination. The lines and fissures in Beth's skin were disappearing, smoothing out. She took a long breath, and another, and the last of the lines vanished.

Beth's eyes focused on Melissa. The brown of her irises seemed lighter somehow, as if a fire burned behind them. "I feel different," she said.

Melissa appraised her. "You are different. You are the only Karta alive who holds two pieces of the soul."

Trey leaned forward, keen interest on his face. "What does that mean?"

"That she's a little bit closer to immortality," Amy said. "The same thing Samantha is trying to accomplish."

"How many pieces does Samantha have?" he asked.

Amy shook her head. "I do not know. Many. She also has the powers of at least one Auseklis, the energy of the mortal souls, and the backing of the underworld. We need a better strategy."

"Have you been talking with Laima?" I asked. "Can she help us?"

The three of them exchanged a look, as if there was something they didn't want to tell me. It was Melissa who spoke.

"Laima gave us one last message for you. But she said not to tell you unless you asked. She's incarcerated."

My jaw dropped. "Did Samantha capture her?"

Amy shook her head. "She said it was Perkons. It's both to keep her safe and to punish her. She is being blamed for not preventing Samantha's rebellion."

Great. Now I felt responsible for the goddess who hadn't been much help to me to begin with.

Trey cleared his throat. "One more thing. Can we help Meredith?"

Oh, Meredith. I turned my attention to her, embarrassed I hadn't thought of her already. "Her wound won't heal." I gestured toward the bandage and looked at Melissa. "How can we help her?"

She leaned forward. "Is it magically infected?"

"No," Trey said, but he sounded less certain. "I don't think so."

"She's a ragana," Norma said. "She should be able to heal it."

"She doesn't know how yet," Trey said, frustration in his voice. "We're a pretty weak team."

"Thanks for the vote of confidence," Meredith growled.

Amy looked at me. "She's still a child. You have the power to nudge her fate."

"She can't do anything either," Trey said, speaking for me. I shot him a murderous glare.

"Come, I'll show you how." Amy stepped to my side and put her head near mine. "You have to see her soul's energy. It will be a light yellow or orange. Can you see it?"

I squinted and crossed my eyes, but nothing appeared. I willed myself to see something. Anything.

"It will come. Just keep trying."

"What do you do when you see it?"

"Summon a vision of her life."

Of her life. The words jolted me like an electric shock. I'd always thought of it as seeing their deaths. But it really was their lives. All the way to the end. "Then what?"

"Then you find a better path, if there is one. If it serves her better to take it, bring it to the forefront of her mind. She still gets to choose, but you brighten the option."

"How do I find a better path? How do I see other options?"

"You'll know," Melissa said. "You'll see all of them. In the blink of an eye. All her futures. All her possibilities."

The idea was mind-boggling, and I pressed a hand to my forehead. "And you don't get overwhelmed?"

Amy turned her attention back to Meredith. "Not when you have hundreds of years of experience to draw upon, no. Let me show you." She locked eyes with Meredith, and then Meredith let out a laugh.

"I know what to do now," she said. "I know what we did wrong."

"How does she know?" I demanded.

Amy gave me a patient smile. "There were really only two choices here. Either she understood how to do the spell, or she didn't. It was always in there for her to know. I helped her remember."

Even as I watched, Meredith unwrapped her ankle. "I have to trace the symbol. I'm the only one who can use the runes." She traced a symbol on her leg and whispered an incantation. Before our eyes, the wound puckered and healed.

"Wicked," Beth said. "Can we do that?"

"No," Amy said. "You are a goddess, not a witch."

"But your powers are pretty cool, too," Meredith said, looking at me.

I grunted. "Yeah. If I can figure out how to use them."

CHAPTER SEVENTEEN

Norma wanted to stay with us while we talked battle plans. Melissa worried the concentration of all of us in one place would attract Samantha's attention, but Amy reminded her that the cathedral shielded us.

"Besides," she said, "Norma isn't immortal any more. It's Beth who is likely to attract the most attention."

I looked at my younger sister, now brimming with the power of two pieces of Karta's immortal soul. I felt a tiny stab of jealousy but quickly brushed it down. The only reason she had the extra power was because I caused her to lose the first one to begin with.

"I've got a question," Meredith said. She was definitely more chatty since healing her ankle. "Samantha was able to reach out to the gods. How?" She held her smart phone in her hand. Her finger stroked the case, and I knew she was desperate to turn it on and pull up a search engine.

"We don't really have a clue how she did it," Melissa said. "Laima probably does, but even if she could reach us, she decides when to contact us and what to say."

"And why is that?" I said, jumping on an issue that had been bothering me for months. "Does she see our futures and decide what information we need to know?"

Nobody had an answer. When I met Trey's eyes, he shrugged.

"The point is, we don't have any way of finding out," Melissa said. "We could go to a library, but there's hardly anything about Latvian mythology. It's obscure and relatively unknown. And we don't have time to fly to Latvia and interview the locals."

"Not to mention we wouldn't be able to speak their language," Meredith murmured.

"Wait a minute," I said, snapping my fingers. Criminy. Why hadn't I thought of this before? "I know a guy!" I pulled my purse into my lap and began digging through it, tossing gum wrappers and pencil stubs and old receipts onto the bench in my search. "Here!"

I placed the business card face up on my thigh for everyone to see. The contents of my purse had changed it so it was no longer crisp and white, but there was his name and his phone number. Professor Kestovely.

"Who is this?" Meredith asked, intrigued.

"This is a professor of mythology who specializes in the Baltic Sea area. I met him at a university in New York." I beamed at them. "He'll have the answers we need!"

Beth brightened, but Melissa shook her head. "Nobody has the answers. Nobody knows."

"We can try," Amy said.

"But I need a phone," I said, holding out my hand.

Melissa gave Amy a wan smile as she slapped her phone into my palm. "I'm starting to think I should just give it to her."

"Might not be a bad idea," Meredith said. "Jayne and I are both journalists. We can find a lot of stuff."

Trey snorted, apparently unable to stay quiet any longer. "Jayne and Meredith are both in high school, just like I am. We're all taking a journalism class."

"Jayne's more than that," Meredith sniffed. "She's an investigative journalist. She gets to work at the editorial office."

I only half listened to their defense or lack of it while I put the professor's number into the phone. Then I hit the call button, anxiety ratcheting up my heart rate and making my throat dry. Would he think I was crazy with my new questions? He'd been very intrigued the first time we met.

He didn't answer, and I was both relieved and disappointed when the voicemail kicked on. "Hi, Professor Kestovely, this is Jayne Lockwood. We met for lunch a few weeks ago. I had questions about Latvian mythology? You said I could call if I had anything else, and I do. I promise I won't take up a lot of your time, but please call me back at—" I slid my eyes to Melissa, and she fed me the digits while I spoke into the answering machine. "Thank you very much."

"Well." I placed the phone on my thigh, hoping he would call soon. "Now we wait. Why don't we all go back to our hotel room? As long as we don't use our powers, Samantha won't be able to find us."

"No powers," Melissa said. "No magic." Her eyes swept sideways to include Meredith.

Meredith nodded. "We'll keep it safe."

I hopped off the bench, and we moved toward the chapel doors. Trey paused, then bent down and picked up a rock. He bounced it in his hand and squinted at me.

"What are you—" I began, just as he chucked the rock at my head.

My arm shot up reflexively, darting in front of my face before I could even think. The rock slammed into my palm with so much force that I cried out. I dropped it and flipped my palm over, examining the blood leaking from the cut.

"Why did you do that?" I gasped out.

Trey's expression was grim as he studied me. "That's the second time I've seen you react to danger instinctively."

"Any normal person would do that!"

"No, any normal person would duck. Maybe cover their head. But they'd also move too slowly and still get hit."

"That doesn't mean you can throw rocks at my head!"

"You reacted exactly as I hoped you would," Trey said.

"Jayne?"

Melissa's voice called my attention. I looked to where she stood in the doorway to the cathedral, phone to her ear.

"Yes, she's here. Let me get her." Melissa stepped up to me and handed me the phone. "It's the professor guy."

I took the phone and pressed it to my ear. "Professor, thank you so much for getting back to me!" I followed Melissa and Trey as I talked, through the chapel and out the entrance. Trey gave a quick scan of the area before ushering us toward his truck.

"Not a problem, Jayne," the professor said, a slight tremor in his voice giving away his age. "I've been intrigued by you since the first time we met. What other mythological questions do you have for me today?"

I took a deep breath. "You mentioned that Karta would sometimes make a deal with the other gods. How would she contact them?"

"Well, I imagine they knew how to reach each other. Perhaps they lived in proximity to each other. Maybe they visited frequently. It's not as if they had cell phones and could text each other." He chuckled.

"Right," I said, giving my own little laugh, but the wheels in my head were already spinning. Text message! Why hadn't I thought of that?

"Of course, at this point I'm simply theorizing. Their ability to communicate with each other is taken for granted, so nothing I've read or heard has given me any indication one way or the other."

I was suddenly anxious to get off the phone, but one thing he said broke through my excitement. "Heard? What do you mean? Hasn't your research been based on historical texts?"

"I wouldn't very much be an authority on the subject if I hadn't gone to the primary sources, now, would I?" He sounded amused. "I've gone back to Latvia and the Baltic region many times over the years. A lot of my knowledge is based on firsthand conversations and interviews with the natives."

I nodded, suddenly confident that I had found the best source of information other than Laima herself, and she wasn't forthcoming, especially not from jail. "You've been amazing. Do you mind if I call you later if I have any more questions?"

We had reached the parking lot now, and Trey held the door of the truck while Beth and Meredith climbed in. Amy and Melissa said goodbye to Norma and came to stand by us. Trey bobbed on his feet, maintaining a vigilant watch on the area.

"Please do. Are you ever going to tell me what this is for?"

I had to smile. There was no way I could ever tell him. "Just satisfying my curiosity."

"That I understand. I hope to have mine satisfied one day also."

I barely registered our cordial goodbyes, my mind already tripping. I looked straight at Melissa and Amy and tried to contain my excitement.

"We contact Laima using a cell phone. We can contact the other gods the same way."

Melissa's eyebrows shot up. "That makes sense. There's just one problem. We don't have any of their numbers."

Trey tilted his head, a glimmer in his eyes. "This won't be hard. The other gods' numbers are probably variations of Laima's."

Trey visibly relaxed when he parked the truck at the hotel. "No magic," he reminded us.

"We won't," I said. I crossed my fingers that Jumis' visit during the night hadn't triggered any magical alarms.

Meredith hurried into the room and picked up the notepad from the day before. She scribbled Laima's phone number across the top as the rest of us filed in. "Okay. I'm just going to write down the letters that correspond with these numbers and see if I can make out a phrase or something pertinent."

"One-eight-hundred-Laima," I said, cracking up.

"Hey, that's an idea," Meredith said. "Let me try to match up her name first." She wrote Laima's name underneath the number. "I got it. The first two digits are five-five, and then the last five digits are the letters of her name." She looked up at us. "I have a file online with all of the gods listed. We can try it to create phone numbers with their names."

"Hey, you're smart," Trey said.

Meredith arched an eyebrow at him.

"What?" he said, tugging on his ear lobe. "It was a smart idea. And you've already got the names, so . . . that was clever also."

"I'm always smart," Meredith said. "I'm one of the smartest kids in my class. But that doesn't stop you from being snotty."

"I'm not always," he said. He shifted his eyes, casting them to the horizon out the window.

"Fantastic detective work," Melissa said, redirecting the conversation. "Let's run with this."

Meredith used the business center in the lobby to print off her list of names. Trey turned the TV back on while she made up numbers for them, and the rest of us sat on the bed and pretended to be interested.

"I've got it," Meredith said, stretching her arms above her head. "A few of them have names that are too long, but most of them I could create a number for."

"Let's test this theory," Melissa said, standing at Meredith's shoulder. "Who should we contact?"

Amy leaned in also, reading the names. "Maybe Mara. Perkons. Zalktis. Ursins or Jumis."

I flinched when she said the last name. Trey glanced at me, but I gave nothing more away.

"Not Perkons," Melissa said. "I'm sure he's aware of the situation and would contact us if he wanted. Not Mara either. Sometimes she's gets so obsessed with winter she doesn't mind a little death."

"The other three, then," Amy said.

"We should make sure the numbers work," Meredith said, "before we ask for help. Make sure it's who we think it is."

"On it," Melissa said, already sending out text messages.

I bit down hard on a nail. I hoped Jumis wouldn't respond.

Melissa stared down at her phone and we all stared at her, obviously waiting for an immediate response. When none was forthcoming, Trey roused himself.

"I'm taking Jayne and Beth to the gym. We need to work on skills."

"Skills?" I sputtered, but he already had me by the elbow and was hauling me out.

"Quit grabbing me," I growled, pulling free.

He used his key card to open the gym door and waited for us to enter. "I want to see what you two can do." He left us standing in the middle of the room and backed away.

I glanced at my sister and then looked at him, arching an eyebrow. "What we can do?"

Trey nodded. "I saw your reflexes take over during the battle. Your sister now has twice as much goddess powers as you do. Beth might reawaken to her past experiences before you do, but I need to see that you're coming along also."

How did he make that seem like an insult? I looked at my sister, and she shrugged.

"I guess you should throw a punch at me or something," Beth said.

"I'm not going to punch you," I scoffed.

She cracked a grin. "You can try."

I grumbled, but I was more worried of looking like a helpless idiot in front of Trey than actually injuring my sister. I threw a half-hearted punch her direction, which she easily blocked.

"Come on," she said. "I saw you hit Samantha harder than that."

"Yeah, she was threatening my sister."

Beth's eyes gleamed. "Pretend like I'm her."

I let out another long-suffering sigh and aimed for her face this time.

She laughed and batted my hand away.

"Jayne." Trey strode into the midst of us, not hiding his annoyance. He made a fist and pulled back his arm, and I readied myself. But instead of aiming for me, he directed the punch at my sister.

The observation was instantaneous, and I knew what he was going to do only seconds before his fist connected with her skin.

Except it never did. Somehow my left hand thrust itself in front of his, shoving his arm away from her. I barely registered the action before he swept the leg behind me, trying to knock me off my feet.

This time it was Beth coming to my defense, her right hand karate-chopping down to slam into the back of his knee.

"Who trained you for combat?" I gloated at him.

"My grandpa," he said, aiming another kick at my sister, which both of us blocked. "What's your excuse?"

Beth grabbed his arm when he attempted to slam his hand into my neck. She twisted it behind him, forcing him onto his tiptoes. To his credit, the only sound Trey made was a little grunt. Beth placed her hands on both shoulders and shoved him into the ground before sitting on his belly.

"I won!" she crowed.

"Great job." Trey shoved her off and sat up. "Two goddesses against one human boy. You should feel proud."

Well, when he put it that way, it didn't feel like much. "But we were fighting," I said. "Isn't that what you wanted?"

"You guys were just goofing off. You weren't reacting—" he paused, his jaw squaring. "There might have been one moment," he said thoughtfully.

"One moment what?" Beth asked.

Trey turned his amber-gray eyes to me. "When I threw the first punch, I was testing Beth's reflexes. But it was Jayne who stopped me. How quickly did you have to think, Jayne, to get your hand in front of mine before I hit her?"

"Were you actually going to hit her?" I demanded. "If I hadn't stopped you, would she have a shiner now?"

Trey shrugged. "I expected one of you to stop me. It wouldn't look so great if somebody saw me hitting you guys."

"You're unbelievable!" I exclaimed, slapping him on the shoulder.

"It worked. I got beat up more than you." He rubbed his shoulder where I had hit him, still studying me.

The gym door opened, and Meredith stood there, her eyes glittering excitedly.

"Guys," she breathed, "we got a response."

Beth shot up and was out the door, but I lingered behind. Trey did also, as if sensing I had something to say.

"I felt something," I said. "That moment when I blocked you. I felt it on the battlefield also."

The triumph sparked in his eyes quickly before vanishing again. "The goddess in you is coming out."

"So I'm remembering?"

"Some part of you is."

"Jayne!" Meredith screeched from down the hall.

Trey clapped a hand on my shoulder. "Let's see what Meredith's got for us before she blows a gasket."

(𝕎)

I studied the text message for the twentieth time, even though we had already analyzed it to the full of our abilities. "So you're sure he's on our side?"

Melissa waved her hand impatiently, half a sandwich in her other hand. She and Amy had hiked out to the local grocery store and purchased a giant sub sandwich for all of us. Spirits were definitely higher now that we had received a positive response.

"That's why he said he's gathering reinforcements," she said.

I read the text one more time.

Message received. Already aware of the problem. Gathering reinforcements. Await instructions.

"It kind of sounds like he's taking over," I said.

"He's not," Meredith said, consulting her spreadsheet. "Ursins' the god of livestock and gives the power of observation and understanding. He's gonna be all about reconciliation."

"And reinforcements?" I said, trying to kill my doubts. "He's aware of the problem?"

"They don't live in separate universes, Jayne," Trey said. "These guys know each other."

"They've probably been watching the dilemma unfold with Samantha," Amy said.

I chewed on my fingernails, still unconvinced. "Then why did we have to contact him? Why couldn't he just find us?"

Trey made a noise of impatience. "Find us how? Who are you to them? Just one of Laima's many minions with a tiny piece of Dekla's soul."

Ouch. "I'm sure they could've found a way," I said stubbornly.

And suddenly, I was there again. There was no doubt in my mind that this was a battlefield as I walked barefoot through the ash-covered grass, a long robe or some kind of cloth twisting around my ankles. I was crying, gut-wrenching sobs as I stepped over the bodies of the fallen. Mortals. *Kaukas* and demigods who had aligned with us. Even godly brothers and sisters whose allegiance had cost them their immortality.

I lifted my eyes to Laima. Tears streaked down her face as well. Behind her, my sister Karta stepped forward. Her expression was grim, face stoic.

"It's time," Laima said.

I nodded, heart twisting within me. I'd be giving up so much. "And Jumis?" I managed to choke out. "What will become of us?"

Laima shook her head. "I'm sorry. The destiny of your love is not as important as the destiny of the human race." She looked at Karta, the dark-haired one of the three of us. "Are you ready?" she asked.

Karta inhaled a deep breath and let it out slowly, and she nodded.

"Why?" The question left my lips before I could think twice. "Why are you not giving up as much as we are?"

The question hurt Laima, I could see that. But as quickly as the pain flashed through her eyes, it was gone. "Somebody has to remember everything. Somebody has to be the guide."

CHAPTER EIGHTEEN

The vision faded, and I was back in the hotel room. The fear and desperation still enveloped me. These weren't my feelings, but Dekla's. And yet, they were mine. For the first time, it really dawned on me what that meant. Her feelings, her emotions, her memories, I carried these pieces with me.

"This has happened before," I said. "And last time we—" I broke off. What had we done? Something desperate. Had it worked? Was that how we won?

"Keep going," Trey urged, his fingers twitching like he wanted to pull the memories out of my head.

I shut my eyes and tried to see more. I willed myself to remember that moment. What were we deciding? But nothing came. I opened my eyes and shook my head in frustration. "I'm going to receive these memories by piecemeal."

"It's all right." Trey gripped my shoulder. "It's coming along."

Amy's gaze never left my face. "You won't remember it all," she said. "Only what is relevant to you. Sometimes I still remember memories I didn't know I had."

"And hers are different than yours will be," Melissa said. "Since your line of descent is different."

Melissa's phone chimed, and we all turned to look at her as she read the text. She looked up and smiled. "Just my boss. Says tomorrow's meeting has been rescheduled for Friday." She lifted her eyebrows. "Which is good, because I don't have tomorrow off. I really need to get these battles over with so I can get on with my normal life."

She said it so calm and matter-of-factly. I stared at her, wondering how she balanced mortal life with these crazy responsibilities.

Of course, life wasn't usually this busy. Usually my jobs as a goddess were a sidenote, background music to the rest of my life.

Right now the background music was trying to take center stage.

Melissa's phone chimed again, and she texted back-and-forth with her boss for a bit. Trey turned on the television, scanning for the news, but I didn't want to hear it. I couldn't stand to think of how many more people were dying.

Melissa stood up, shoving her phone into her purse. "That last text was from Ursins. He said he's got his regiment assembled." She actually looked excited. "He knows where Samantha is and wants us to challenge her."

"Do you have a location, Melissa?" Amy asked.

She waved her purse. "Follow me."

Meredith sat still as the rest of us made for the door, and I paused.

"Are you okay?" I asked her.

"Yes." But her face was stiff and pale, and she hadn't moved from the bed.

"How's the leg?" Trey asked her, placing a hand behind her shoulder

167

blades and urging her to her feet.

"The leg's fine." She arched her shoulders just enough that he dropped his hand.

"What is it?" I asked.

Meredith bit down on her lower lip, tears filling her eyes. "What if that vision I saw is going to come true? What if all those humans under Samantha's control are going to die?"

I exchanged a look with Trey, and then slipped my arm around her waist. "It's not going to, okay? We don't know where that vision came from. But even if you were seeing the future, remember it can be changed. We influence people's lives so that something different happens. You don't have to be a goddess to do that."

"As long as they have two paths open," she said. "What if they don't? What if they only have one choice?"

"There's always another choice," Trey said.

Was there? Samantha had taken away their free will.

We followed Amy and Melissa in Trey's truck for nearly an hour.

"Where are we going?" I asked after forty minutes.

"Maybe Samantha is taking her show out of town," Meredith said. "So she can conquer the next city and build onto her army."

"A thought, but I don't think so," Trey said.

"Why?" Meredith fired off at him, her voice testy. "Just because you want to disagree with me?"

"No," he said. "Because Samantha wants to own you guys. So I don't think she'll move on just yet."

"She knows we'll follow her."

"Guys," I said. "You both raise excellent points. The fact is we don't know what she's doing because none of us are mind readers. That would be an excellent power, if any of you should develop the ability. Let's just follow Amy and Melissa and see where they're taking us."

"You're the one who asked," Meredith grumbled, crossing her arms over her chest and falling silent.

Amy finally pulled off the interstate and entered a suburban area. We drove through the blocks of houses for several minutes before her car pulled alongside the curb and stopped.

Trey stopped also, and I climbed out of the truck, gawking at the small single-story house with beige siding that looked like it hadn't been washed since it was put on sixty years earlier. Identical houses dated the block all the way to the end of the street. Melissa and Amy walked back to join us.

"What are we doing here?" I asked.

"I don't know," Amy said, voice soft. "This is where Ursins said to go."

"Why?" I furrowed my brow. "Do some of the *kaukas* live here?" After our battle in the parking garage a few weeks ago, Laima had taken us to one of the sprite's houses in the country. He lived just like a human, so it wasn't an unreasonable assumption.

"Must be something like that," Meredith said. "Certainly we wouldn't be fighting the battle here."

"No, of course not," I said, even as I worried we were.

"And why not?" A man strode down the sidewalk toward us, his arms muscular beneath the sleeveless tunic he wore that concealed nothing. Weapons were strapped to his back and along a belt that cinched his tunic. Between that and his shoulder-length blond hair, he looked like Thor's long-lost brother.

My jaw dropped. I nudged Meredith anxiously and hissed, "That's not Thor, is it?"

She rolled her eyes and elbowed me to give herself some more space. "No, Jayne. Wrong pantheon."

Of course. This must be the guy we'd been talking to. I frowned at him as his words caught up to me. "What do you mean, why not? We can't have a battle in a suburb around all these houses. People will get hurt."

He met my gaze with steely blue eyes. "Do you hear yourself? People will get hurt. People are already getting hurt. The time will come when the mortals must take a stand and join one side or the other." He paused as if for dramatic effect. "But that day is not today. Unless the mortals choose it to be."

The bodies. Mortals cut down before their expected ends. Destinies never realized.

"The humans will die if we involve them," I said.

He strolled past me as if I hadn't spoken. He rapped on the door of the aging house in front of us. A short man with crinkly eyes and wavy brown hair opened it. His nose was slightly too large for his face, and if he'd had pointed ears, his elfish appearance would have been complete. I recognized him immediately as a sprite, one of the *kaukas*.

"Gather your people," the Thor-guy said. Ursins, I reminded myself.

The little man nodded and disappeared back into the house.

More cars pulled to the curb around us, and women and a few men piled out of them, some young, some older. I recognized a few familiar faces from our last battle. The others I didn't know, but I deduced from their resolute, grim faces that they were part of our army.

Doors to houses up and down the street popped open, and *kaukas* streamed out of them. They came from around the block, filling up the sidewalks as they approached. At least three hundred, like too many clowns popping out of a circus car. They each brandished stoic, determined expressions.

Ursins turned to me. "Now is the time to get rebel girl here," he said.

My stomach tightened. "Here? I thought we weren't going to involve the mortals just yet." Since when did I refer to humans as mortals? I had a heightened sense that they were different than me. Weaker, yes, but that didn't make them inferior. If anything, it made me their protector. I glanced at the remaining houses around me, feeling the desire to check on the people inside, going about their business with no idea the Apocalypse was about to take place in their backyard. I wanted to look at their lines, make sure their lives still had a proper ending.

"Not here." He pointed over my head. "There."

I turned to see what he meant and spotted a wide-open field between two subdivisions. A sign out front listed, "For sale — 140 acres — subdividable."

I shook my head. "We're too close to the people."

He met my eyes, and a flash of recognition jolted me.

170

"Like I said," he said, "the mortals will have to pick a side soon."

Déjà vu. He and I had had this argument before. Rather, he and Dekla. He was close to her, like a little brother. I glowered at him.

"Where is your ragana?" he asked me with a familiarity that both disturbed me and put me at ease. We knew each other. Our thoughts and our conversations moved in a familiar pattern, and my ire with him faded away.

"Ragana is here." I gestured to Meredith.

"What is her element?"

If someone had asked me that question ten minutes earlier, I would've just given them a blank stare. But I didn't hesitate when I responded, "Wind."

Meredith gave a start and shot me a look of surprise. "What?"

I turned to her, explaining something I hadn't even known I'd known. "Every ragana has mastery over a natural element. She can manipulate the other elements with help, but it's a learned art. Only one will come easily to you, and yours is wind."

"How do you know all of this?" she breathed, staring at me as if she didn't know me.

Maybe she didn't.

"She's remembering." Trey slapped his hands together and grinned like this was all his doing. "See? You don't even realize when you're remembering. The memories just become a part of you."

"Yes," I whispered, feeling a surge of triumph. I could do this. I was going to succeed without anyone's interference. Without having to marry someone.

"So the whole time I was trying to make lightning bolts and fireballs, that's just not something I can do?"

I shot Meredith a smile and took her arm. With my finger, I traced the symbol for fire. "Draw that symbol and try your fireball."

Understanding lit her features. "Like when I healed my ankle with the symbol." She retraced the rune, took a deep breath, and whispered a few words. From the middle of her palm, a tiny finger of flame erupted.

"Oh!" She closed her hand, immediately extinguishing the flame, but not before I saw her excited face.

"Can you get us a funnel cloud right above that field there?" Ursins asked, interrupting our excitement over the discovery.

I shot him an annoyed look, much like I would my younger brother—if I had a younger brother. "Give us a second." I turned to Meredith. "Ready for this?"

"Why am I doing this? Calling a tornado down on these people?"

"We're not just telling Jods we're here. We're issuing a challenge. You fought and lost your last battle. This one we will win," Ursins said. He tapped his wrist and murmured to his arm. I tilted my head. Was he performing an incantation?

"Jods?" Meredith asked. "Not Samantha?"

I ground my teeth together. "Samantha is only a tool. This is Velns' doing. He's the mastermind behind Jods and Samantha. It's always been Velns versus Perkons. We have fought this war many times, and it's time to quiet his demons for a few more centuries."

"Who are you?" Meredith said, staring at me.

"No kidding," Beth said. "Are you still in there, Jayne?"

She sounded genuinely worried, so I flashed a smile. "I'm still here. I'm just understanding more and more of myself."

"Of Dekla," Ursins said.

"Am I going to start to remember a bunch of stuff too?" Beth asked.

"Yes," Trey said. "And it will probably happen faster than with Jayne because you have two pieces of the soul."

Ursins cleared his throat. "Funnel cloud?"

"Meredith?"

"I'm on it. I can do this?"

I gave her an enthusiastic nod. "Yes. This one should come naturally to you. Just like walking. You don't think about lifting your foot up, you just walk." I knew I was asking a lot. Babies don't go from crawling to walking all at once.

She whispered to herself and began to swirl her hands around each other. Beth elbowed me.

172

"Jayne, look."

I turned my face toward the field and wasn't surprised to see a black cloud forming into a funnel shape, just like the one Velu Mate had used to bring the demons from the underworld during the last battle. "This isn't another portal to the underworld, is it?" I asked, getting nervous.

Ursins shook his head. "Not to the underworld. Ragana can open the gates to hell, but not this way."

His answer begged another question, but before I could ask, he cleared his throat and looked out over the *kaukas* and people who had gathered.

"On me," Ursins shouted, and he strode off with absolute arrogance and authority, presuming we would follow him.

Which we did, naturally.

But first we had to cross the street. We waited at the stoplight for our green signal, and we received more than a few stares from cars driving by. I imagined our Thor look-alike with his three hundred midgets garnered more attention than the rest of our motley crew.

"Is this our army?" one of the other women asked Ursins, and I heard the same disdain in her voice that I felt. "I thought you were gathering forces. This is all you could get?"

He turned and gave her a condescending look. "I only had a few hours. My brothers will come. I haven't called the mortals yet. That's your job."

Her eyes rounded. "My job?"

"Aren't you a goddess of fate? Plant the desire to fight for us in their minds and bring them here."

I could read the thoughts flitting behind her eyes because they were the same as mine. Change the mortals' destinies. Bring them to the battle, where most would die. For us.

Was I capable of that?

The light changed, and we crossed the street. As if sensing my eyes on her, she turned and faced me. Her gaze swept over me from head to foot. "So you're Jayne."

She said it without emotion, very calmly, almost a little sadly. I cocked my head. "How do you know me?"

The fleeting smile she gave me was definitely tinged with sadness. "We all know you. You and your sister. You're the ones chosen to lead this battle."

Amy and Melissa had said that also. "Why do you think that?"

"Laima foresaw it. She told me to do all I was capable of to help you succeed."

My throat clogged. "Why us?"

She shook her head. "I don't know. I didn't summon a vision of your life."

The finger of Meredith's funnel cloud dipped toward the ground, the clouds rolling back. The wind kicked back our hair, throwing grass and trash at us even though we stood hundreds of yards away from it.

"That's enough," Ursins said.

Meredith put her hand out and stopped the cloud before it became a tornado. Cars skidded to a halt in the street, flipping around or backing away. A van from the weather channel pulled over at the intersection, and a crew piled out. I glanced behind me toward the subdivision and noticed the humans gathering, filming the event or gawking open-mouthed.

Ursins saw me watching them. "This event is definitely going to capture their attention."

I could only imagine. "How will Samantha get here? Where is she keeping her army?"

"The funnel is an open doorway. We've invited them to us. Wherever they are, they can create a pathway and come out here."

My newfound knowledge failed me. None of what he said made any sense, and I was still trying to figure out which question to ask first when a beam of light appeared at the bottom of the funnel cloud, like a spotlight. It shone straight down to the ground, and tiny beings began dropping to the ground.

I revised my original analysis. It wasn't like a spotlight at all. It was more like a transporter beam from Star Trek.

"Get ready," Ursins said, and he moved into a fighting stance, reaching behind him and removing a long bow.

CHAPTER NINETEEN

I imitated Ursins, copying his fighting stance. But the way my weight shifted to the balls of my feet and how my arms moved up to protect my face, it didn't feel like I was imitating at all.

The tiny figures continued to fall to the ground like ants plummeting from an anthill. But they didn't stop when they landed; instead they were instantly racing across the field toward us. And more were coming.

Suddenly, the ground trembled like tiny micro earthquakes shook it. Or a stampede of elephants. Or a herd of thundering horses?

I couldn't believe my eyes as hundreds of horses tore through the surrounding houses, stopping traffic as they raced to the empty lot.

A grim smile set on Ursins' lips. "My horses. Go!" He pointed toward the figures, growing larger by the second, and horses whinnied, shaking their manes and bowing their heads before galloping forward.

"First line of defense. Raganas!" Ursins yelled, redirecting my attention.

My heart stammered in fear for Meredith. Several women lurched forward, whispering and drawing runes in the air. I did a quick head count. We had seven now, which was more than yesterday. At Meredith's bewildered look, I pushed her forward also.

"Just use your element. Take them down."

"Samantha's people are going to die."

Of course. She was thinking of her vision. A hopeless feeling gripped me around my chest, constricting my heart and making it hard to breathe. Unless I got their souls back into their bodies, our only options to defend ourselves were to incapacitate them or take them prisoner. And then what? Tie them up and leave them in the bathroom of our hotel room?

"Do your best to just knock them out," I said, trying to ease my conscience as well as hers.

The other raganas weren't holding back. Fireballs burst through the approaching army, and my heart hurt as the human figures fell to the ground, some of them with flames burning their bodies. Lightning struck out of Meredith's funnel cloud, collapsing more of the army. A wall of dirt sprang up in front of the approaching line and buried several others.

"No," Meredith gasped. "I can't do it."

I didn't blame her in the least. I wanted to tell everyone to stop also. Was Stephen in that army? Aaron? My head throbbed. He had to be all right. All of this was for nothing if I couldn't save him. I didn't even want these powers. I just wanted to live a life with Aaron.

And then, right before my eyes, *vadatajs* burst through the wall of dirt, faces distorted and twisted. Their swords chopped the wall to bits. They did not run at us; they marched, lopsided and slow, as if nothing we did could stop their approach. Behind them the jackal men emerged, the long two-pronged staffs held in front of them like knives.

Meredith exhaled. "These guys I don't mind killing."

"Second line of defense. *Kaukas!*" Ursins yelled.

With a roar that surprised me, the three hundred or so of them charged forward, their hands going to their belts. They pulled from them what look like conductors' batons, but as they withdrew them from their belts, the batons grew, until they held pointed bayonets in their defense.

Three of them converged on a *vadatajs* to my right, and after several slashes of their weapons, he went down. For a moment I felt a surge of hope. Until I saw how many more there were.

Another emerged right behind his fallen comrade, and with a lift of his sword, he slashed through two *kaukas*. They collapsed to the ground, blood spilling from their torsos and staining the grass.

I sucked in a breath, suddenly struggling for air. The *vadatajs* hadn't just stolen their powers. He had killed them.

From behind the demons, another enemy emerged: the humans.

At the same time, a low buzzing filled my ears. I pulled on my earlobe, trying to clear my head, but it didn't go away. I shifted and noticed a dark, shifting cloud moving toward us at rapid speed.

"What is that?" I took a step backward as the black mass neared.

"My bees," Ursins said, steadying me with a touch to my shoulder. "These are the ones from my personal gardens. They drink from celestial nectar, and their stings can incapacitate even the demons."

The keeper of bees and horses. I remembered now. "You called them?"

"They will give their lives for me. They only have one sting in them."

Sadness rang in his voice, and pride, but I thought of the mortals. "Will they kill the humans?"

"Yes," he said without pause. "Multiple stings will kill them." His eyes met mine. "The humans are not the target, but when we are under attack, the bees will protect."

There was a challenge in his voice, and I remembered Trey's words: *Who's side are you on?* I faced forward, watching the black mass break apart and streak into the opposing side. Bile burned the back of my throat.

The humans ran toward us, their faces blank behind their helmets.

"Third line of defense: mortal goddesses and their protectors!" Ursins yelled.

"Jayne!" Amy slid into position beside me, already breathless. "This is your chance to save them. Find their life path like I taught you. Alter what they're about to do. Change their next steps."

"I haven't been able to summon a vision yet," I said, feeling sick and useless. "I don't know how to change what they're going to do!"

"You have to try. Or else we have to stop them physically."

Translation: change their fate or take them down.

I faced one of the soldiers racing toward me, smaller of stature and most likely a teen. I met his eyes but saw only blankness there. Could I even alter the destiny of someone not in charge of his own will?

The boy did not tear his eyes from mine. He raised his staff as he got close to me, and I was forced to block the blow.

"Ouch," I said. But I had no time to even rub the spot where he had hit me before he was lifting his staff again. Where was Trey? Wasn't he supposed to be protecting me? And Beth? I poked my head around and spotted both of them locked in combat.

The staff came down on the back of my head with a mind-jarring blow. I squinted against the tears filling my eyes. I turned around to face him, cursing my bad luck. I should be at school worrying about my next physics test. I grabbed the staff in the middle and had a tug-of-war with the zombie boy before I let go. He stumbled backward, crashing into the grass and knocking out two of his comrades in the process.

I gave a grim smile, but my rush of victory was short-lived. The human jumped back up and lunged at me. This time, the other two joined him.

I groaned within myself. Three at once? I bent my knees and grabbed the first staff that came at me. With superhuman strength, I yanked it away and shoved it into the stomach of my attacker. I spun around to fight the others just as a *vadatajs* lifted a sword to bring me down. My eyes went wide with alarm, and I smacked him upside the head with the staff.

He didn't die. I couldn't kill him this way. But he did stumble and fall, momentarily losing his grip on his sword.

The humans were still coming at me, and I panicked. Reaching down, and I grabbed the *vadatajs'* cursed sword. Before I could second-guess myself,

I plunged it into his gut.

He stopped moving, and his red eyes went gray. I yanked it out and swiveled to face the humans on my flank.

They advanced on me, taking swipes at me with their staffs. One of them pulled a dagger from his belt.

My heart raced. I had to defend myself. But I did not want to hurt them.

The first stepped up on my left, and I jammed the staff into his throat, thrusting him backward. *Don't die*, I pleaded, cursing myself for being such an ineffective goddess of fate. But I couldn't worry about him, because the one with the dagger was taking cheap shots at my arm. Chances were all he needed to do was scratch me, and I'd lose my powers.

I pulled the sword back and stabbed at his dagger. He came at me again, and I spun and parried, battle moves kicking in. He lifted the dagger high. I ducked and rolled, then flipped around and thrust my sword into the back of his leg.

It was meant to cripple him, but as soon as I removed the weapon, I knew from the amount of blood that I'd done more than that. It gushed outward, coating the leg of his jeans.

"No!" I cried, something crumpling within me.

He collapsed to the ground, not trying to rise again.

"No!" I sobbed out the word, tears choking my throat, and I fell to my knees beside him. I dropped the sword and pressed my hands to his wound, trying to ebb the flow of blood.

The third man came at me with his staff, but I grabbed it from him and walloped him in the temple, knocking him unconscious. Then I turned my attention to the dying human in front of me. My shoulders shook with my tears, and I took his hand, staining it with his own blood. I stared into his eyes and tried to summon a vision. I didn't even know if he was a youth, but I had to do something.

"This isn't how you're supposed to die!" I cried. "Not by my hand!"

He stared emptily up at the sky. Who was he? Had he been someone's husband? Someone's father? Someone's boyfriend?

His fingers were stiff in mine, and his breathing stilled. I had killed him.

"Jayne! Jayne Lockwood!"

My name bellowed across the battlefield, so loud that everyone paused their motions. I lifted from the ground, trying to draw breaths against the horrible pain in my chest.

Jumis stood directly beneath the funnel cloud, arraigned in brilliant gold armor. Something tugged at the back of my stomach, something instinctive. He was beautiful, but he was more than that. He was gentle, and compassionate, and tender.

I hardened my heart. "Not to me," I whispered.

And then he lifted an arm and pointed to a soldier locked in battle with three *kaukas*. They stood unmoving, two *kaukas* with staffs lifted to knock them into the back of his neck, and one of them with a dagger extended and pointing at his belly.

"This war is raging around you, Dekla, and you have the power to stop it! Do something!"

I was in no mood for this. I clenched my jaw, my fists trembling. I took several steps forward, and nobody stopped me. Both armies had frozen.

"I can't!" I screamed at him. "If I could, I would have already!" I wiped angrily at the tears that rolled down my cheeks. "You've picked the wrong Dekla!"

Jumis stepped up to the soldier. He placed his hand on top of his head and gave a sharp jerk. I cried out, terrified he'd just broken the man's neck, until he lifted the helmet and dropped it onto the grass.

"Aaron." I uttered his name without thinking, despair rising in me.

"Save him, Dekla," Jumis said. "Only you have the power." He closed the distance between us. "The battle still rages. The moment I release you, you'll be swept back into it. And he will die, like all of these other humans unknowingly sacrificing their mortal existence because you're not strong enough to stop Samantha." He halted in front of me. "I'm trying to help you."

"Help me save Aaron so I can be with him?" I raged. Because I knew that wasn't true. I knew Jumis far better than that. "This is not about me. This is about what you want."

180

His hand snaked out and grabbed my wrist. "I want you. That's all I've wanted, for a thousand years. You wanted me too, you've just forgotten. I'll give you everything. Your powers, your memories, I'll even save Aaron. I'll fight by your side, and Jods and his entourage will crumble to the dust before us."

I wavered, telling myself to stand strong. "I'm starting to remember on my own. I'm getting the power."

"You'll never get it back fast enough." His voice whispered over my head. "You know it. By the time you get it back in a month, in a year or ten, this battle will have ceased for another century. How many people will die before then? How many lives will you take?"

His words stabbed my heart. I clutched my chest, aching.

Jumis glanced over his shoulder at Aaron. "Let him live, Dekla." His voice took on a tender tone. "I know you love him. I accept that, and I offer this to you. Let him live."

I stumbled toward Aaron and stopped in front of him. I stroked his face, those eyes that were once so blue now black and expressionless. "What will you do if I agree?"

"I will remove his body from this battlefield immediately. It is the only way I can guarantee his life."

"And then what?"

"You will have access to your memories. Whatever you need to know, you'll find it."

"And you and me?" I said, bringing the conversation back to what really mattered.

He cocked his head at me, and although a part of me hated him for his manipulation, another part of me sighed at the empathy in his eyes. "Come to me when this battle is over. You will remember how."

I nodded, not trusting myself to speak.

He extended his hand. "Do you swear?"

A chill ran through me, and I swallowed hard. "What am I swearing to?"

"To follow through on the commitment you made to me a thousand years ago. To be my wife."

When I did not immediately respond, his eyes darkened. "I am not saving this boy's life for my benefit. If you ask this of me, I ask that of you."

I closed my eyes. No other option presented itself to me, and I didn't have time to delay. I opened my eyes. "Okay."

His hand shook in front of me. "Swear it."

"On what?"

"On your mortal soul."

Sounded awfully ominous and trapping. My hand trembled as I took his. I realized it didn't matter what I thought because he knew I would try to get out of this, which was why he was making me swear. And if I couldn't get out? Was I willing to do this? For Aaron? For all of humanity?

Yes. I was.

His fingers tightened around mine, sending a current of comfort through my skin. "It will be all right, Dekla," he said.

I clung to those words, that feeling. "I swear it."

"On your mortal soul."

"On my mortal soul," I repeated.

A rope shot upward from the ground, winding itself around my wrist and then around his. It glowed bright white for an instant, burning me with heat, and then sank into our skin and vanished, leaving only a gold tattoo entangled around my wrist and fingers.

He released me. "It is done." He closed his fist and then opened it, revealing the ball of fire he'd tempted me with before.

I didn't snatch it, not yet. "What is done?" My heart hammered in my throat. "We're not married now, are we? Because I'm in high school, and my mom would kind of have a cow."

He made a noise in the back of his throat that was undeniably a laugh. "No. Not yet. There will be an official ceremony."

I hid my relief. Forcing back my misgivings over what I'd just done, I wrapped my fingers around the little ball in his hand.

What happened next was so instantaneous that I didn't even have the chance to react. I threw back my head as memories rolled over me. They collided in my mind, brilliant, fast, as vibrant as if they'd happened yesterday but with the hue of history, the veracity of ancient fact.

The three of us stood on the ash-covered meadow, Karta, Laima, and me. The cries of the dying echoed in my ears, the pain of the cut-off lives pounding in my heart. We put our hands together as three sisters. Ragana stepped over, the wind picking up her silky hair and whipping it around her face, though I didn't know if it was a wind she had created or a natural one. She placed her hand over the top of the three of ours, and I closed my eyes while she murmured.

A fire started in my navel, pushing outward, expanding to my limbs until it exploded from me, from my fingertips and my head and my ears, from every piece of me. I lost the ability to stand. My hand slipped away from my sisters, and I couldn't even keep my eyes open as I smacked into the ashen grass beneath us.

Laima's plan had worked. The pieces of my soul were still shooting out of me, and I felt my body, my perfect, immortal body, aging in moments what should've happened over centuries. I gasped for breath, and a hand stroked my forehead.

"Dekla," a male voice moaned, his tone soft and mournful.

Jumis. I wanted to see him one last time. I forced my eyes open, caught sight of his beautiful face, the angry tears glistening in his eyes. My ancient heart beat with all the passion it had left. *I'm sorry*, I thought. *Sorry I couldn't fulfill my promise.*

His hands cradled my head, and he said, "I will find a way. I will make it happen."

His lips on my face were the last thing I felt before I left my fading mortal body behind.

The vision vanished, but I remembered so much more. My mind automatically shoved the memories aside, too many to rifle through, to internalize. But the feelings emerged in my soul, changing me. I opened my eyes and found Jumis staring at me.

"You remember," he said, hope and expectation in his eyes.

"I remember," I confirmed. And now I understood. But it was not the time. "Return me."

He didn't hesitate. He waved his hands, and the world around me unfroze. The rage and roar of the battle filled my ears at the same time that Jumis wrapped a hand around Aaron's wrist. The two of them vanished in a swirl of smoke.

Well, I wouldn't be going that way. Now I knew so much, so much. I didn't even have time to think about all I knew because I had a battle to win.

CHAPTER TWENTY

The demons with their wicked swords were all around me, and I couldn't take the chance of one of them touching me. I needed Auseklis. I turned around and ran back to my army, cursing my body for not having the speed of a goddess. My fighting instincts were honed and ready to go, though, and this proved useful several times as a few of the stupid mortals attempted to take me out.

Trey's eyes were focused on me as I skidded to a halt in front of him. I took his wrist and turned it over, examining the heavy chains tattood there.

"Let's break these, shall we?" I said.

"Quickly, if you don't mind," he replied.

"Beth!" I said, but I didn't just call her. I knew now how to tap into the core energy that was my sister goddess. The two pieces of Karta in Beth drew me right to her. I found her in an instant, locked in hand-to-hand combat with three goblins. In her hands she held the bayonet of a *kaukas*, and she used it to skewer two of the *vadatajs*. I tugged on her energy. She whipped her head around, surprise on her features.

"Beth!" I called again as she came closer. She stumbled forward.

"Did you do that? Did you pull me here?"

I patted her face. "Sorry. I didn't mean to make it so strong. Where's Ragana? I mean—Meredith."

"She's there. Using wind as a shield to protect those fighting." Beth pointed just a few yards away.

"Then we go to her."

"Remember I don't have my powers," Trey warned. "If we walk through these armies, we'll be exposed."

"Let's tread carefully."

Beth held onto Trey's hand, and I fended off any approaching soldiers.

"Meredith!" I shouted as we neared her. "We need you! Just for a moment." I placed her hand around Trey's wrist. "Beth, put your hand on top. It's time to free his powers."

"You know how to do this?" Meredith asked.

"Not me, you. You need to break the chains that bind him." I opened my hand, showing the star burned into my skin. "I have his power. But it can't get back to him."

"How?" she whispered.

"Use the symbol for breaking." I drew it on her hand, then closed my eyes and searched for Trey's energy source. It was caged inside of me, shaking against the bars, desperate to get out.

"Free it, Meredith," I whispered.

I opened my eyes and watched as she traced the symbol on her wrist.

"With this power of mine, I set free the power of thine," she whispered. The symbol glowed blue for a moment before fading.

I focused on Trey's energy source and put my hand, star-down, over his.

The power grew stronger and larger until the proverbial cage around it swelled.

Trey sucked in a deep breath, his hand trembling where it was sandwiched between mine and Beth's. And then all of that caged power burst out of my hand, blowing me backward like a fuel-powered jet pack. Trey's hand flipped around lightning-fast, grasping my wrist and holding me on my feet. For a moment his entire body glowed, and then only his eyes. I looked down to see the chains had faded.

"Step back," he said, and I did so. What was he going to do?

"Jayne," he said, meeting my eyes, "turn the tide. I'll protect you."

Turn the tide. I cast my gaze about and spotted several of Samantha's mindless humans fighting with Ursins' army, or what remained of it. The jackals and *vadatajs* gathered too close for comfort, but I ignored them, trusting Trey. My eyes scanned Samantha's soldiers, finding one with the yellowish-orange aura Amy had told me about. I could see it as clearly as a spotlight glaring behind him.

"Look at me," I said. I didn't shout or try to get his attention; I just directed my words toward his mental energy.

He looked at me, and I was so surprised I almost didn't follow through. Black, empty eyes stared into mine, and I worried there would be nothing for me to influence, no soul. But I summoned a vision anyway, just as I knew I could.

I saw the battle through his eyes, but there was no emotion. He acted on instinct, destroying the enemy like a mindless drone. I saw his comrades fall around him, many of them dead, but he didn't react. There was nothing.

It gave me a moment's pause. I knew the proper course of action was to find a better future and plant the first step in his head, and then leave it open for him to choose. Whatever his fate should be of his choosing.

But this man no longer had the ability to choose. He could only obey.

In which case, I had to do something different. I had to give him orders.

This was new territory for me. I had to find whatever Samantha had done and change the command. I searched the emptiness in his body for the commands, for a source of understanding. For anything left of his soul.

I almost didn't find it. It flickered like a burning ember ashed over, black on the outside with sparks of orange attempting to burst through. I held it gently with my mind, catching my breath as it went from blistering heat to unexpected coldness. It seemed he would turn me to ice. I gripped the frozen energy source, cupping it between both hands. The pain was intense, searing through me, and I screamed.

But I also succeeded. The black outside melted away, revealing a shimmering, blue crystal. It only had one command: destroy the life sources. I gave it a new one: lay down your arms and go home.

Immediately I withdrew, breaking eye contact with a ragged intake of breath.

Someone supported me, and I turned my head to see my sister holding me up.

"You screamed," she said, her eyes bright with worry. "Are you okay?"

"I'm okay." I pushed myself to my feet and looked for the soldier. Just as I had ordered, he had put down his staff. He turned on a diagonal and began walking.

"Where's he going?" Beth asked, her eyes on him also.

"Home," I said, a rush of relief warming my chest. "He's going home."

"Does he remember?"

I shook my head. "He doesn't know anything. But at least he'll get home alive. His family can figure out what to do with him until I get his soul back to his body."

"Can you do more, Jayne?"

I turned my attention to Trey and noticed for the first time the way he stood in front of us, arms pushed outward as if holding up a wall. Sweat dripped down his face, and his arms trembled with fatigue.

"What are you doing?" I asked.

"Protecting you," he said with a grunt.

"He's created some kind of field that the demons can't get through," Beth said. "The humans can still pass through, but Meredith and I have been handling them." She brandished a staff that one of the zombies must've left behind.

Then I spotted the human bodies lying around her, eyes closed, with metal helmets over their heads. A few wore armor, but most were dressed in street clothes.

"I can't hold this forever," Trey said.

"Why do you need to hold it at all? The visions are instantaneous."

"Not this time," Beth said. "You weren't moving, and then you screamed."

The news startled me. Usually during a vision, time didn't pass. But to know that I had been standing still, helpless while I manipulated Samantha's orders—suddenly Trey's role felt even more important.

"I know what to do now. It won't take me as long." I turned my attention away from them and focused on the next soldier with the orange glow. *Look at me*, I thought again, and the soldier swiveled.

It was a girl. The realization surprised me, though I knew it shouldn't. Samantha had collected without bias. As soon as our eyes connected, I initiated the vision. This time I knew right where to go, looking for the icy blue rock covered in black.

I found it, but the cold emanating from it was so strong that I hesitated. This would hurt. But I had no choice.

I gathered what I could of my own firestorm into my mental hands, warming them. Bracing myself, I wrapped my fingers around the black ice.

Again the cold stunned me, so sharp it burned. I might have screamed again, though I tried not to. My teeth chattered as I plugged myself in and issued a new command. *Drop your weapon and go home.*

Immediately I withdrew, shaking and looking for my own warmth.

"Are you sure you're okay?" Beth asked, her voice hesitant.

I shook my head clear, getting myself back into the present situation. My fist clenched and unclenched even though there was no physical chill. "I can do this."

"Then do it quickly," Trey said. "You've done two, and there's a whole army out here. Meredith and I can't hold them forever."

I took just a moment to look around, and my heart sank. They were maybe half of the *kaukas* left fighting, and only seven remaining goddesses and their entourages. Horses littered the ground, and the bees were gone. Ursins was fighting also, giving out orders and encouraging at the same time. My heart filled with gratitude for him, and I could only hope the fallen were injured and not dead.

I also noticed the piles of human bodies, and the total was still rising. My chest knotted. How close was this to Meredith's vision? If I wanted the destruction to end, I had to act.

I found the next adolescent, and this time I didn't hesitate when I found his icy core. It hurt, but the pain passed quickly. I moved from him to the next, and the next, and the next.

I lost count of how many freezing rocks I held in my hand. My breathing came harder, faster, and I stumbled forward, searching for the next one.

I tried to get the attention of another soldier, but the soldier didn't answer me. Was I losing my power? *Look at me*, I directed. Instead, the soldier walked right past me.

"Jayne. Jayne. Up now."

I hadn't even realized I was on the ground until Trey's hands heaved me to my feet.

"They're in retreat." Ursins placed an arm around my waist, lifting me away from Trey.

"Where were your people?" Trey snarled, anger flashing in his eyes. "Where are the other gods?"

Ursins shook his head. "They have decided only to watch. For now." He caught my gaze. "The right person might be able to change their minds."

"Don't they know what's at stake?" Trey continued to rage. "Samantha is after their immortality! How many pieces of the goddesses has she collected now?"

"I know."

I struggled to get my feet under me and walk without their assistance. My eyes raked over the fields, the carnage. The bodies.

"We lost so many," I whispered.

"On both sides," Ursins said, his tone grim.

"No," I said, anger and desperation choking me. "On our side. All of

190

them are on our side."

We retreated back to the safety of our vehicles. I watched Meredith's storm cloud suck itself back into the sky, and only then did I notice a series of television vans along the road.

"How many people saw that battle?" I asked, rubbing my palms together. I still couldn't seem to get warm.

"It was broadcast live," Ursins said. "The mortals know now."

"What does that mean?" Not that I'd been under the impression what we did was a secret, but I couldn't imagine the rational part of the world accepting what was happening.

"Oh, the government will come up with a logical explanation," Trey said, his eyes still simmering. "They always do."

"And the death count?" I couldn't see the battlefield from here, but in my mind's eye I pictured all of the bodies, and I wanted to cry.

"Disease. Drugs. Bees gone wild. Whatever they can come up with."

"There will be some who see the truth," I said.

"Absolutely," Ursins said. "Those will be the mortals who choose to stand and fight with us next time."

Next time. This wasn't over. "How will they find us?"

Ursins shrugged. "I do not know. But they always manage to."

"It's us."

I turned my head to see one of the women looking at me. I recognized her power as identical to my own, which made her a Dekla also. She finished bandaging the head of her ragana, and now she faced me. "We are goddesses of fate. If they get it into their heads that it's their fate to help us, they will find us. And they will fight for us."

"Jods has gone too far," Ursins rumbled. "When we fight again, it will be bitter."

I snorted. "Because this last battle was sweet? I can't wait to see bitter."

Trey closed his hand on my arm. "Let's get back to the hotel. We have preparations before then."

"How can humans fight with us?" Meredith asked as we climbed into the truck. "What can they possibly do?"

Die, I thought, but I kept the morbid thought to myself.

Beth turned to her. "We're human too. And we are out there fighting." Her eyes swiveled to me. "Jayne? You've remembered stuff, right? How does this work?"

I was suddenly too foggy with sleep to dredge up a memory. It tickled the back of my mind, an awareness of how this had been done in the past. "They'll answer a call. They'll be ready. They'll be trained."

"How can they be trained for something they didn't know was coming?" Meredith asked.

I leaned my head back against the seat, letting my heavy eyelids slide closed. "It's their destiny."

Silence met my proclamation, and then Meredith said, "Well, that's twisted. That's like saying this war with Samantha was fated to happen."

I didn't have the strength to answer, but I felt the truth to her words. All of the possible futures were right there in front of us. I used to think the path I saw before me was inevitable, that it was the only one. But I was starting to understand there were many paths, and the only thing inevitable was that we had to choose one.

Which one being the magic question.

CHAPTER TWENTY-ONE

I slept the entire hour back to the hotel. My sleep was not restful. I knew I was dreaming, but I sat in a dark room, unable to see anything, even myself.

"Turn on your light," Jumis' voice said from somewhere in the blackness.

I did, turning my palm up and calling for the ball of flame he had given me. The energy pulled up from my core, coalescing in my hand.

The light illuminated Jumis standing in front of me. Shadows flickered across his face as the fire danced and balanced majestically.

"Where are the souls?" I asked, my throat achy as I spoke past a lump.

"In the underworld, along with Aaron. When will you come for them?"

"Tonight," I said. I couldn't wait another day. There would be no more battles with human casualties, not if I could help it.

I sensed him in my head, probing my thoughts, searching for my secrets. I slammed up a wall so hard that he physically reared back.

"Yes," I said with a smile, "I remember how to do that now."

His hand came out and stroked my forearm. "And us? Do you remember us?"

I did. I remembered the strength of their love. But it wasn't mine, it was Dekla's, and she lost him. My heart belonged to someone else, and I would do whatever it took to free him.

But I wasn't going to reveal that. Not until Aaron was safe.

"I do," I said. "I remember."

His fingers tightened around my arm, and I didn't need to read minds to feel his immense relief. I felt sorry for him, because I knew he loved me—no, Dekla—and he had done all of this to fulfill his promise to her.

"Tonight, then," he said. His hand slid off my arm, and I woke as Trey shook my shoulder.

"Come on, Jayne," he said softly. "We're at the hotel."

I blinked and looked around. Beth and Meredith were already gone. I swung my legs out of the truck and planted my feet on the concrete.

Trey came around the truck and placed his hands on my shoulders, forcing me to meet his gaze. "What happened out there?"

I frowned. "What do you mean? I did exactly what I was supposed to do. I got my memories back and figured out how to change the soldiers' immediate future."

His grip tightened on my shoulders. "What you did wasn't natural." When my frown deepened, he quickly added, "It was amazing. And I've got my powers back. But you should never have been able to remember all of that so quickly. You did something."

It wasn't a question. It wasn't even an accusation. It was a statement. And as I met his amber-green eyes, I realized it was a loaded statement; he expected an explanation.

How much could I tell him? If I told him I planned on saving Aaron and the other souls and then refusing to marry Jumis, Jumis could read his mind and find out. I couldn't risk it. I would just have to tell him the plan and let him put his own pieces together.

"I made a deal with Jumis."

"Jumis. Escort to the underworld. I knew you were still seeing him."

The way he said it made it seem as if we were dating or something. Which, well, considering the circumstances . . . I ignored the insinuation in his tone. "He gave me back my memories."

"In exchange for what?" Trey tilted his head, looking at me suspiciously.

"Not just my memories, but all of the souls of Samantha's army," I said, anxious to show him how sweet my half of the deal was.

Trey's suspicious look didn't go away. If anything, his eyes hardened. He took his hands off my shoulders and stepped back.

"Including Aaron," I said, now desperate for him to support me in this decision.

"In exchange for what?" he repeated.

I sighed. That was how these things worked, wasn't it? Never something for nothing. "I have to go down to the underworld to get the souls."

"And?"

My lip twisted, and I lowered my eyes. "And stay with him."

The silence between us only lasted ten seconds before Trey blurted out, "And stay with him? That makes no sense."

I swallowed hard. "Apparently Dekla promised to marry him. He wants me to make good on that promise." I found the courage to lift my face, and then I wished I hadn't.

Trey's eyes widened, his pale skin going from white to pink to purple. "Are you crazy? How could you agree to that? You realize you're human, right?"

I tugged on his arm, desperate for reassurance. "There's another way, isn't there?" I remembered what Trey had said earlier about choices. There was always another way.

Trey turned away from me, shoving his hand through his hair before

195

spinning back. "I'm not sure I can protect you from this one. You promised. Did you swear it?"

Tears pricked my eyes. "I had to! People were dying! Aaron — Aaron could've died!"

A flicker of compassion lit his eyes before he extinguished it. "What did you swear on?"

My lip trembled. "My mortal soul."

He looked at the ground and shook his head, the hopelessness evident in his expression. "I don't know, Jayne. Maybe there's not a way out of this one."

There was absolutely no part of me that wanted to tell Beth and Meredith about the deal I'd made. But Trey insisted.

"I'll take you down to the underworld tonight. And I'll do what I can to bring you back. But if I can't, they have a right to know why."

"Trey —" I began, but he wasn't done.

"Beth will have to come with us. By yourself, you can only free the souls of minors, children and teenagers. We need Karta's power to free the adults."

I hadn't thought of that. My body flushed cold.

"Don't worry about her," Trey said. "I'll keep her safe."

With Beth's involvement, I had no choice but to tell them about our descent. Meredith freaked out, begging us not to go before she finally accepted I had no choice.

"There's more," he said, giving me a steely glare.

I sighed, wishing I didn't have to spill this part. "I made a deal with Jumis. Me in exchange for the souls."

Meredith wrinkled her nose. "What does that mean, you in exchange for the souls?"

When I didn't immediately respond, Trey did for me. "She has to marry him."

"What?" Meredith shrieked. "What about Aaron?"

I swallowed hard. "I'm doing this for him."

"I don't think he's going to thank you!"

196

Probably not. "I had to agree to it," I whispered. "Jumis gave me the knowledge to fight in the battle today."

Tears filled Meredith's eyes, but Beth studied me shrewdly, her calculating gaze very unlike that of my little sister. "Is there a loophole?"

I shrugged. "The original Dekla, she was absolutely in love with him. She wasn't looking for a loophole. If there is one, I'm not aware of it. And you should know, Jumis can read minds."

My sister and Meredith exchanged glances.

"I'll do some research, see what I can find," Meredith said. "And I'll avoid talking to him at all costs."

"Don't tell me anything you find out either," Trey said. "I'll be accompanying them tonight, and he'll know if he sees it through me."

Meredith gave him a disdainful look. "I wasn't planning on telling you anything anyway."

Beth turned her serious brown eyes to Trey. "Why are you going with us?"

"Because the underworld is a dangerous place, and I'm a protector against the evil and shadows that reside there. You're still mostly mortal."

His words struck a chord. I had sworn to Jumis *on my mortal soul*. If only there were a way out of that.

I looked at Beth. "If you get home before me, tell Mom what happened, okay?" I wasn't sure I would make it home at all, not if I was stuck with Jumis. But I didn't tell her that.

She gave me a scornful look. "You're not getting out of this that easily. You get to come home and tell Mom you married the grim reaper all by yourself."

I laughed, and then I wrapped my arms around my sister and held her tight.

I spent the afternoon in the business center researching with Meredith until she kicked me out.

"You're depressing me," she said. "Go buy a chocolate bar."

I did. Then I returned to the room and took a hot shower to calm my nerves, but it didn't work. Meredith ordered Chinese food for dinner, and I picked at my lo-mein with my chopsticks, stomach twisting nervously.

"How does this work?" I asked Trey.

"We've been to the stairs before, right?" Trey met my eyes over his chow mein noodles.

I squinted at him. "Only in my dreams."

Meredith gave him a curious look. "You guys dream together?"

He waved her off. "It's one of the ways I have of communicating. You were dreaming, Jayne, but your soul was already finding the path. Now we have to find the path with your soul *and* your body."

Another thought struck me. "If I was already dreaming about this before I ever met Jumis—does that mean making this journey was part of my destiny?"

"Aaron is in the underworld. If you were ever going to save him, making this journey was part of your destiny. Remember, our destiny is made up of our choices and desires."

I nodded, latching onto his words and hoping I could remember that in the days of confusion yet to come. "So how do we get there in real life?"

"She'll have to open the door for us." He gestured at Meredith. "We're all a team here, as I'm sure you've figured out. I can create the path, but she has to open it."

"How do I do that?" Meredith asked.

"Ask Jayne. She'll have to tell you the symbol."

Even as he said the words, the image came into my mind. The symbol for travel—two lines intersecting, like a cross, but with arrows pointing outward on all four ends. "I'll help you, Meredith," I said.

She cast me a sideways look. "Your new-found confidence is kind of sexy."

"Maybe you should be more confident in your abilities," Trey said.

Her face turned bright red. "Maybe you traded in your confidence for conceit," she said, her voice laced with poison.

Trey blinked at her sudden onslaught, and then his own face turned pink behind his freckles. "I didn't mean it like that. I was just saying, confidence looks good on everyone."

"I heard you loud and clear," Meredith snapped. "We all did."

"I think you better just step out of this one," Beth said to Trey.

Trey held up his hands in a gesture of surrender. "Fine. I was just gonna say, ragana's powers are stronger at night. The witching hour and all that."

I arched an eyebrow. "That's a real thing?"

"It's a real thing."

"Midnight, then." I looked back and forth between Trey and Meredith, my stomach tying itself in knots even as I felt better having a plan. "We'll leave at midnight."

Trey turned on the television, searching for the news. I wanted to ask him to turn it off, but I also desperately wanted to know what was going on.

He didn't have to search long. It was all over, reports of a debilitating disease that could seize control of the victim's mind, making them go crazy before killing them. The string of bodies dropping from New Jersey to Kentucky was blamed on this, as well as the field of death from this afternoon. A video clip showed of our battle, but it was skewed. It showed Meredith's funnel cloud and the humans and horses, but none of the demons or goblins or *kaukas*. I knew Beth and I were in that battle somewhere, but I couldn't make out individuals.

"We have encountered a few people who seem to be surviving the disease, although they can't tell us anything about it." The camera flashed away from the newscaster's face to a reporter walking along the street. The reporter kept trying to talk to a young man. The boy didn't answer, his gaze steadfast on the road in front of him. I recognized him as the boy I'd ordered to go home; his body, anyway. His mind and soul were still far from him.

"Can you tell me your name?" The microphone stayed ready in front of the mouth of the boy-zombie, but he said nothing.

"Where are you going? Where did you come from?"

He got no response. The boy just kept walking, only one goal in mind: get home.

"Good job there," Trey said. "Sending them home. Smart thinking. A piece of him is still in there, or he wouldn't know which way is home."

I shrugged off his compliment. I hadn't done much.

199

"But while we don't know what's causing this disease, we do know new victims are being struck every day," the newscaster said, her pretty face marred by concern. "City officials suspect it may be connected to the string of suicides a few weeks ago. As loved ones and citizens continue to report those who are missing, more than four hundred people have vanished from the Illinois-Kentucky border." A map appeared on the screen, with the border and the affected area circled in red.

"She's moving west," Trey said. "She's hightailed it out of here and is collecting more people."

"It's a moot point," I said. "By tomorrow, we'll have freed their souls, and every single one will be heading home to their families."

"That won't stop her from getting more," Trey said.

"I think my fiance will help me out," I said, trying to be glib, but I nearly choked on the word.

A stark silence fell, before Meredith broke it by saying, "Do you think the New Jersey police saw us fighting today?"

I tilted my head and considered the question. If I knew Lieutenant Bailey . . . "Yes. I'm sure they've been watching everything unfold. I'm sure they saw it all." What did he think of me now? We had a tentative trust between us before, even if my powers had made him weary. Now? He probably wanted to lock me up with all the other mutants in a special jail.

Oh, wait. Wrong comic strip.

I coughed back a laugh. Someone needed to write our story. It would be new, original, groundbreaking.

The news finished up, and Trey put on a sitcom. None of us slept. I kept checking the digital clock on the nightstand. 9:50. 10:20. 11:16.

The witching hour was approaching.

I closed my eyes and fought against the nervousness by dredging up memories of Aaron in my mind. The first time we met, when I refused to meet his eyes because he reeked of lemons, and that meant I would See his death. How he didn't let that deter him from pursuing me endlessly, how his sense of humor and easy-going attitude won me over. He pulled me out of my heartbroken stupor over Stephen.

200

Then I thought of how we had drifted apart over the past two months, and how it was mostly me being insecure and immature, demanding more of his time than he was able to give right now. I clung so hard that I pushed him away, so far away that he was willing to go back to England to ease the troubled feelings between us.

But it wasn't because he didn't want me. His last words to me, even after he broke up with me, were, "I love you. Whatever happens, remember that."

My throat closed up at the memory. Had I even said it back? He'd followed me to Maryland, broken up with me, and declared that he loved me, all right on the heels of telling me he was leaving me to go to England. My brain had been so whiplashed I hadn't been able to think straight.

The bed jostled, and I opened my eyes to see Meredith sitting by my head. "It's time."

I sat up, my eyes seeking Trey. He stood by the closet, opening and closing the door that held a handful of hangers and not much else.

"Ready?" I asked, although I had no idea what came next.

He closed the closet door. "Ready." He took a deep breath and released it slowly. Then he put his hand on the closet door and closed his eyes.

"No way," Meredith said, disbelief in her voice. "That's not possible."

Trey straightened up and released the door. "The path is formed."

Beth bounced off the bed. "I have to see this." She stepped over to the closet door and tried to open it. It wouldn't budge. She shook the handle.

I stood up and wandered over to the closet. I wrapped my hand around the door knob and twisted it in my grip, but it wouldn't even turn. I let go. "I can't open it."

Trey inclined his head and waved his hand toward the other bed, where Meredith still sat. "Ragana?" He kept his head lowered as if the word itself weighed him down.

Meredith pushed off the bed and stepped over, her eyes uncertain as she looked at him, but he just beckoned her forward.

"The symbol, Jayne."

"Right," I murmured. I traced the cross on Meredith's arm and gave her what I hoped was an encouraging smile. Meredith's fingers copied the tracing.

"Just do what you think will work," Trey said, also attempting a smile.

Meredith put her hands on the door much as he had, paused a moment, and then whispered a few words.

The door knob glowed red. She took a step back, and I stepped forward.

"It's all yours, Jayne," Trey said, his tone weary.

I took a steadying breath and focused on the door. I didn't make eye contact with Meredith or Beth, just stretched forth my hand and grabbed the knob.

The heat scorched my skin as if it would melt the flesh right off my palm, and my first reaction was to jerk my hand away. But I couldn't. My skin and the doorknob had become one.

CHAPTER TWENTY-TWO

I rattled the knob, frantic, desperate to get free and bolt away. But instead, the door slid open.

My hand fell from the knob as if they had never been attached, as if it hadn't just scalded me. I looked down at my flesh and saw the star, the brand of Auseklis, glowing orange.

This was the only way.

Any residual doubt dispelled. I stepped into the closet, my foot going into the blackness that threatened, no, promised to swallow me up with each step.

I took two more before realizing I was alone. Quickly I swiveled, panicking, expecting to find the closet door closing on me. But it was still open, and Trey murmured a few words to Beth before turning and gripping Meredith's arm. Beth stepped beside me as he spoke to Meredith.

"You did good. You know how to do this. Stay safe until we get back."

Meredith nodded, her jaw clenching. Tears glistened in her eyes. "The same to you. Keep them safe."

Trey hesitated a moment longer, and just when I was about to call out to him, he dipped his head and kissed her.

My jaw hit the stairs in surprise.

"That's unexpected," Beth said, her tone delighted.

I waited for Meredith to pull back and slap his face, but instead her arms wrapped around him, curving her body to his, and I had to turn away from the passion in their embrace.

He separated from her with an audible smack, and I could only stare at him as he entered the staircase with me.

"Um—" I began, but then he pulled the door closed behind us.

Instantly we plunged into darkness, and I forgot anything else I was going to say. My hand slapped out, finding a wall coated in some kind of grime. How was it possible this wall could be filthy as if from centuries of mold and dust when Trey had only created it minutes ago?

He touched my back between my shoulder blades. "I'm here, Jayne, Beth. Go forward."

My panic dissipated at his nearness. "Beth?"

"You won't be able to see her or hear her in here. You're both too mortal. But I've got a hand on her also."

"I can't see anything."

"Use your light."

Use my light. That was what Jumis had told me. I held my hand in front of me and called my energy source to my fingertips. The little orb of fire lit the narrow corridor, showing a descending staircase with walls enclosing us.

There was nothing behind me but a dead end.

The stairs were steep, and I measured each step carefully. "What about Beth? Can she see?"

"No. She can hear me, though. She's trusting me to guide her. I'm using your light."

My heart squeezed for Beth, and I wished I could reassure her. At least we had Trey. "What is this place?" I asked as we went down, down, down.

"The pathway to the underworld." Trey's voice followed right behind me, his touch light on my back. "It can be called forth when it's needed."

"How do you know how to do all of this? Is there a school for Latvian gods in training and their protectors?"

"Sort of," he said, surprising me. "The knowledge is passed on from parent to child, even before we inherit the power. We have to be prepared. But some things are forgotten when they aren't used. My grandfather never had to create a pathway to hell, and I wasn't even sure if I would be able to do it."

"But you did," I said with grudging respect in my voice. Trey continued to amaze me, and I realized how lucky I was to have him on my team. "What should we call our little quartet, anyway? Team Flash is taken. And Team Arrow. Team Jayne?"

He laughed, a soft sound in the darkness around us. "Team Freedom. That's what we're fighting for."

The freedom to make our own choices, to live out our own destiny and death. "Yeah. That sounds about right."

I fell silent as we continued down. Trey's hand fell from my back, but I felt him close by. Sometimes I heard him murmuring to Beth. I lost track of time. One moment would seem to take an eternity, each sound magnified, from the intake of my breath to a drop of water somewhere to Trey's footstep behind me brushing across the top of the stone. It would seem we moved in slow motion, several lifetimes passing from the time I lifted my foot off of one step and brought it down on the next. Moments later we would seem to move in quick speed, the steps blurring beneath my feet, taking corners and switchbacks at breakneck speed. These moments disoriented and frightened me, and I would reach my hand back for Trey.

Each time his fingers clutched mine. "I'm still here, Jayne."

"Do you feel it?" I whispered. "The way time passes strangely?"

"I feel it. Time for the gods does not flow the same as it does for us. We with our mortal minds can't comprehend it, so it plays tricks on our brains while we try to make it fit in our world and reality."

Those words did not comfort me. "How much time has passed?"

"I don't know."

That was all I got from him.

My hands grew sore and achy as we descended, my joints stiffening. The air got older and musty, thick enough to taste. A strand of hair fell over my shoulder, and for second I thought it looked white, but when I picked it up to examine it, it was brown. Out of the corner of my eye I saw the flame in my other hand leading the way, but my fingers appeared to be skeletal, white bones supporting the suspended, flickering light. My eyes turned to them, but it must've been another trick of the light. Or of the darkness, or of the heavy feeling pervading the air. My normal fingers were there, flesh and blood wrapped around bones.

"What is this place?"

"All of time. Yesterday, today, the future."

His voice sounded faint, distant. I turned around and saw no one behind me. Instantly I stopped walking, and the light in my hand trembled, nearly extinguishing.

"Trey?" I called. Where was he? Fear thundered in my heart, thundered in my ears, as loud as a herd of elephants storming across a tin roof. A measuring beat, steady, steady, louder, louder. "Trey?" I called again, my voice arcing in fear.

"Jayne?"

The voice came from behind me, and I whipped around. There, about twenty steps below me, was Trey. I shivered, hating this place, fear pounding in my throat.

"How did you get down there?" I demanded. He'd never walked past me.

He shook his head. "Come, Jayne." He held his hand out to me and didn't lower it until I reached him and slipped my fingers into his.

"Don't let go."

His simple command, said without fanfare or drama, filled me with the knowledge that something sinister surrounded us.

We continued down, my fingers clenching Trey's, each step feeling like a year. From time to time I caught a glimpse of my hair drifting across my shoulder, white as snow. But any time I looked at it, it appeared normal. The moment I took my eyes from my hand, in my peripheral vision I saw the glistening reflection of light on bone. And I knew this wasn't a trick of the light.

"Are we dead?" I was afraid to ask, but I had to know.

Trey's fingers squeezed mine, warm and alive. "No. But the living do not belong here."

A year seemed to pass, then another, then a decade. We passed through time without speaking until I asked, "Will we ever get there?" Would the world we'd left behind be obsolete by the time we did?

The floor beneath our feet smoothed out, and Trey stopped walking.

"Dekla." A voice boomed from the inky blackness, warm and affectionate and immediately dispelling my fears.

"We are here," Trey said, but he didn't let go of my hand. Instead, he drew me closer, shielding me behind him.

A light appeared from somewhere above us, illuminating a grand hall. It was decorated as if for a banquet, though no food sat on the table and no one else appeared. If Jumis hadn't brought the light, we could've been in a darkened cave. Beth appeared in the yellow glow clutching Trey's other hand, and she gave a little cry when she saw me. She threw her arms around me, and I felt her tremble.

"I'm sorry," I whispered. "Sorry you've been sucked into this."

"You may go, Auseklis," Jumis said. "Your job here is done. Thank you for bringing them safely."

Trey hesitated. "They'll need me to see them out."

"Dekla is not going back."

Trey tightened his jaw. "But Beth is."

"What about the souls?" I said, fighting to keep my head clear.

Jumis nodded. "I know where Jods is keeping them."

"You promised to release them. They'll need me to ascend," Trey said.

His voice held a challenge in it, as if daring Jumis to go back on his word. Or make him leave.

"Stay, then, so you can guide them to the world of the living." Jumis looked at me, eyes like liquid pools of ink. "Dekla, release his hand."

My fingers opened, moving away from Trey's without me telling them to. I choked back a gasp of astonishment. "How — ?" I began, but then I remembered. I belonged to him. He could command me.

And then my knees went weak, because I knew this was not a binding I could break. I belonged to him.

Trey moved to steady me, but Jumis got there first. He caught me, cradling me. "Don't fight this, Dekla. This is how it was always meant to be. You and me. The bringer of death and life and the goddess of fate. Together forever."

I closed my eyes, tears threatening as the futility of the situation weighed on me. His words struck me wrong, sounding like a happy song gone mad.

"Where are the souls?" Trey asked. I opened my eyes to see his gaze locked on Jumis, a muscle twitching in his cheek.

"They are being kept in a cage. I do not have the right to free them, but with the goddesses' powers, we can release them all. And then you can guide them back to the living. If the three of you felt the effects of the pathway even with your godly powers, it will be that much worse for the souls that are entirely mortal."

I found the strength to stand up, preferring my own two feet to Jumis' arms. "And when they return to the world above? How much time has passed since we began our descent?"

Jumis turned his dark brown eyes on me. His features were as lovely as ever, but this time I saw nothing enticing about them. I felt as if I'd been trapped, manipulated. I might have promised with my own words, but I had only done it because I'd been coerced to. There had been no other choice. And for that, I despised him.

"No time has passed," Jumis said, his tone gentle. "When Auseklis returns to the land of the living with the souls, it will have been moments since the three of you left. Only Aaron has his physical body here. The other souls will disburse to find their bodies the moment they exit the pathway. Aaron will be in the care of Auseklis."

I turned to Trey, determination strengthening me. "You have to get Aaron home. Don't stay here. Make sure he gets home safely." *Don't fight for me*, I pleaded.

Tray hesitated. "My duty is not just to you, but to your sister. And Meredith—"

"I am sacrificing everything to make sure Aaron lives!" The anger that shook my words was more than just mine. Dekla's power radiated in my veins, and I looked down to see flames lighting between my fingers. I tempered my voice when I spoke again. "Auseklis, your kind have always been trusted servants. I am trusting you now with one of my most precious treasures. Take him home." Authority rang in my words.

Trey nodded. "I will get him home safely."

I flung my arms around his neck. "Thank you."

He hugged me back, but he didn't speak.

"Come, Dekla." Jumis' hand closed around my wrist, and I fought the urge to fling it off. "Come," he repeated. "I need you and your sister to set them free."

CHAPTER TWENTY-THREE

Jumis led us down a dark, dripping hallway. Then we went through a doorway into what appeared to pass for the outdoors in the underworld. A vast lake stretched out in front of us, tall, mossy trees and bushes with beautiful, exotic flowers surrounding it. Strange creatures with misshapen faces and lumpy appendages swam in the water's depths.

"What are those?" I asked, a shiver running down my spine.

"You remember, Dekla," Jumis said calmly, and even as he said it, I did remember.

The souls of the damned. Once they had been men, and then they were *vadatajs*. And then finally, when they lost all sense of humanity, they became nothing but hideous creatures. I looked away from them. "Where is Aaron?"

"I hid him with the other souls. I knew Jods would not look for him there."

"Why is Jods in charge of these souls and not you?" Beth asked.

Jumis spared her a glance. "I am not the god of the dead. It is not up to me to guard the souls. I have been escorting them to the underworld in Saule's place, but it is my job to begin the cycle of life, not end it. These souls are not dead, but neither are they living. Jods has captured them in this unnatural in-between state. By freeing them, you will be restoring balance."

He led us around the lake and into another corridor. The light followed him. My flame had extinguished, and I was tempted to call it back. Doors lined this passage, and I heard voices, some of them desperate, crying, others merely curious, speaking to us as we walked by.

"And this?" I asked, waiting for the answer to reveal itself in my memory.

"You tell me," he said, amusement in his voice. Like this was a game to him, watching me uncover the memories of my predecessors.

"Waiting," I said. "They're waiting for judgment so they can leave for their final resting place."

"That's right."

Jumis pushed open a door, and we stepped into a room. What looked like a giant gilded birdcage sat in the middle of the floor. Figures whirled within it, and I caught glimpses of a face, a hand brushing the bar, eyes turning toward me, before they all swirled together into a misty mass.

But then the body standing at attention in the corner caught my attention, and I ran forward. An invisible barrier blocked me three feet before I got there, and I smacked into it hard enough to bounce onto my backside.

"Aaron!" I cried.

"He doesn't have his soul back yet," Jumis said. "Let us release them."

I took a hesitant step toward the golden cage, but no barrier stopped my approach. "Beth," I said, and she came to my side.

"What do we do?" she whispered, her eyes wide and uncertain.

I could easily pick out those under my jurisdiction; the orange orbs flitted and bounced against each other and the cage, eager to get out. I had no idea how to help Beth see them. I turned to Jumis.

"She doesn't remember. She doesn't know how to do this. Can you help her?"

He looked at her, and I saw him calculating what he could gain from this. I placed my hand on his arm before he could think of something else to leverage against me and said, "I'll stop fighting. I promise."

He turned his eyes on me, and I realized I'd underestimated him. Naked vulnerability and hope shown in his expression. All he wanted was my love.

He closed his palm, and when he opened it again, an orb of energy danced there, identical to the one he'd offered me, but blue instead of orange. Beth's gaze landed on it, and there was no mistaking the hunger in her eyes. He extended it to her, and she snatched it quicker than I could blink. In a moment it dissolved into her fingers, and she closed her eyes and inhaled. When she opened them, the blue light flickered in their depths.

"I know what to do now," she breathed, excitement and certainty in her voice.

"Then let's begin," I said. I focused on the souls in the cage and began seeking out individuals, one by one. Once again, time seemed to stand still. But it didn't drain me like it had on the battlefield. An eternity passed and still, Beth and I were side by side, looking into their souls and offering them a choice.

There was no lock on the cage; they had been bound only by their inability to decide to leave. Once they decided, the cage couldn't hold them. They slipped through the bars and crowded around Trey like ethereal beings.

The last one got free of the cage, and I took a step back to get my bearings, to fall back into my own body, my own soul.

The feather light touch of Jumis' hands on my waist made me turn toward him.

"One more, Jayne."

It was the first time he had called me by my given name since the battlefield. There was a tenderness and compassion in his eyes that I didn't expect, and I didn't want it. I looked in the direction of Aaron's body, still lying prone on the ground.

"Jayne," Beth said. She held out in her hand a shimmering mist. "This is Aaron. I thought you might want to be with him when I release him."

I nodded, too emotional to speak. Jumis held out his hand for mine, and I accepted, eager to see this end.

He stepped to the barrier, but when he tried to pull me through, my hand would not pass. He looked at me, blinking, and I saw a flicker of confusion pass over his face. He studied our entwined hands and tried again to tug me in after him. "Why can't I pull her through?"

Trey shook his head. "I don't know enough about what created this to answer the question."

"I passed through the barrier unhindered."

I rattled my hand in his, but the wall bumped between our fingers. "Well, why can't I get through?"

"Dekla, come to me," Jumis commanded.

My body tried. I smashed up against the invisible barrier, but that was all.

"How can this be stronger than a binding?" Jumis asked Trey, his voice sounding more puzzled than angry.

"I'm not sure. But if Jods created this, he may have intentionally made it so no mortal could pass through."

"As if he knew we might try," Jumis said. "Then Jods knows the human boy is here." He looked at me. "But if she cannot go through, I cannot keep my promise to her."

A note of desperation entered his voice. If he couldn't keep his promise to me, I was not expected to keep mine. For a brief moment, hope surged through me. I wouldn't have to marry him. I would be free of him.

But then I realized what that would mean, why I had even agreed in the first place. I wanted Aaron set free. No matter what the personal cost.

"Can't you get him?" I asked.

Jumis shook his head. "He won't leave without his soul, and I can only retrieve the souls of the dead. I cannot put his living soul back in his body."

"I can set his soul free," Beth said. "Then he'll be able to walk out of his own choice."

213

"No," Jumis said. "The soul is immortal but still tied to mortality. It won't pass through either. One of the goddesses of fate must return it to him."

"Try it," I told Beth. Maybe he was wrong.

She looked at the mist swirling in her palm, and then it lifted away from her and spread out against the barrier like a raindrop on a windshield, dispersing before coalescing into a hazy circle.

Aaron. That was Aaron's soul, trying to get into his body. I turned to Trey, my desperation matching Jumis'. "There must be a way to get me through."

"You would need the powers of immortality," Trey said.

"Is there a way to give me them?" I demanded.

"Not without Deivs—" Trey began. And then he stopped and met Jumis' eyes.

There was another way. I saw it in their expressions. But from the look on Trey's face, he didn't like it.

"What?" I demanded. "Whatever it is, I have the right to know. I have the right to make that decision."

"You can marry me now," Jumis said.

I jerked, nearly pulling my hand free from his. "Is that meant to be some kind of joke?"

"No," Jumis said, locking his eyes on mine. "It is an offer."

"If you marry him, his immortality extends to you. As long as you are his wife, you can cross the same barriers he can." Trey said the words softly, somberly.

"It is not how I planned it," Jumis said. "But you knew a wedding was going to happen. If we do it now, we can free him. Before Jods discovers we're here. It is something I can offer you."

I couldn't breathe. My eyes were frozen on Aaron, the man I had once hoped to spend my life with. And yet it seemed in order to save his life, I had to pledge my life to another. "How?" I asked, hearing how my voice trembled. "How can this be done now?"

"Auseklis can do it for us."

I spun to face Trey, unable to hide my surprise. This was something I hadn't known, even as Dekla. "You? Aren't you a man of many talents."

He looked rather sheepish. "It's not done often," Trey said. "In fact, I don't know when was the last time it was done."

"Because most of us married eons ago," Jumis said. "In the presence of Deivs or Perkons. I am one of the few who was left alone after the last war."

After Dekla chose mortality over me and left me alone.

I heard the words he didn't say and made my choice. "Will you do it then?" I asked Trey.

He looked at me in disbelief. Then he nodded. "I'll need help remembering the words."

"I can help you," Jumis said. "For more than a millennia those words have echoed through my head, as I've longed for the wedding day I was deprived of."

The pity welled in my heart against my will. When the sisters split their powers, Dekla had known it would hurt Jumis, but she'd never expected him to pine away for her for hundreds of years. "You should've moved on," I whispered.

"I couldn't."

I shut my eyes, feeling sorry for him, and sorry for me, because the Dekla that loved him was no more. I carried those memories, I knew the love they'd shared, but he was not mine, not in my heart. I opened my eyes. "What are we waiting for?"

Jumis stepped out from the barrier and took my other hand, holding both of them in his own.

"Are you sure?" Trey asked. Behind him, tears trailed down Beth's face.

I returned my gaze to Jumis, refusing to overthink this, refusing to imagine what this meant for the rest of my life, for the rest of eternity. Criminy. "Do it."

Trey exhaled and straightened his back.

"Ask me my name," Jumis said.

"What is your name?" Trey said.

"Jumis. Ask me my desire."

"And what is your desire?"

"To join with Dekla, whom I love. I promise not to seek to do her harm and to repair any harm done and to seek to be honest . . ."

The words continued while I fought a wave of dizziness, heat rushing up to my head. This was really happening. And then Trey spoke to me.

"What is your name?"

"Jayne."

"What is your desire?"

I nearly choked on the words. "To marry Jumis."

Trey looked at Jumis for help, but he shook his head.

"Skip the promises. She has already given me the most important one."

Trey nodded and spoke to us both. "Cross your arms and take each other's hands."

We did so, my hands clammy in Jumis' grip. Trey put his hand above ours, and the binding Jumis had imprinted on me when we made our deal lit up, sparking orange and green.

"Now you are bound one to the other with a bond not easy to break. May the infinite light of Deivs and Saule shine upon this union," Trey said, his voice solemn. When Trey withdrew his hand, a golden ray of light wrapped around our wrists, pulsating brightly for a moment before vanishing.

I licked my lips, tasting the saltiness of tears trailing down my cheeks.

"It is done," Trey said softly, his voice holding a note of mourning.

Beth let out a sob. She reached for me, but I ignored her, facing Jumis. "We free him now."

"Take his soul," he said, nodding at the swirling mist beside us.

I held out my hand, and the mist surrounded my fingers, caressing them, feeling so tender I wondered if Aaron wasn't aware of who I was and what I'd done.

Jumis took a step backward through the barrier, his hand still holding mine. I took a step forward to follow, and this time I met no resistance. I passed through the barrier with him, Aaron's soul entangled with my skin.

As soon as we crossed over, the mist disentangled itself and rushed to

Aaron's body. Within moments he took a deep, shuddering breath, at the same time that the entire cavern trembled around us.

Jumis' hand closed on my shoulders. "The barrier. It must have been an alarm. Jods knows we are here. We must leave."

Aaron sat up, blinking his eyes as a shaky hand pressed to his forehead. I pulled away from Jumis and knelt by his side, one hand reaching out to join his, my fingers trembling as I brushed the hair off his face, my chest aching when my skin touched his.

He lifted his gaze. "Jayne?" His eyes flitted around the room, taking in Trey and Beth and Jumis, the cage, the door.

But all I could do was stare at the blue in his eyes, no longer black and empty from Samantha's spell. I drank in the dimple in his chin, the little curl across his forehead that refused to stay where it should.

"Jayne," Jumis said, his voice authoritative, and Trey added, "He's right, Jayne. We aren't prepared to fight down here."

"Time to go." I took Aaron's hand and helped him to his feet.

"Where are we?" he asked, one arm going around my shoulders in a natural, familiar gesture. My throat burned.

"I don't know what you remember," I said, moving us toward the door. Whatever barrier had been there was gone, or maybe it was only to keep mortals from getting in. "A lot has happened. You were being held captive here in the underworld. But now you're free." I offered him what I hoped was a bright smile, but hot tears pricked my eyes.

"What's wrong?" he asked, concern in his expression. One hand cupped my face, his thumb running along my jaw. I closed my eyes, relishing the touch.

"Nothing," I said, my chest constricting.

"Is it because I broke up with you?" He smiled, though he looked a little confused, as if still trying to place his memories. "I didn't mean it. I did it to save you." He glanced around as we walked out. "You said we're in the underworld? What's going on?"

"Don't worry about it. Everything is right now." I walked him over to Trey and then slipped out from under his arm. Trey met my eyes, and a look

217

passed between us. I knew I could trust him. He would take care of Aaron.

"Come on." Trey moved faster down the corridor. "We have to hurry."

Jumis moved beside me, not touching me, but I felt the weight of his presence. "We'll ascend a different way. But let's watch them get to safety."

Beth turned and squeezed me tight. "I love you. I'll see you soon."

Aaron had started after Trey, but he stopped at Beth's words. "Jayne?" he said. He held out his hand. "Aren't you coming?"

My throat closed, the tears flowing freely down the sides of my face. "I can't," I whispered.

Aaron took two steps back to me. The confidence of his former self was returning, his expression firm. "Why not?"

I couldn't tell him. So I just shook my head and stared at him. The one I would never have.

He took my hand, apparently not accepting my silence as an answer. But before he could pull me forward, Jumis put a hand on my shoulder.

"She cannot go with you."

Aaron turned a fiery gaze on him. "You can't hold her hostage!"

Jumis opened his mouth to defend himself, but I interrupted. "He's not holding me hostage. I made this decision." My voice cracked on the last word, ruining my attempt at bravery. "It was the only way."

Aaron turned his eyes back to mine. His grip tightened on my hand. "I didn't sacrifice myself so you would give yourself up for me."

The irony of the situation had not been lost on me. "It's different. You saved me from losing my powers to Samantha and becoming her slave. I had the opportunity to save your life, and I took it."

"So you could be his slave?" he demanded.

"She's not my slave," Jumis said, lifting his chin. "She is my wife."

Aaron's face paled and then went scarlet. "Wife?" he snarled, and of all the fights and arguments we'd ever had, I'd never seen such fury leap over his expression. He grabbed my face and tilted it toward him. "Jayne. Say it's not true."

The urgency in his voice broke my heart, but I couldn't deny it. When I didn't say anything, he bent his face to mine and kissed me, his lips hard enough to bruise, his mouth hot and furious. He crushed me against him and I melted into his embrace, holding him as close to me as I dared, knowing this was the last time.

Jumis jerked me away, and then he shoved Aaron hard enough to send him slamming into the opposite wall as he were nothing more than a bean bag.

"Take him, Trey!" I shouted, terrified that Jumis might lash out at Aaron again.

"Jayne!" Aaron said, getting to his feet.

Trey grabbed his arm, somehow holding Aaron in place. "I will. I promise, Jayne—"

"Go!" Jumis roared, and the cavern shook again, pieces of rock and debris showering our heads.

Trey didn't wait. He forcibly moved Aaron down the corridor. Beth cast one last glance my way before running after them.

"Will they make it?" I cried out. "Will they be safe?"

Jumis put his hand on my arm and pushed me into the room we'd just left. "Auseklis will get to the surface. We must go also." A stairway had appeared behind the cage, and Jumis prodded me up into it. He came behind me, then closed a door and the passage sealed shut as if there had never been a door. "Move quickly and quietly. Jods cannot reach us once we reach the realm of the celestial gods."

We did not speak as we climbed. The ascent felt very different from the descent, with no wacky time warps or loss of direction.

Finally he said, "I kept my end of the bargain."

Was he insinuating that I had not kept mine? That there was something more I needed to do? I swiveled to face him, meeting his eyes head on. "And I kept mine."

"Yes, you did." He closed the distance between us and held his hand out. "Come."

I didn't budge. Would he command me if I didn't? As his wife, I would have to do his bidding. "Where are we going?" To fight a war, I hoped, and not hop a cruise ship for a honeymoon.

He tilted his head again, that playful smile returning to dance about his lips. "Why, Dekla, don't you know? We have a war to win. The war council is already waiting for us above." With that, he stepped past me on the stairs, leaving me no choice but to walk in his shadow.

Get all 4 Goddess of Fate Books!

  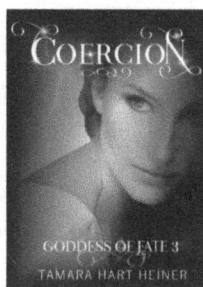 

Preview of DESTINED

"Jumis and Dekla, come forth," Perkons boomed.

I nodded, remembering the real reason I was here. Jumis offered me his hand, and I took it.

"We still skip the official vows, as they have already been said," Perkons said, electricity shooting from his head. "But we must anoint your bride."

"Anoint me?" I started to say, but no sooner had I opened my mouth than a girl holding a bowl stepped forward. She smiled at me, dipped her finger into the bowl, and removed something glossy and golden. Questions rattled around in my brain, but I wasn't given the chance to ask. She touched her finger to my lips, leaving the heavy substance there. My tongue darted out and tasted the substance. Honey.

"May your words to your husband always be sweet and your heart full of charity," she said.

"Kiss her and make her yours, Jumis," Perkons said.

Kiss me. My heart skipped a beat. Thus far we'd avoided any unnecessary touches. But Perkons was watching, and Jumis didn't hesitate. He leaned forward and pressed his lips to mine, warm and confident. Then he drew back, his gaze eager with anticipation. My mouth buzzed, my lips stunned from the turn of events.

"You may remove the wreath," Perkons said.

A bonfire appeared in front of the throne. Jumis placed both hands on either side of the wreath on my head, and then he tossed it into the fire. Another girl stepped forward and handed a white cloth to Jumis. His mouth curved upward in a smile, and he settled the cloth on top of my head.

"We wish you happy long years," Perkons said, and the wedding party took up the chant.

We had already married, but this felt far more official than the ceremony Trey had performed in the underworld. Jumis took my arm and led me to a table overlaid with bread and fruit, but I suddenly remembered Laima. I pulled away and swiveled her direction.

Perkons had risen from his throne and stood next to her. People moved out of my way and I approached them. He spotted me and gestured me forward.

"I have brought Laima here on your request." He turned his eyes back to her. "While it was your idea to split Dekla and Karta's souls into mortals that caused the trouble we are in now, it did indeed provide us the element we needed to win that war. However, there should have been more policing on your part, more analysis of character before you allowed just any mortal to accept the responsibility of even a part of your sisters' souls. That is where I see your failure, and because of that, the girl called Samantha got a taste of immortality and ran rampant with it."

Again he paused, and this time Laima spoke. "You are correct on all accounts. I can assure you when this war is over, nothing like that will ever happen again."

"I believe it will be your intention to prevent it, but I'm not sure you have the ability to do so. And if you do not, the pieces of our souls cannot remain with humans."

She did not respond, though Perkons gave her a moment to. Lifting his chin, he said, "I need your assistance in this war. I need you to undo the harm caused by the rebel girl. Do you accept?"

Laima's eyes glittered. "With all my heart, even without you asking. Samantha—" she spat the name out like it tasted vile, "has defiled our mission and our purpose. She has twisted into her own image something sacred, and I will not stop until she pays recompense for her deeds."

The venom in her words shivered down my spine, and I added a small prayer of gratitude that I hadn't given in to Samantha's offers when she invited me to join her side. I definitely didn't want to mess with these guys.

"Then I set you free, but I counsel you not to leave this realm. We can protect you best here." The golden chains around Laima's wrists evaporated the moment he spoke the words. "You will be summoned to the war council tomorrow."

Someone else had approached to speak to him, and a few people fluttered to Laima's side to whisper words of encouragement and comfort. I remained where I was until she gave me her attention.

"Congratulations on your nuptials, Dekla," she said.

I scowled at her. She knew I was not her. "Just call me Jayne. What's going on? You seem awfully calm about everything."

She patted my head. "Jayne, I am glad you're here. All will be well."

With that she walked past me and entered into a conversation with another wedding guest, leaving me wondering why I had fought so hard to get her freed. She wasn't going to give me any more information in the immortal realm than she had in the mortal world.

Bibliography

Alcott, Frances Jenkins: *Wonder Tales from Baltic Wizards: Pagan Mythology, Shamanism, and Magic from Finland, Lapland, Estonia, Latvia, and Lithuania*. Compass Rose Technologies, Chicago, IL., 2010.

Baltic-crossroads.com/symbols.php

Eldermountaindreaming.com/category/latvia-traditions/latvia-symbolism/ Forthisjoyousoccasion.com/ceremony-with-wiccanpagan-handfasting.html

Grimes, Algirdas J.: *Of Gods and Men: Studies in Lithuanian Mythology*, transl. Milda Newman, Indiana University Press, 1992.

Machal, Jan: *Slavic Mythology*. Mythology ebooks, 2010.

weddings.traditionscustoms.com/lithuanian_wedding

Did you enjoy this book? Please consider leaving a review! Once I have 50 reviews I will begin work on the next series!

Want to join my fan club?
Text TREADER to 33777!

About the Author

Tamara Hart Heiner is a mom, wife, baker, editor, and author. She currently lives in Arkansas with her husband, four children, a cat, a rabbit, a dog, and several fish. She would love to add a macaw and a sugar glider to the family. She's the author of over twenty published books in genres varying from kids books to nonfiction.

Connect with Tamara online!
Twitter: https://twitter.com/tamaraheiner
Facebook: https://www.facebook.com/author.tamara.heiner
blog: http://www.tamarahartheiner/blogspot.com
website: http://www.tamarahartheiner.com
Thank you for reading!

www.ingramcontent.com/pod-product-compliance
Lightning Source LLC
Chambersburg PA
CBHW011353010726
47494CB00008B/2300

* 9 7 8 1 9 4 7 3 0 7 3 0 8 *